RAMSAY AND THE SMUGGLING RING

A RETIRED SLEUTH AND HIS DOG HISTORICAL COZY MYSTERY

ONE MAN AND HIS DOG COZY MYSTERIES

P. C. JAMES

Copyright © 2024 by P. C. James

All rights reserved.

No part of this book may be reproduced in any form or by any electronic or mechanical means, including information storage and retrieval systems, without written permission from the author, except for the use of brief quotations in a book review.

Important Notes:

1. While the **places** named in this book are **REAL**, the **people and events** are **NOT**.

2. This is a work of **fiction** and any **resemblance to real people** then or now is **entirely coincidental.**

❀ Created with Vellum

1

NORTH RIDING OF YORKSHIRE, ENGLAND, OCTOBER 1964

IT WAS A BRISK OCTOBER MORNING, a clear sky for once, a stiff breeze blowing in from the sea where white crests topped each wave crashing on the beach. Standing at the foot of New Street, the principal street of Robin Hood's Bay, where the land met the ocean in an ancient slipway, retired Inspector Ramsay and his dog Bracken watched fishing boats out in the bay rising and falling as three-foot-high waves rolled under them.

"I'm glad I'm not a fisherman," Ramsay said, shuddering at the alarming vertical movement of the smaller boats. Bracken who was seated beside him, the cobblestones cold and damp beneath his furry behind, didn't respond. He didn't approve of what he could see was a cold, wet time ahead of him.

"The tide's on its way out and the day looks fine," Ramsay said. "We'll walk to Ravenscar over there," he pointed at the Raven Hall Hotel atop the 600-feet cliffs that rose from the scar, and the flat rocks that ran out from the base of the cliffs into the sea, about two or three miles away. "We'll climb the cliffs, it says in the guidebook there's a path, and we'll have our lunch in the hotel. What do you say, Bracken?"

Bracken didn't like getting sand in his paws, was afraid of the sea and those crashing waves, and his expression in answer to Ramsay's question said so, as clearly as if he'd spoken.

"It'll be fine," Ramsay said, correctly interpreting his young dog's opinion. "You'll enjoy it, you'll see." He stepped off the cobbles and onto the flat rock, then a few steps later, onto the sandy beach.

Bracken dragged along behind, thoroughly disgusted until a seagull sheltering from the wind on a boulder at the foot of the cliff caught his eye. Barking, he ran at the bird who rose, shrieking obscenities, and perched on a ledge higher up the cliff, well out of Bracken's reach.

Smiling, Bracken trotted back to join Ramsay only to see drumlins scooting along the shore searching for food. He raced across the sand, scattering the birds into flight. Panting he trotted back to Ramsay who said, "I told you it would be fine." Bracken ignored this and kept his eyes scanning the beach for more dangerous birds who might harm his dear friend, Ramsay.

"Even the wind's dropping," Ramsay said, "and the sun feels warmer. What a day to be alive. Autumn really is the best season."

Above the cliffs, trees and bushes had taken on their yellow and gold coloring. The sky was blue, except for a band of dark cloud appearing above the high ground to the west, and the sea was deep blue with sparkling white crests. Ramsay's heart lifted with the joy of being alive.

"No more putting ourselves in danger," he told Bracken, whose puzzled expression rightly reprimanded Ramsay. "You're right," Ramsay said. "None of that was your idea."

Thirty minutes later, a sharp squall of rain pattered on them, and Ramsay looked again at the bank of cloud now covering half the sky. He looked back at Robin Hood's Bay and then forward to Ravenscar and frowned. They were both an equal distant, but the climb up the cliffs at Ravenscar on wet rocks, mud, and grass would be slow and dangerous.

"We should turn back," Ramsay told Bracken. The squall returned with even more force this time and a blustery wind drove it sideways into his face. Ramsay stopped and unslung his rucksack from his back; he'd bought it especially for this trip despite being so dismissive of all those backpack hikers he'd seen in the Lake District. From the bag he pulled out waterproof leggings, a jacket, and a hat, all in a shocking yellow hue. When he had those on, the rain was now steady, and Bracken was pressing against his leg for comfort. Ramsay pulled out the jacket he'd bought for Bracken and tried to put it on him.

Bracken was having none of this. Whether it was the matching yellow he disapproved of or just the discomfort of its elastic straps around his legs. It reminded Ramsay of dressing a baby who didn't like clothes. A momentary mental image of him dressing his first born, when he'd had no idea how to dress him, sent a painful jolt through Ramsay that had him gasping for air. Ignoring this out-of-nowhere sensation, he persevered and finally Bracken and waterproof coat were joined in a grudging acceptance.

The stabbing pain he'd felt bothered Ramsay for they were becoming more frequent. He rather hoped they were symptoms of an incipient heart attack but was afraid they were symptoms of the grieving process he'd so ruthlessly suppressed when his family had been killed by a German bomb in World War Two. Since his enforced retirement, these moments were happening often and he wasn't sure he could push them aside so easily now, when he didn't have work to deflect his thoughts.

As he considered these new experiences, torrents of rain were blocking out the view of the beach to the north and south and the waves were once again growing, they thundered on the beach making Bracken start and shudder in growing alarm. Ramsay looked about hoping to see shelter.

"There's a rock overhang," Ramsay said, pointing to the low cliffs at the top of the beach. "We'll shelter under that until this squall passes. Rain like this never lasts too long."

The rock overhang gave some shelter, but the blustery wind continued swirling plenty of rain in on them. Holding the rain hat close about his face, Ramsay searched for a better place and saw a narrow vertical crevice in the rock nearby. He edged slowly to it, trying to keep under the rocky overhang, and peered through the gap. It was too small for either of them to get through but there was a cave behind it. He looked at the crevice in puzzlement. It wasn't a natural break in the rock; it looked more like a door.

Ramsay slid his fingers inside and investigated. It was a door. He pulled at it; the door opened further until the gap was wide enough for him to slip sideways through. Inside smelled rancid, and he put his handkerchief over his nose and mouth. It was a smell he recognized, decaying dead meat. Probably a sheep who'd fallen in from a crack higher up the cliffside.

"Come in here, Bracken," Ramsay said, signaling Bracken to join him.

Bracken shook his head and backed away.

"Come on," Ramsay urged. "The smell will clear now that the door is open." He pushed to make the gap even wider. It was heavy and the hinges stiff. "All this salt air has rusted them," Ramsay grumbled to himself, and he put all his weight to the door. It finally swung fully open. "Now, it will be better," Ramsay told Bracken who stayed where he was, shivering.

Ramsay turned to peer into the cave. With the door open, and light filtering in, he could see it was more like a tunnel than a cave. "It will be a tunnel associated with the old alum mine they mention in the guidebook," he called to Bracken.

The door, he decided had been put in place years before to prevent visitors from exploring shafts that were now likely dangerous. Some shift in the earth and rock must have sprung open the door recently and because the storm had brought him to the overhang, he was the first to notice. He'd have to alert the authorities, when he got back to the village. Ramsay stepped farther into the tunnel and peered at the paper-strewn floor deeper within, and the odd-looking mound lying tight against the wall. His heart sank. It looked awfully like a body and not a sheep's body. A human body.

Hoping he was imagining things, the smell probably had set the thought in his mind, he walked a few more cautious steps until he could see. It *was* a man's body, lying on its left side with the flesh already decaying away from the bones. Ramsay had seen such sights many times in his police career but every time it made him feel sick. His first thought — that someone had crept in here to get out of the cold and become trapped — he had to dismiss. The right side of the man's head was broken, the eye socket was missing the outer bone and the temple beside it too was depressed. "Our old friend the lead pipe," Ramsay muttered to himself.

He turned away to examine the papers on the floor. They looked like bills of lading. He picked up the nearest and read it. It recorded a shipment of 'machine parts' transporting from Germany to England via Rotterdam, and it wasn't centuries old, it was only two months ago. He picked up another, but the lettering was faded with damp and the light too dim for him to read. Once again, he thought how useful it would be if he smoked and therefore carried matches or a lighter. He replaced the paper carefully where he'd found it and made his way back to the door. He removed his handkerchief and gulped in wet, salty fresh air. The rain, he saw, was easing off.

"Soon as this downpour stops, Bracken," Ramsay said, "we must get to a phone."

Bracken's head nodded in misery. He was cold, wet, and the smell of putrefying flesh was the worst scent he'd ever experienced. He'd happily leave now whatever the weather.

Ramsay pushed the door closed and wedged a rock at the base to prevent anyone seeing the gap and entering to investigate.

They stood mutely observing the downpour, water dripping from their waterproof clothes. The squall was easing off. Ramsay could see both ends of the bay now, though low clouds still hid the Raven Hall hotel, perched as it was on the cliff edge.

Looking north, Robin Hood's Bay could be dimly seen through the rain. Its whitewashed walls and red roofed houses clustering around the slipway looked very far off in the swirling misty weather. From his years in Newcastle, Ramsay knew that sudden squalls were a feature of life on the coast but generally they didn't last long. This one had already outstayed its welcome, in Ramsay's mind.

Finally, the rain eased off and Ramsay could see the sky above, blue now that the squall was passing away. "Let's go," Ramsay said, stepping out into the thin rain and gesturing

Bracken to follow. The waves, whipped up by the squall, thundered on the sand, and Bracken flinched at each, straining on the leash in his hurry to reach dry land. Dispirited, they trudged back to Robin Hood's Bay, heads down and shivering with the cold.

"Hot baths for us when we get back to the guest house," Ramsay said. Even Bracken, who wasn't an enthusiastic bather, seemed to nod his agreement.

2

INFORMING THE AUTHORITIES

THEY MADE their way straight to the police house in the village where Ramsay was pleased to find the village constable accepted immediately what Ramsay told him. He'd expected some skepticism because that had been his experience whenever he'd given local police information about their 'patch'. This time was different, and he expressed his gratitude for the hearing he'd been given.

"Well, sir," Constable Storm replied, "we had a local man go missing around the middle of August, and there's been no sign of him since. He wasn't lost at sea because, while he owned fishing boats, he'd stopped going out after an accident left him too lame to be safe on a small boat."

"You say fishing boats," Ramsay said, "but did they ever do general transporting of goods?"

"They might, I suppose," Storm said, thoughtfully "but I never heard they did. Why?"

"Because there are papers strewn across the floor beside the body. Some look like lists of fish prices and some like bills of lading for goods. They may not have anything to do with the body, of course, but it seemed likely."

Storm considered this for a moment. "I've been looking into a possible smuggling ring operating from around here. This may be the first real evidence there is one. I'll phone Whitby and get an ambulance and forensic people here. Meanwhile, we should go at once to this cave, in case someone else tries to take shelter there."

Ramsay looked down at Bracken who was still shivering and said, "I need to get my companion warmed through before he falls ill."

"Leave him here," Storm said. "We have a spaniel and she and my wife would love to coddle your collie for an hour or so."

With that agreed to by Mrs. Storm, Ramsay led the policeman along the beach toward the cave.

As they walked, Constable Storm said, "We don't get a lot of visitors this time of year. Are you staying long?"

"I thought a week," Ramsay responded, "depending on the weather and how far I want to walk."

"The weather's changeable in the autumn, right enough," Storm agreed. "Are you a big hiker?"

Ramsay laughed. "I only began this summer. For the past twenty-five years I've spent most of the days sitting down, which is why I was unsure. I only retired earlier this year. I was invalided out of the force, you see."

"I'm sorry to hear that, sir," Storm said, sympathetically. "You seem fit enough now though."

"I spent some of the summer climbing up and down Lakeland Fells," Ramsay continued. "My first efforts were pitiful but I'm much fitter now. Maintaining fitness was part of my idea behind this trip. With winter coming on, I'll likely be sitting by the fire instead of behind my desk."

"You can always do some sightseeing to break up your

hiking days," Storm said. "We've a lot of places for people to see in this neck of the woods."

Ramsay nodded. "I know. I bought a guidebook and plenty of people told me of things I had to see. I'll probably do as you suggest, particularly if we have more days like this one."

"It's a beautiful part of the world," Storm said. "I say so and I've lived here all my life. I'll never leave. It's part of the appeal of the job, being able to wander around this area every day and get paid for it."

"How big is your patch, Constable?"

Storm outlined the boundaries — which was no help to Ramsay because he'd never heard of any of the places mentioned — finishing by saying, "They've given me a motorbike, a Francis-Barnett, to travel the complete area. Most of my time, though, is here in the village where I can walk it."

"Here we are, Constable," Ramsay cried. He'd been growing anxious that they seemed to be walking and walking and never arriving at the place. He'd become frightened he'd missed it. Now bathed in bright sunshine, the still-wedged door looked too obvious to have been hidden. Opening the door, they entered the tunnel together, with the policeman's powerful lamp leading the way.

"I'd heard rumors there was a tunnel from the beach to the old alum mine," Storm said. "But I never heard that anyone had found it."

"It may not go all the way up to the alum mine," Ramsay said. "Here the cliff is low, only fifty feet or so. The wagons from the mine could have come down the hillside and only entered a tunnel for the last little bit. After all, a gradual descent to the beach in a tunnel is a lot easier than getting the alum down that last fifty feet to the beach by a crane."

Storm's flashlight shone a wide beam across the back of the tunnel, exposing the body, the fallen rock that blocked further passage, and the papers on the floor. Covering their mouths and noses, the two men made their way to the back of the cave where the torch starkly illuminated the scene Ramsay had witnessed earlier through only the dimmest of daylight.

"With luck," Storm said, "the forensic experts can tell us if any of those papers are connected with the body." By now they'd reached the dead man and Storm examined it dispassionately.

"It could be Harry Peacock, right enough," he continued. "It's hard to tell but he looks the right height and his hair's the right color."

"Did Harry have any distinguishing marks?" Ramsay asked.

Storm nodded. "But they were of the kind that are lost now. The pathologist will do better from his bones and teeth."

"How long until the others arrive?" Ramsay asked.

"By the time they've rounded them up and driven over from Whitby, at least an hour. Then they must make the trek along the beach with their equipment. Say another hour." Storm glanced at his watch. "We've been an hour now, so I'd guess we'll see them making their way here soon."

"Tell me about Harry Peacock and your smugglers," Ramsay asked conversationally, hoping to learn something of the background to this murder before senior officers arrived and shut down communication.

"There's not much to tell," Storm replied, as they stood at the entrance to the tunnel gazing at the beach where people were once again walking or playing. "We all got a notice from Scarborough Police to be on the lookout for smuggling. Bottles of foreign booze were turning up throughout Scarborough and the neighboring towns and villages."

"You hadn't seen any of that in Robin Hood's Bay?"

Storm shook his head. "But you know how it is in a small community, everyone knows the local copper. Anything shady is kept well away from prying police eyes."

Ramsay grinned. "It's like that in cities too. Even new officers are soon well-known and avoided, if possible. So, watching the fishermen wasn't because of anything you saw here?"

Storm frowned. "Yes and no. I'd felt for some time something was odd about Harry Peacock and his boats and smuggling might explain it. But until we got the notice, I had no reason to watch anyone."

"What made you think something was odd?"

"You'll know, I suppose, that fish stocks in the North Sea have been declining for years now?" Storm asked.

Ramsay nodded. "I'd hear that from trawler captains in Newcastle but, to be honest, I took it with a pinch of salt. Farmers, for instance, claim the weather is getting worse, colder every year, and they can hardly make ends meet. Thing's growing worse is a common theme of everyone who makes their living from the land and sea, I find."

Storm laughed. "I know what you mean. But with Harry Peacock it was different. When other fishermen had had enough and were looking to get out, Harry always had money to buy their boats and equipment."

"He wasn't suffering from a declining catch the way they were," Ramsay said, nodding.

"Exactly," Storm replied. "Now, to be fair, he was a great fisherman and knew these waters better than anyone else.

You see, I had some suspicion about his success but not a solid reason why he was successful."

"It's often the way," Ramsay said. "Success often seems to favor one individual over others and it's hard to put your finger on the difference. Did you learn anything after you started surveillance?" He continued gazing out to sea but from the corner of his eye he watched the beach to the north where the forensic team would come. He could still see only dogwalkers, but his nerves were on edge, knowing he had to get everything he could from Storm before the police arrived.

Storm shook his head. "No. Harry's boats left the bay, stayed out all night and returned with fish next morning. I even asked to see the catch once or twice, trying to make it friendly, neighborly, like, but there was nothing to see. Just fish."

"How did he catch fish when others couldn't?"

"Like I said, he knew the waters better than anyone but..." Storm hesitated. He seemed to be struggling for the right words. He continued, "there was one time, when he wanted to buy his third boat, when he seemed about to lose it all. He couldn't pay his crews."

"And what happened?"

"Out of nowhere, he got a business partner. A Geordie called Armstrong, Sam Armstrong. He arrived in the village, took a house on the Whitby road, and Harry had money to buy the boat he was after and send them all out to sea again."

"Did you look into the background of Mr. Armstrong?" Ramsay asked hurriedly, for he could now see a party of men and equipment leaving the slipway at Robin Hood's Bay.

"I did but there wasn't much to go on. He'd had a business in Newcastle then, when his wife died, he sold up and moved to Robin Hood's Bay. He has no convictions, not even a speeding or parking ticket to his name. An honest citizen, by all accounts."

Ramsay laughed. "They're the ones you have to watch."

Storm nodded, grinning. "I agree but it was what I was told by those who should know so I had to accept it. Anyway, Harry's fishing business has continued steadily ever since. It hasn't grown larger but neither has it shrunk."

"And the memo from Scarborough didn't cause you to dig deeper?" Ramsay could see the police somewhat clearly now and he knew Storm soon would as well and wonder if he'd been wise sharing so much with a stranger, even an ex-policeman such as himself.

"It would have done, only Harry Peacock went missing and my focus changed to organizing searches, alerting local police and the newspapers and radio, and all the paperwork that goes with such a search. I couldn't say it was murder, of course, but I treated it as such so if it turned out that way, I would have plenty to show how seriously I'd taken it." His attention was caught by the police experts and officers who were now in hailing distance, and he stepped out from the shadow of the cliff and waved to catch their attention.

Ramsay frowned. He'd learned all he could in the time available, and it went without saying he wasn't going to investigate, but it was intriguing -- and so soon after his adventure with Sophia and Alastair in the Lake District. Was rural England such a hotbed of crime, or was he causing it by the magic of his presence? He grinned at the thought of himself as a 'pied piper' of crime leading the country's criminals to commit their crimes when he arrived in the neighborhood.

Constable Storm led the forensic team to the cave as Ramsay tried to start a conversation with the police sergeant who approached him.

"I'm Tom Ramsay. I found the body."

"I hope you didn't mess with the crime scene," the sergeant said, ignoring Ramsay's offer of a handshake.

"I was an Inspector with Newcastle police for about a quarter of a century," Ramsay replied. "I do know my way around a crime scene and what not to do when in one."

"Well, they're putting someone from Scarborough in charge of this one, so we won't need your help."

Ramsay was puzzled. Such hostility before he'd done anything they could complain of seemed over-the-top, even by a frustrated sergeant's usual attitude. He shrugged and said nothing.

The sergeant too had decided silence was the best policy for he made his way to the tunnel and called for Constable Storm to join him at the entrance. There was a hurried conversation, with regular dark looks toward Ramsay, before the sergeant re-joined him.

"Storm tells me you were asking questions about the case," the sergeant said, his expression grim, almost menacing. "You're not in the force now and you have no role to play here. Forget what Storm told you and continue your holiday without interfering, or leave early. Just be sure you supply us with your home address before you go."

"Is there something wrong, Sergeant? I seem to be missing part of this conversation," Ramsay said.

"Your fame has preceded you, Mr. Ramsay," the sergeant replied. "You had us running around looking for a missing girl only a month or so back. Only, she wasn't, was she? Now, the Inspector won't be here for another hour or so, he says. I suggest you go back to your hotel, which is it by the way?"

Ramsay told him the name of the guest house and agreed it would be best if he went there. With that, he set out back along the beach to the village.

3

A VOLUNTEER ASSISTANT SIGNS UP

ARRIVING AT THE SLIPWAY, he walked toward the small cafe at one side of the main street. He was about to enter when he immediately felt guilty at leaving Bracken to fend for himself while his owner drank tea and ate pastries indoors. Sighing, he continued walking up the increasingly steep street.

He stopped and looked in the bow window of a small gift shop, its small, thick glass panes distorting everything inside. Opposite was a greengrocer, W. Wilson, selling fruit, vegetables, flowers, and homemade fruit wines, blackberry and elderberry making up the bulk of the bottles. Ramsay continued and passed another tiny shop selling beach items, shrimping nets, buckets and spades, windbreakers, beach balls, all entirely unsuitable for a north-eastern seaside town in October. He assumed some people must still buy these items but there'd been no one on the beach sunning themselves either of the two days since he arrived. A shop selling jet, Whitby Jet, was next. It too had seen better days. Nobody had bought jet jewelry since Queen Victoria died and the shop's appearance confirmed it. What would have been a goldmine when Victoria was mourning her beloved Prince Albert, and the court and country were following her lead, was now a forgotten business in a small fishing village.

Higher up, another teashop called to him and this time he succumbed to its siren call. This one was a little upmarket from the one at the water's edge and it had been a steep climb. He needed a refreshing, calming drink after the day's horrors. It even allowed pets inside. He ordered tea and a scone before taking up a chair and table near a window looking out to sea. He had his choice of spots to sit, on this cold autumn day.

Out at sea, he could see small fishing boats, though they didn't seem to be fishing. He'd noticed others just off the slipway, bobbing in a deeper pool near the flat rocks that reached out into the sea. Did some fish by day and others by night? He must ask Mr. Armstrong when he spoke to him, which he wasn't going to do. None of this was Ramsay's business.

His tea and scone arrived, and he thanked the young woman who brought it. She nodded and was about to leave, then changed her mind.

"Are you the one who found old Harry's body?" she asked.

"I found a body," Ramsay said, guardedly. "But I've no idea whose it is."

"It'll be old Harry," the young woman said, confidently. "He was always going to be murdered sooner or later."

Ramsay laughed. "One of those cantankerous old men, was he?"

"You could say that," she replied, grinning. "Or you could say he was a miserable old sod without a good word for anyone."

"You didn't like him?"

"He was all right," the server replied. "I didn't mind him, but lots did. I don't think they appreciated being called names whenever he spoke to them."

"Names?"

"He always addressed me as 'trollop'," she said, "because I once dyed my hair. He never forgot."

"And what *is* your name," Ramsay asked. "I'm Tom Ramsay."

"I know who you are," she replied. "Percy Storm has told everyone. You're a celebrity, see?"

"I didn't know," Ramsay said, puzzled. "When did he have time to tell everyone?"

"He didn't but he told his missus and that's the same thing."

Ramsay grinned, shaking his head. "The village information machine is the fastest in the world, I find. It puts all that radio and television news to shame. You still haven't told me your name."

"Eliza," she replied, "Eliza Danesdale."

"Is that short for Elizabeth?"

She nodded. "My mam was besotted with Princess Elizabeth at the time she had me," Eliza said. "It could have been worse. It could have been Margaret Rose and there's nothing good you can do with either of those names. I didn't fancy Liz or Bessie and I love *Pride and Prejudice* so Eliza it is."

"Didn't you get teased a bit at school? It's very grand sounding."

"People might once maybe but I made sure they didn't do it twice," Bess said, grimly. "Do you like *Pride and Prejudice*? You'd better say yes because it's my way of sorting the wheat from the chaff."

Ramsay shook his head. "When I was a boy, I did read

fiction but usually, the authors from my own country, like Walter Scott, Robert Louis Stevenson and John Buchan. Then later," his face darkened, "I didn't want to read about wars or conflict. Now, I only read non-fiction."

"Jane Austen talks about men preferring non-fiction," Bess said, sympathetically. "I suppose I should give you a passing mark on my test."

"Otherwise, it would be difficult for you to serve me tea?" Ramsay suggested.

"Perhaps," Eliza said, loftily. "I'll consider you on a probationary period for now. Maybe, *Pride and Prejudice* isn't a good marker where men are concerned." She frowned. "I know so little about men, you see."

"Well, Eliza," Ramsay said, changing the subject in case the conversation became embarrassing, "as you seem to have been on speaking terms with at least one man, the late Mr. Peacock, maybe you could tell me more about him?"

The café door opened, the overhead bell rang, and an elderly couple entered. Eliza left Ramsay with a quick, 'maybe later' and went to greet them. They were clearly local regulars.

It was some time before he could catch her attention again, as the couple, Eliza, and the proprietress of the teashop were soon in a conversation about the couples' new granddaughter, their son, the upcoming Whist Drive, and sundry other local events.

When he did catch her eye and she returned to the table, Ramsay asked, "I heard you call the lady in the kitchen your mam. Is the teashop your family's?"

"Yes. Mam does the cooking, I serve at the counter and tables, and dad does the books, except in summer when it's really busy, and then he does the books and helps me serve."

"You're a hardworking family," Ramsay remarked.

"You have to have more than one job or business in a place this small," Eliza said, "or you'd starve."

"Which is why I suspect smuggling may be behind Harry Peacock's death," Ramsay said. "Not on an industrial scale like in a bigger port, but larger than the bottle or two of cheap spirits that everyone smuggles in whenever they travel abroad."

"Nobody around here is driving Rolls-Royces," Eliza said, disbelievingly. "If there is smuggling, it's only Harry's fleet and they're hiding the money somewhere."

"The crews on Harry's boats would have to be paid well to keep quiet. Have any of them bought anything surprising in the past months?"

"Only Fred Ramsbottom who bought his son a motorbike so he could get to college in Scarborough easier."

"Isn't there a regular train?" Ramsay asked.

"That's what everyone asked but Fred said his son was doing evening classes there too, and the trains weren't convenient at night," Eliza replied, "and he's right. If you want to go to an evening event in Scarborough or Whitby the train service is hopeless. People often hire a bus, if there's enough going."

"That must cramp the style of you young folks," Ramsay said, laughing.

"Not as much as it must have done before there was even a train," Eliza replied, her face crinkling in a smile that made Ramsay feel the sun had suddenly appeared, "but most people marry locally so it all works out." She saw a raised hand at a nearby table and said, "I'll be back," and hurried away.

When she re-appeared at his side, Ramsay asked, "It's too busy to talk properly. Where can we meet later to talk?"

Eliza thought and said, "The Seaview Hotel after we close for the day. Say seven o'clock."

"You won't mind being seen with a notorious celebrity in such a public place?" Ramsay teased her.

"It's why I chose the Seaview," she replied. "I want everyone to know I'm assisting you with your enquiries."

Ramsay was taken aback, saying, "I'm not making any enquiries and I have an assistant, my dog Bracken."

Eliza dismissed this feeble effort to put her off with a wave of an imperious hand. "Nonsense. Bracken can't go in the Ladies Room. Or any ladies-only places. I can."

"True," Ramsay admitted, "but I don't need any of that because I'm not making enquiries."

"So, you're actually asking me out on a date?" Eliza laughed, making the older couple stare in disapproval.

"I'm just intrigued about Mr. Peacock, that's all," Ramsay protested.

Eliza considered carefully before saying, "It's different strategy, asking a girl out to talk about a corpse but maybe that's how it was done when you were younger. It will have to include dinner, if it's a date."

Ramsay was about to say forget it but took a deep breath and recovered his wits instead. "I'd like to talk to you about Harry Peacock over a quiet drink. That's all."

Eliza smiled. "Pity, I've always wanted to have dinner at The Seaview Hotel. We can't afford such high-living, you see."

Seeing she wasn't going to talk about the victim without paying her a quite frankly outrageous bribe, Ramsay smiled and said, "I'll make a reservation for seven-thirty. Will that give you time to change?" When Eliza assured him, it would, he added, "Where do I meet you?"

"At the hotel, seven-thirty, and don't be late."

Ramsay said goodbye and left the café to continue his climb, first he'd need to rescue Bracken from the police house and then on to the guest house. He was still chuckling at the artful way he'd been led from a sixpenny-piece drink to a five-pound-note meal when he arrived at the police house to be greeted by an ecstatic Bracken and equally excited spaniel.

His welcome at the guest house, when he asked the proprietress for The Seaview Hotel phone number and the reason for his call, was anything but ecstatic. The proprietor, Mrs. Golightly, was horrified.

"Oh, Mr. Ramsay," she said, "you shouldn't. Eliza Danesdale is a nice girl in her own way but wild, you know. She may embarrass you there just for the fun of it."

"They won't refuse to serve us, will they?" Ramsay asked, mildly alarmed.

"Oh no. I doubt they know who she is," the landlady said. "No, I'm afraid of what she may do when they seat you for dinner."

"Is she so bad? Aren't her parents around to restrain her?"

"They are and I'm sure they do," the landlady said. "Her father is a clerk in the Ravenscar Fishing office and a very genteel man. And her mother is a respectable woman, but you know how it is with young people today. They're always rebelling against something, usually the upper classes and Eliza has been known to make wild speeches at inappropriate times. Like last summer's village fete when she protested the use of seaside donkeys."

"I'm sure we all wonder how well the donkeys are treated when they're not carrying small children on rides along the beach," Ramsay replied.

"We may indeed, Mr. Ramsay, but consider, if those

donkeys can't make a living for their owners, they'll be put down. There's no other use for donkeys today. How is death better than a boring life taking children on rides?"

"I take your point," Ramsay said. "I'll try to keep her focused on my interest in Harry Peacock and away from protests."

"Are you investigating his death?" his landlady asked. "Has Percy Storm asked for your help? I'm sure he should, a man with your experience."

Ramsay shook his head. "I'm leaving this to the police. Only, I can't help but have an interest, you know."

"I see, yes. Well, don't forget what I said. Be wary of Eliza. She doesn't mean to do harm, but harm is often the end result."

"Like those donkeys?" Ramsay hazarded to guess.

The woman nodded, unhappily. "All slaughtered for animal feed when summer ended."

Ramsay looked at Bracken, waiting patiently at his feet and he felt anger rising in his chest. "I'll be sure she behaves herself at The Seaview Hotel, Mrs. Golightly. I don't want to be slaughtered any time soon." He paused, then asked, "Surely the donkeys weren't killed because Eliza protested against them?"

She shook her head. "It wasn't just Eliza, but the protests helped focus the council's mind on the subject. They introduced a lot of new bye-laws about donkeys, their welfare, their droppings on the beach, and so on, for next summer."

Ramsay nodded. "It probably wasn't a hugely profitable business then."

"I imagine not, and you have to keep the donkeys without any income for about eight months of the year," Mrs. Golightly said. "We have a short summer season here."

"The death of a prominent fisherman and the beach

donkeys all in a few months," Ramsay said, thoughtfully. "Quite an upheaval I imagine in a place as small as Robin Hood's Bay."

Mrs. Golightly agreed but added, "To be honest, not many people liked Harry Peacock despite all the employment he provided, and not many liked the donkeys either. Kids liked them, adults much less so. But there's no connection between the deaths. The donkeys were owned by the family that runs a small scrap yard just outside the village. For all his 'man-of-the-people' blather, Harry looked down on the Cuthbert family with great disdain. They're barely getting by you see and he'd made it."

"Self-made men do tend to be dismissive of the struggles of others," Ramsay agreed. "I've noticed that over the years."

* * *

AFTER THE DINNER reservation was made, Ramsay retired to his room to think and rest. Walking along the beach hadn't been anything like as strenuous as climbing the Lake District fells but he found it had left him weary.

"Probably that soaking we got this morning, Bracken," Ramsay grumbled, slumping into an armchair.

Bracken, seeing rest was in the immediate future, lay down beside Ramsay and — worn out chasing, and being chased by an excitable spaniel — fell asleep. Ramsay thought about the rest of his vacation. *I should keep away from the beach and even the village for the next days, so I won't be, or won't find myself wanting to be, dragged into investigate. This was strictly police business.*

He'd go inland and walk among the dales. And there was one modern wonder of the world he'd been told he had to see, Fylingdales Early Warning Station. He'd even been shown photos of it, and it was truly dramatic. However, he'd crossed it off his list when he'd learned more. War and all its horror held no attraction for him. Not since his wife and family had been killed. Now it seemed, he may have to at least walk by the place if the weather at the coast was anything like today. This rather depressed him and he too dozed off, only to be woken thirty minutes later by a discreet knock on the door.

"Yes?" Ramsay called.

"It's the police station," he heard Mrs. Golightly say. "An Inspector Baldock wants you to meet him and give him your version of events this morning."

Ramsay groaned. However, he felt he should because Constable Storm hadn't impressed him as being a man who would accurately relay to the inspector what Ramsay had told him. Ramsay roused Bracken and made his way downstairs where his coat and hat were hanging next to Bracken's leash. He dressed and clipped the leash to Bracken's collar before setting out for the police house.

4

A DANGEROUS ENEMY MADE

AFTER HANDING Bracken once again into Mrs. Storm's care, Ramsay was introduced to Inspector Baldock.

"I've given a full statement to Constable Storm," Ramsay said, as the Inspector ushered him into the interview room. It was late in the afternoon, and he'd only just warmed up in the guest house. Being called back to the police house was not what Ramsay had wanted or expected. Detective Inspector Baldock, seconded from nearby Scarborough, had been assigned to the case and he wanted to hear from the man who'd found the body, as he told Ramsay when they shook hands.

"We always have more questions," Baldock replied, brusquely. "I'm sure you know how it is."

"Of course," Ramsay said carefully because he didn't like the man's tone and he was puzzled to explain it. "I'll do anything I can to help."

"I'm glad to hear it," Baldock said, "after the run around you gave us all over that 'missing' girl."

Here it was again. Had the search for Sophia, only a

month or two before, really reached all the way to the East Coast? And caused so much resentment?

"I don't know what you mean?" Ramsay said, at last.

"I mean you allowed half the police in the country to search for someone you were keeping hidden," Baldock replied, towering over the now seated Ramsay in an intimidating fashion.

"It was best she remained lost," Ramsay said, maintaining his calm. "Anyway, if I'd betrayed her, she'd have run away again and may never have been found alive."

"So, you say, but here's what I say," Baldock replied. "If you're holding anything back on this case and I find out, you will be charged with every offence I can find in the book that fits. Is that clear?"

"Very," Ramsay said. "But as I know nothing about this case nor the people involved, you can be confident I'm not holding anything back."

"Then walk me through your movements this morning and leave nothing out," Baldock said, dropping heavily into the chair opposite Ramsay across the old desk. He was a heavy-set man with dark features. He looked like a boxer gone to seed. His hair, once black, was now streaked with gray.

Ramsay recounted the story again, while Baldock followed it in Ramsay's written statement, asking occasional questions but generally letting Ramsay speak.

"And you've never met the deceased?"

"Never. I've never actually been to Robin Hood's Bay before."

"Never?" Baldock asked.

Ramsay shook his head. "Whitby is as far south as I've been on this coast."

"And being a detective in a port city like Newcastle,

you'd know nothing about smuggling or smugglers, I suppose?"

"We had smuggling through the port," Ramsay agreed, trying to remain calm, "but it was big time stuff on merchant ships, not bottles of brandy on trawlers."

"And your visit to Whitby," Baldock said, innocently, "five years ago, was it? Just a holiday jaunt?"

"You know very well it was in connection with a smuggling operation I was investigating," Ramsay replied.

Baldock nodded. "And you liaised with Len Pritchard?"

"I did," Ramsay replied. "He and I investigated a number of leads I'd gathered."

Baldock smiled. It wasn't a pleasant smile. "Pritchard was an officer who was later thrown out of the force on suspicion he was the smugglers' inside man."

"So, I heard," Ramsay said. "All I can say is I had no suspicion about Inspector Pritchard while we worked together."

"And now you find the body of a suspected smuggler, here in Robin Hood's Bay, not six miles from Whitby."

"As I said," Ramsay replied. "I'd never seen the man before, to the best of my knowledge, and I didn't recognize the name Constable Storm suggested."

Baldock nodded. "For now, I'll accept that, but I should warn you, I'm having a copy of the files from that smuggling case you worked on with Pritchard sent down to me and if there's even a hint in there you knew this victim or the people Constable Storm has been watching, I'll have you."

"You're letting the search for the recent runaway cloud your judgment, Inspector," Ramsay said, finding it hard now to maintain a steady voice.

"You're forgetting Whitby, Pritchard, and the recent

amazing coincidence of you just happening to find the runaway girl and now this body."

"Coincidences do happen in life," Ramsay retorted.

"Not this many," Baldock growled. "And a smuggling case with ex-Inspector Pritchard, who we know was an informer, and who might yet be something more than just their informant, maybe even the ringleader, is a coincidence I'm not disposed to believe in."

Ramsay's patience snapped. "I could concoct the same story about you. You work in Scarborough, a police station only a few miles down the coast. I'm sure you've worked on smuggling cases and maybe even with Pritchard. And how hard would it be for an experienced inspector to get himself assigned to a smuggling case that he was maybe involved with?"

Baldock's face flushed an angry red. "Get out before I forget you were once one of us," he shouted. "How dare you suggest I'm corrupt. Get out!"

Ramsay rose to his feet and turned to go. "Likewise, Inspector. How dare you suggest I was?"

Ramsay left the room, fuming. He'd have to watch his step for the length of this inquiry; he was sure Baldock would implicate him, if he could. He gathered up Bracken from Mrs. Storm, where Bracken had already become a popular visitor, thanked her and exited the building.

As he returned up the steep hill out of the village to the guest house, he considered the interview and the future. "It maybe wasn't wise to suggest he was a bent copper," he muttered to himself, before quickly looking around to see if anyone had heard. There was no one near and he sighed with relief before quietly lapsing into his faint, remaining, Scottish dialect. "Mebbe I should nae talk to meself oot loud for a while," he continued, breaking the resolution he'd just made.

Bracken nodded, shooting him a sympathetic glance, before signaling his wish for a walk by heading immediately to the entrance of a grassy trail running along the edge of the cliff, leading out to Ness Point.

Ramsay fondled his dog's ears and said, "Could I have a cup of tea before we go?"

Bracken's expression was severe.

Ramsay grimaced. "Very well but if we get soaked again, it will be on your head, my lad," he said, accepting his fate and following Bracken along the path.

When he was sure they were alone, Ramsay commented, "I know I said we were going to enjoy cliff walks, and beach walks, and if the weather stayed dry, we'd finish it all by doing the Lykewake Walk over the moors. And I also said I wasn't going to get involved with this murder we discovered, but..." he paused, and Bracken gave him a despondent look that said: 'I'm guessing already that '*but*' is going to be bad news.'

"The thing is, Bracken," Ramsay continued. "I've made a terrible mistake. It shouldn't have happened. After all, I've used the same technique myself to get a witness to lose their composure and say something that opens up the case. Only, Baldock was unpleasant from the outset, and he got under my skin."

Bracken's ears were drooping by now. He didn't want to hear anymore.

"Anyway, I must solve this before Baldock provides an answer that buries me in dirt. I've made a bad enemy there."

Bracken marched on, following a rabbit scent that seemed new enough for a chase.

"What's your opinion of Constable Storm, Bracken?

He'll have been told not to talk to me but is he the sort of man who'll be so unhappy at having his opportunity to shine taken away from him that he'll help an amateur sleuth?"

Bracken stopped and looked sternly at Ramsay. His expression clearly said, 'Are you kidding me?'

"I agree," Ramsay said. "I think he'll be happy to let Baldock get on with it, preferably without a constable's help, which means he won't help me either."

As Ramsay had now said what Bracken would have suggested, Bracken returned to straining at the leash in hopes of catching up with that rabbit.

Ramsay sighed and let himself be pulled along until a rabbit shot out of the tall grass at the side of the path and Bracken set off in pursuit.

Ramsay hauled him back. "There's a long drop to the beach that way, Bracken. We'll keep to the trail, if you don't mind."

Bracken thought: 'I do mind but I'm happy enough I got to startle that rabbit, so I'll skip the stern look this time.'

Ramsay looked at his watch and sighed. "We can't go too much farther, Bracken. I have a date I must get ready for."

This stopped Bracken in his tracks. 'I don't understand *date* but I do understand *too much farther*.'

Ramsay and Bracken stared at each other for a moment, then Ramsay said, "It's no use looking at me like that. I have a witness I need to interview and somehow discussing it over a drink became dinner out." Bracken's expression suggested he didn't approve. Ramsay felt guilty.

"You'll be fine with Mrs. Golightly. You know how she spoils you."

Bracken's expression said: Secondhand affection is no

replacement for the bond between you and me, Ramsay.'
And Ramsay felt even worse.

"I don't care what you think," Ramsay said firmly to Bracken, and also to himself. "It's even more important I learn about the victim now. It's a race to the solution between Baldock and me. And if Baldock wins, you won't like it any more than I will."

Bracken set off again heading to Ness Point, but Ramsay hauled him back. "We wasted so much time talking, our time has gone. We'll come this way tomorrow, I promise."

If I'm still free to roam and not in a police cell, Ramsay thought gloomily.

5

FIRST INTERVIEW

"You're here in good time," Ramsay said, as he turned into the short drive of the hotel to see Eliza waiting at the door. He was surprised to see how well-dressed she was in a smart, new, blue frock and matching jacket. Not at all the waitress of an hour or so ago. Even her auburn hair, that could hardly be contained under the waitress cap, was now elegantly styled away from her face. It came to him she'd been waiting for this evening for quite some time.

"A gentleman shouldn't keep a lady waiting," she replied.

"Sadly, I'm not a gentleman," Ramsay said, grinning. "Just another grumpy old man."

Eliza took his arm, and they entered the hotel, Eliza still teasing him about his timekeeping and Ramsay protesting he was, in fact, five minutes early.

Their table, however, was ready and they were seated almost at once at a small table at a window overlooking the bay. Ramsay looked about the room, noting the white linen, polished glasses and cutlery, with flowers at each table. A comfortable place for the well-to-do of the neighborhood to while away an evening.

"What do you want to know?" Eliza asked, her face buried in the large menu. "I don't want to spoil dinner by talking about murder all the way through it."

"I want to know everything you know about the man and his business, as well as anything you've heard about how others saw Harry," Ramsay replied.

"I don't know what I know," Eliza said, briefly emerging from behind the menu and grinning at him. "Maybe, if you asked questions, it would help me to remember."

"Very well," Ramsay said, "who might have a grudge against Harry?"

"Half the village, I should say," Eliza replied. "He didn't believe in manners, so far as anyone could tell."

"I was looking for something a little more murderous than hurt feelings."

"My dad says every time you forget your manners, someone gets murdered," Eliza said, primly. "I'm sure he doesn't mean it literally, but I share his view. Hurt feelings are surprisingly strong emotions."

"I agree with your dad too, in general," Ramsay said. "But let's think of more compelling motives first. Business rivals..."

"He bought them all out," Eliza interjected.

"Maybe one of them took that badly?"

Eliza shrugged. "Maybe, but they had to sell. There's no fish left out there, so they say."

"What about personal relationships?" Ramsay asked.

"He had none," Eliza said. "His wife died years ago, and he's stayed single ever since."

"No lady friends?"

Eliza laughed. "Not around here anyway. Everybody knows him too well."

"What about quarrels, grudges, general dislike among Harry and the village men?"

Eliza placed the menu on her plate with a dramatic sigh. "He quarreled with everyone, there were even some fights in the past, but nothing of that sort recently."

Ramsay stopped the questions when a waiter came to take their order. With that settled, he continued, "I don't understand how he came to be murdered. According to you, everyone tolerated him, and no one wished him harm. It sounds unlikely, don't you think?"

Eliza flushed pink. "I didn't say that. I just don't know of any strong motive recently, that's all."

"Well, have your 'little gray cells' been stimulated enough now to tell me about him?"

Eliza nodded guiltily, like a schoolgirl caught out in a prank. "Dad says," she stopped, then asked, "do you know my dad worked for Harry Peacock?"

"I'd heard rumors," Ramsay said.

Eliza nodded. "He looks after the company books and, in his view, the company is in a bad way. He didn't tell me, of course; I heard him telling mam there might be hard times ahead if the company went belly up."

"What about the partner, Armstrong?"

"Dad says he only started taking an interest in the business when Harry disappeared," Eliza replied.

"So, someone with a strong motive you'd forgotten," Ramsay said, accusingly.

"I was going to tell you over pudding," Eliza said, "which, for some daft reason, they call dessert here. No wonder we locals eat at other places."

Ramsay thought *the prices may be the bigger deterrent.*

Even he'd been surprised, and he'd stayed at a posh place in Keswick only months ago. He couldn't help noticing how Eliza had slid dessert into the meal, as well as the starters she'd just ordered. He smiled. Ramsay liked people who didn't pick at food like a bird.

"What does your dad think of Armstrong?"

"He thinks he's a hard man and working for him might actually be worse than working for Harry had been."

"Does you dad have any sense the business has revenues that don't appear in his books?" Ramsay asked.

Eliza frowned. "I've heard him once say he didn't know where some money came from but then Armstrong came on the scene, and he thought that explained it."

"I was thinking more of every week's revenues, rather than a one-off."

"You're thinking smuggling?"

Ramsay nodded. "It might explain why Harry was killed and how the company keeps going when catches are down."

Eliza shook her head. "Well, dad doesn't know anything about it. I'm sure of that. He's a stickler for honesty in everything. He says accounting makes you that way."

Ramsay didn't disillusion her with tales of policing in the wider world, he just said, "I imagine there's another set of books for that side of the business, if there is a 'that side of the business.'"

"There's been rumors but no one can ever point to evidence," Eliza said. "Maybe we can solve the murder and expose the smugglers."

"We?" Ramsay asked, amused.

"You'll need local knowledge to get to the bottom of this," Eliza replied, tartly, "and I'm your only volunteer right now."

Ramsay shook his head. "Harry Peacock was brutally murdered. You should keep well out of it."

"It's because he was brutally murdered, I have to do my best for him," Eliza said. "When I said he wasn't much liked in the village, I told the truth. Where I wasn't entirely truthful was letting you believe that I shared the village's opinion. He was a miserable so-and-so, but I liked him."

"Even though he called you a trollop?"

Eliza grinned. "It was just his way."

"He didn't frighten you, though," Ramsay suggested.

Eliza shook her head. "With dad working for him, we saw more of Harry than most. He was always kind to me, and he put up with my childhood nonsense better than a lot of others did."

Ramsay laughed. "It seems you and he had a soft spot for each other."

Nodding, Eliza said, "I think we both felt like outsiders much of the time and saw that in each other."

Ramsay asked, "I gather Harry was a big man around here. Employer, curmudgeon, successful businessman, best fisherman, and so on. Have I got that right?"

Eliza nodded. "Compared to everyone else here, he was a giant." She laughed before adding, "And he roared like one when things weren't to his liking."

Ramsay took a few moments to consider. When he'd helped the runaway Sophia and brought the culprit to justice, he'd relied heavily on Sophia and Alastair's local knowledge. This time he wasn't helping a local; he was getting himself out of a scrape. Was it right to involve an inexperienced outsider in his trouble? Keeping Sophia hidden had kept her safe. Letting Eliza help him may put her in danger.

"If it helps," Eliza said. "You can accept me as your

assistant, or I start investigating on my own. Harry was a friend. I want his murderer found and dealt with."

"All right," Ramsay agreed, concerned she was just wild enough to do what she'd threatened, "we'll be partners on this investigation but with one condition, and I mean this. If at any time you sense danger, you get out of wherever you are as fast as you can."

"I'm not stupid," Eliza replied. "I want to live forever, not die young and have a good-looking corpse."

"Then your first task is to get me and your dad together for a talk," Ramsay said. "He may know something he couldn't say before."

"We'll talk to him tomorrow, I promise."

The server arrived with their shrimp cocktail starter. "Are these local shrimps?" Eliza demanded of the waiter.

"They are, *madam*," the man said, snootily. "All our food is fresh and local."

Satisfied, Eliza picked up her fork and started.

"I'm not sure old Harry hasn't passed his spirit to you," Ramsay said, smiling.

"I told you we were alike," Eliza said, between mouthfuls. "The servings are small, aren't they?" she added, noting her starter was already gone.

"That's so you have space inside for your pudding," Ramsay said, sternly, feeling a bit like a parent and immediately regretting it when the now regular stab to the heart happened. His family seemed to be creeping back into his life the more he left the carefully cloistered world he'd created for himself at work.

"Pah!" was Eliza's articulate rebuttal.

"You can tell me more about what's been happening here these past months," Ramsay said, slowly lifting a shrimp to his mouth despite Eliza watching every movement.

"Nothing ever happens here," Eliza said, loweringly.

"You'd be surprised how, whenever police go to some horrendous crime those are the first words they hear from witnesses. All the events that led up to the crime, were missed or dismissed."

"Oh, all right," Eliza said, as the server came to take away the starter plates, and her hopes of the next course rose. "Where should I start?"

"Start somewhere and things will come back to you as you talk," Ramsay replied.

"All right. About a year ago," Eliza began, "a young man arrived here with a new boat with all the latest in fishing tools. It had sonar, like submarines use. Even Whitby and Scarborough didn't have boats like that."

"It must have caused quite a stir," Ramsay agreed. "Is he still around?"

Eliza shook her head. "Harry said only people who couldn't fish needed stuff like that, and it turned out he was right. In six months, the boat was for sale. People weren't too surprised because the man knew nothing about the sea or fishing. What was a surprise was Harry bought the boat. After all the sneering and derision, he bought it."

"Was that when Mr. Armstrong came on the scene?"

Eliza nodded. "It was. Harry seemed to be struggling to raise the price being asked and he was trying to negotiate it down and then, suddenly, he had the money."

"And Armstrong arrived," Ramsay suggested.

"Not right away," Eliza said. "He appeared only after the boat was bought and in Harry's fleet. Harry began introducing him to influential people as his partner."

"Have I understood this correctly," Ramsay began,

"twelve months ago a stranger arrived with a state-of-the-art fishing boat. Six months later, he gave up fishing and put the boat up for sale. Harry began negotiations to buy the boat and maybe a month after he found the money. About a month after that, say four months ago, Armstrong arrived as 'Harry's business partner.'" Two months ago, Harry is murdered."

Eliza nodded. "That's right. Oh! There's something else. Harry gave up skippering his boat around that time too. He said he was feeling his age."

"Did that sound right to you?" Ramsay asked.

Eliza shook her head. "It didn't. If anyone had suggested it to him, he'd have bitten their heads off and, anyway, he didn't act old or weary."

"How often does your father meet Armstrong?"

"Nowadays, daily. Up until Harry's disappearance, barely at all," Eliza said.

Their main course arrived and for a few moments, there was silence, before Eliza began again. "Harry had a son who didn't take to fishing and left the village years ago. He fell out with his father over it, and we haven't seen him since. It's years since I've seen him."

"What sort of man is this son?" Ramsay asked.

"Arthur Peacock's no sort of man at all," Eliza said scornfully. "That's what Harry said, and he was right. He wanted to be a pop star."

Ramsay laughed. "I thought that's what every youngster wanted to be now."

Eliza smiled. "But this was years ago, not now. It was the time of the dinosaurs, Cliff Richards, Marty Wilde, people like that."

Ramsay who could vaguely remember the entertainers she mentioned and who were now entirely eclipsed by new ones, like The Beatles, was as unimpressed as no doubt Eliza expected him to be. "Did Arthur Peacock have any success?"

"Have you heard of him?"

"No, but he may have a stage name I have heard of," Ramsay responded.

Eliza nodded. "True, but he hasn't. We heard he's now a manager of entertainers rather than an entertainer himself. People have such unrealistic ambitions, don't you find?"

Ramsay thought this a very adult observation for a nineteen-year-old but didn't say so. His experience was, at that age, people were touchy about such matters. He also didn't point out Eliza herself may be indulging in an unrealistic ambition as a sleuth. "At least he seems to be making a go of the entertainment business. It's not an easy place to work, I'm told."

"From what we hear, he's at the sleazy end of the business," Eliza replied, scornfully. "Drink, drugs, wild parties, brushes with the law, you know the sort of thing."

Ramsay had little experience of the youth side of the entertainment industry. Newcastle wasn't a place where such things happened, he was pleased to say.

"Do we know where he lives?" Ramsay asked.

"I don't but dad might," Eliza responded. "You think the son was angry when he found Harry had taken on a new partner and maybe cut out his useless son?"

"If he did, he may well have been," Ramsay said, "particularly if he spends his money the way you say and, what is more suggestive, is the son might know where the tunnel was. Boys have a way of stumbling on places like that, whereas Armstrong certainly wouldn't unless he'd been shown it."

"By whom?"

"By Harry, of course," Ramsay replied. "There were a lot of papers in there, more than you'd expect if it was just a case of dumping a body. I think Harry was using it as a warehouse for the secret side of the business."

Eliza frowned in thought. "If it's as you say, Harry's son must have found the tunnel when he was alone. A gang of boys wouldn't have kept it secret."

Ramsay nodded. "You're probably right. Maybe Harry's son used it as his own secret place and then abandoned it when he grew older."

"You think Arthur may have killed his father for the business?" Eliza asked.

Ramsay nodded thoughtfully. "If he's strapped for cash, he might well have done that. But it's all just guesswork right now."

"Dinner isn't and it'll get cold if we sit here talking all night," Eliza responded, tartly.

6

SECOND INTERVIEW

RAMSAY AND ELIZA walked back to her home in companionable silence, until they reached her garden gate, where she stopped and said, "Thanks for dinner. I've wanted to go there for so long and now I have. A dream come true." She smiled and added. "We have smaller dreams here, you see." She quickly kissed Ramsay's cheek and turned away, calling back to him, "I'll have dad ready to talk tomorrow morning, if you're up early."

Ramsay laughed. "If you're successful in persuading him, come to the guest house at seven. I'll be up."

He walked slowly to the guest house, pondering all he'd learned and imagining Bracken's enthusiastic greeting when he arrived there. His reception from Bracken when he did arrive, however, was chilly. Bracken sat and stared coldly as he removed his coat.

"It's not what you think," Ramsay explained, stroking Bracken's head. "I learned a lot tonight. It was worth the extravagance." Bracken didn't seem convinced.

"And we have a new assistant," Ramsay said, encouragingly. "Like Sophia. You liked Sophia, didn't you? You'll like Eliza."

Bracken's expression said: 'I'll decide for myself who I will like, thank you. And for me to forgive tonight's desertion, the price is going to be high.'

Ramsay sighed and led the way into the sitting room where Mrs. Golightly was knitting.

"Did she behave?" Mrs. Golightly demanded. Her normally genial expression now tinged with suspicion.

Ramsay nodded. "She was every bit the lady. She and I spent an enjoyable and informative evening."

"Hmm," Mrs. Golightly said, rising. "I expect you'll be wanting some tea. They serve only coffee at places like that."

Realizing he had two injured souls to soothe, Ramsay agreed he'd love a cup of tea. While Mrs. Golightly fussed in the kitchen, Ramsay worked on Bracken, patting, scratching, and stroking until, finally, Bracken forgave him.

When Mrs. Golightly returned with a tray, she asked, "And what did you learn?"

"I learned a lot about what's happened here in the village over the past year."

"You think a girl, barely out of school, can tell you about village life?" Mrs. Golightly cried. "Like all children, she knows only what she sees, not what adult people felt or experienced."

"Well," Ramsay replied, in what he hoped was an encouraging tone, "she's only the first person I've spoken to. Perhaps, you could tell me what you saw, felt, and experienced."

"Me? I'm too busy running a guest house to spy on other people."

"But you go into the village to shop every day," Ramsay

protested. "You're a member of the Chamber of Commerce, I remember you saying, and the Women's Institute, the Parish Council, not to mention the events committees you serve on."

Mrs. Golightly was taken aback at this recounting of all the things she'd told him and hadn't quite appreciated they would come back to haunt her. "It's true, I'm active in village life but I'm sure I didn't hear or see anything that would explain a murder."

"Nothing about smuggling, perhaps?" Ramsay asked.

"There are always rumors and gossip but that isn't evidence."

"No smoke without fire, they say. What were the rumors you heard?" Ramsay probed.

"People wondered how Peacock's boats could keep catching enough fish to survive when other fishermen were selling up," Mrs. Golightly replied. "Particularly after Harry Peacock stopped fishing when his claim had always been that he knew the waters and the fish better than anyone."

"Why did he stop going out on his boats? Do you know?"

"He said he'd an old injury that was playing up and he needed to rest for a while," Mrs. Golightly said. "But he showed no signs of injury and the new man who he took on to replace him as skipper of *Ravenscar Lady 1* wasn't local and couldn't know the waters or the fish."

"Up until then all his boats had been skippered by local men?"

"At first, but over the last years, they were replaced by outsiders," Mrs. Golightly replied. "The local men didn't like it, there was even talk of a strike, but they settled down after a time."

"The skippers were removed, and the crews kept," Ramsay mused out loud.

"Not entirely," Mrs. Golightly said. "The most active in

objecting were replaced by others, though they were usually replaced by more desperate local men. The decline of fishing out of Bay had left several men unemployed, and it isn't easy to get to work in other places from here."

"With this changing of the guard, I see why smuggling became a rumor," Ramsay said, slowly. "The cast-off men would want to harm the business that dumped them."

"Precisely. They were understandably bitter, but they could provide no evidence. The men working on the boats said it was nonsense, just sour grapes."

Ramsay asked, "What did people think about Harry quitting after all these years?"

"I think most people were surprised at first but then we all thought it was time," Mrs. Golightly said. "A lot of people don't know when it's time for them to stop. Haven't you seen that?"

"And when Harry disappeared?" Ramsay asked, sipping his tea and not answering her question. "What did people think then?

"Some said he'd scarpered with the loot. Anyway, searches were organized. They combed the village, the beach, and the clifftops for days without finding anything."

"Giving credence to the running off story?" Ramsay asked.

"Exactly. It became known the business was struggling, catches were down, and debts were due. There seemed every reason to believe he'd taken what he could and made a run for it. I believe Percy Storm alerted the police at ports and airports to apprehend Mr. Peacock, if he should try and leave the country."

"It seems the village has been a hotbed of upsetting events and talk these past years," Ramsay said.

"Oh no," Mrs. Golightly cried. "I wouldn't want you to

think that. It's just village gossip and there's always plenty of that. No, no, nothing ever happens here."

"If I wanted to speak to the two opposing groups of fishermen," Ramsay began, "who would you recommend I speak to? I'm looking for a sensible spokesman to give their side of the story."

"That's not an easy question to answer, Mr. Ramsay. There was a lot of anger at the time. Of the men who wouldn't continue with Harry Peacock's boats, I'd say, John Robinson. He's a steady, quiet man who thinks. For those who stayed on, I don't know. They're the sort who enjoy fighting in pubs after a few drinks." She shook her head, "I can't say who you should talk to, and that's a fact."

"What about Mr. Armstrong? What do people think about him?"

She frowned. "He's a man who doesn't join in village life and what little anyone can say of him is he doesn't seem a nice man. However, Harry Peacock was much the same sort of character and we got along with him for nigh on fifty years."

Ramsay laughed. "Businesspeople, particularly successful ones, are rarely the life and soul of any party and they often struggle to behave in ways that lead to friendships. Does anyone know anything real about him?"

"They say he was pressing Harry for money. Repayment for some of the loan, you understand," Mrs. Golightly said.

"He too may have bills to pay," Ramsay said, thoughtfully, wondering if he dared phone his old colleague Morrison for background on Armstrong so soon after promising not to do it again at the end of the kidnapping case in the Lake District.

Mrs. Golightly nodded. "Bills are the one true constant

in life, I find. If it wasn't for bills, I wouldn't have any correspondence to speak of."

"I can confirm that experience," Ramsay said. "My pension check arrives, I put it in the bank, and then I write cheques to pay for the bills that roll in every day. By the end, I've little to show for my years of work and my mailbox has nothing in it I want to read."

"You have no remaining family?"

"There are some Ramsay's back home in Scotland, or at least that's where they were when last I knew of them. I haven't seen or heard from them since before the war. My parents are both gone and my wife and children too."

Mrs. Golightly sympathized. "I have children. One lives in London and one in Coventry. It's where the work is and I'm glad they have good jobs, but they're both boys and not regular correspondents. They phone occasionally, of course, but telephone calls are so expensive, aren't they?"

Ramsay smiled. "They are, indeed. I've learned a lot more from our chat, Mrs. Golightly. Thank you for that. I hope to meet Mr. Danesdale tomorrow; Eliza has promised me she'll have him here at seven in the morning. He may have a suggestion on who to talk to."

"A nice man, Mr. Danesdale, but not a very strong one," she replied. "I hear he's struggling to work with the new owner, Armstrong. He'll likely be laid off soon."

"Maybe that will mean he'll talk freely," Ramsay said, rising to his feet. "Thanks again for the tea and chat but it's time for Bracken's evening stroll, followed quickly by my bedtime."

If Eliza's dad is frightened for his job, will that make him more, or less, willing to talk, Ramsay wondered as he and Bracken wandered the quiet lane that ran beside the rail station. If there was friction between Armstrong and Peacock, Eliza's father would be the one to know, but would he say?

7

THIRD INTERVIEW

NEXT MORNING AT SIX-THIRTY, Ramsay and Bracken were outside the guest house trying to look like dog and walker, and not a sleuth waiting for Eliza and her father to appear, which they finally did.

"We can't talk outside," Mr. Danesdale said, after he was introduced to Ramsay. "Someone is sure to see."

"We'll go to my room," Ramsay replied, looking about them. The street was empty of people, too early for workers to be heading out, Ramsay imagined.

"What is it you want to know?" Mr. Danesdale whispered, when they were in Ramsay's room with the door firmly closed.

"You're concerned if Mrs. Golightly hears us?" Ramsay asked, quietly.

"My position at Ravenscar Fishing is hanging by a thread," Danesdale replied. "I'd rather no one knew we talked and certainly nothing of what we said."

Ramsay nodded. He saw why Mrs. Golightly called Eliza's father a 'weak man.' He was slender, stooped and gray, the result of a lifetime hunched over a desk and books, no doubt. Even his face, which would normally be weather-beaten in this northern coastal village, was gray, lined, and his expression depressed. He seemed to be trembling and that too was suggestive. Had Eliza bullied him into coming to speak to Ramsay? He glanced at her, but she seemed comfortable enough to meet his gaze. He hoped she couldn't divine his thoughts about her father.

"As I'm sure Eliza has told you," Ramsay began, "I'm interested in what happened to Harry Peacock."

"And as I told Elizabeth," Danesdale interjected, "that's police business and no one else's."

"Quite right," Ramsay said, casting a warning glance at Eliza to prevent her angrily closing her father down. "And I will, of course, inform the police of any findings but you know, I find that once you start along the path of solving crimes, it's almost impossible to cure yourself of it. I'm just too involved to stand idly by you see."

"I don't want my daughter placed in any danger, Mr. Ramsay," Danesdale said, in what was the firmest voice he'd used since they began speaking.

"I don't either," Ramsay said, "between you and me, I'll see she goes nowhere near danger. Strictly, running errands or researching in the local library, I promise."

Eliza looked about to explode but before she could speak, her father said, "We don't have a library, only a library van that comes around on Thursdays."

Ramsay was pleased to see Eliza had decided to say nothing, but he had no doubt he'd hear more about it when they were next alone.

"You say your job is hanging by a thread," Ramsay said, "is that because the fishing business isn't doing well?"

"Partly," Danesdale said, "and also I get the sense Mr.

Armstrong may sell the boats and business to get his money out and maybe even make a profit."

"I see," Ramsay said, nodding. "You don't think he's committed to Ravenscar Fishing?"

"I'm sure he's not. I can't help feeling he loaned Harry the money to buy that last boat so he could get control of the company, which makes me suspicious about Harry's death."

"Don't you think that would be too obvious?" Ramsay asked.

"I know what you mean but he loaned the money, took a fifty percent share in the business and now he's in control."

"Who did Harry leave his fifty percent to?" Ramsay asked.

"I don't know," Danesdale replied, wringing his hands in apprehension of his future.

"Can you find out?

Danesdale shook his head. "His will isn't in the office, I've looked. It must be at his home or at his lawyers, Martin and Son in Whitby."

"I'm sure the police have already been there," Ramsay said, "so we may know soon enough. If he left it to Armstrong, then there's nothing to be done. The company is his to do as he pleases with."

Danesdale nodded miserably. "That's what I fear."

"Has he said anything to you about the future?"

"Only that the catches aren't coming in and economies will have to be made," Danesdale said. "He means me, of course."

"Are the revenues down so much?"

"Not really," Danesdale said. "They fell when Harry stopped going out on the boats, of course, but they haven't grown any worse than that."

"Why did Harry stop fishing?" Ramsay asked. "It seems out of character."

Danesdale looked perplexed. "I asked him, and he said it was time. Only, the man he brought in to replace himself showed up the next day, which means Harry had already hired him without telling me or anyone."

"Would he normally tell you?"

"I do the payroll," Danesdale said, "and all the hiring documents. It was a scramble to have them ready before he sailed that night, I can tell you."

Knowing men like Harry, this sudden hiring may be significant of something or only a whim, Ramsay thought, before saying, "You said earlier Armstrong might want to sell off the boats. Is the company in such poor shape?"

Danesdale shook his head. "It's getting by as things stand, only it wouldn't sell for much as a going concern. He might sell the business, but more likely the boats."

"Would he make money doing that?"

"He only put in money to buy the one boat, *Ravenscar Lady 4*, so all the others would be pure profit."

"If I wanted to speak to one of the crew members," Ramsay asked, "who would be the most reasonable to talk to?"

"None of them," Danesdale replied, even more quietly and glancing at the door. "But if you must talk to one of them, choose Thornton Duck. He's been with the company all along. He keeps his head down and says nothing but, if you talked to him away from the village, he might be more forthcoming."

Ramsay glanced at his watch as he could see Danesdale's knees were twitching so much even with his hands on them he couldn't hide his trepidation. "I know you have to get to work but is there anything you can think of that might shed some light on what happened to Harry Peacock?"

Danesdale shook his head.

"For instance, do you remember the last time you spoke to him? Was it the day he disappeared?"

"It was," Danesdale said. "When he stopped fishing, he began coming into the office every day. That day, Harry told me he was going to the bank in Whitby. That's why, when I informed Constable Storm, the rumors started about him running away with the company's cash."

"Did that seem likely to you?"

Danesdale shook his head. "There wasn't a lot of money in the account. He would have had to have some pressing reason to run that day when we were expecting our money from Pilgrims Limited, the company we sell most of our fish to, on the following day."

"What time was that; do you remember?"

"About nine o'clock," Danesdale replied. "He planned to get the nine-thirty train, getting to the bank early enough for it to be quiet."

Ramsay pondered this. He could ask the stationmaster if Harry got on the train that day only, he was sure Constable Storm would have done that already. Maybe Storm would tell him, or would he tell Eliza in casual conversation -- not knowing Eliza was Ramsay's sleuthing sidekick?

"One more thing," Ramsay began, "did Harry ever mention his son?"

Danesdale's expression grew even more distraught. "He didn't like what he heard from Arthur, whenever they spoke on the phone. Arthur boasted of what sounded like orgies, though I can't believe half of what Harry described."

"Was he going to cut Arthur out of his will over this behavior?"

Danesdale shook his head. "Harry and Arthur didn't see eye-to-eye, but Harry believed in family. He once said to me that Arthur would settle down when he had the business to run."

"Had he told Arthur this?"

"I don't know," Danesdale replied. "He might have done. Then I imagine he wouldn't need to. There was only Arthur to leave it to, until Armstrong came along."

"Hmmm," Ramsay began, only to be stopped by Danesdale.

"I have to go, Mr. Ramsay," Danesdale said, rising from the chair. "Being late may be enough to push Armstrong to fire me."

"I'll stay," Eliza said, as her father was leaving. "I'm sure Mr. Ramsay has some ideas to follow up on."

When Danesdale was safely out of the house, Ramsay began, "Could you..."

"Never mind that," Eliza cried, "what's this 'research in the library' rubbish?"

"We had to re-assure your father," Ramsay said, grinning. "Now, could you find out from Constable Storm if Harry Peacock got the train that day?"

"We already know," Eliza said, distracted from the rant she'd planned to deliver. "There are no secrets where Percy Storm and his missus are concerned."

"And?"

"He didn't," Eliza said. "So far as Percy knows, my dad was the last person to see Peacock alive."

"Nobody saw Peacock walking from the office up to the station?" Ramsay asked. "It's a narrow road with houses on both sides?"

Eliza shook her head. "Nobody claims to have seen him."

Ramsay was thoughtful. "How confident are you that Constable Storm was telling the truth about what he knew and how much was conjecture by Mrs. Storm?"

Eliza laughed. "You won't have to be here very much longer to know how easily the Storm's talk about everything, no matter how secret it's supposed to be."

"Now we need to know when he was killed," Ramsay said. "Was it that day or later?"

"Your question about him being seen," Eliza said. "He should have been. Unless he didn't go up through the village but down to the beach and on to the tunnel."

Ramsay nodded. "He wouldn't have to go far along the beach before, to an observer, he was just another man out walking."

"Still, you'd think someone would see him," Eliza said. "I wonder if Percy asked that?"

"He didn't know about the tunnel and nor did anyone else, apparently."

"If Harry was killed there, someone knew," Eliza replied.

"We don't know he was killed there, and I don't see Inspector Baldock sharing that information with me," Ramsay said, ruefully.

"So, it's all down to me grilling Percy to share the dope," Eliza said, putting on an excruciatingly awful American accent.

"If what you just said means you're going to engage Constable Storm in harmless conversation about what's happening, then yes. It's your first serious assignment."

"Like Mata Hari, I'll use my feminine wiles to get the truth out of him," Eliza said, lapsing now into cinema speech. She was clearly relishing the chance to play the world-weary spy.

"Don't do anything to make him suspicious," Ramsay pleaded. "Just be the Eliza he knows and loves."

"Loves!" Eliza cried. "He took me into custody when I protested the treatment of local donkeys. That's how much he loves me."

"And then it was the rack and thumbscrews at the police house, I'm guessing," Ramsay said, sarcastically. He'd heard these tales before.

Eliza reddened. "Well, tea and scones with Mrs. Storm actually, but still, it shows I'm not beloved by Percy."

Ramsay shook his head, smiling. "Just be yourself to either of the Storms and find out when Harry was killed and if anyone saw someone who looked like Harry on the beach that day."

HAVING SET his assistant off to investigate, Ramsay and Bracken walked out, following the cliff path they'd taken the afternoon before. It was a clear day and Ramsay could see the Raven Hall Hotel on the clifftop at Ravenscar across the bay as if it were nearby. In the bay, some small fishing boats were working, and, on the beach, he could see dog walkers and a couple of hikers. He stopped, much to Bracken's disgust. That rabbit was still around, he could smell it.

"I wonder what sort of day it was that day," Ramsay said to Bracken. "Could someone enjoying the view from that bench I see ahead of us, have seen Harry on the beach? If they knew him, of course.

"And," Ramsay continued, "if there is smuggling going on, surely anyone up here could see where those trawlers land the goods if it isn't at the slipway?"

Bracken gave him a look that said: 'Can't you walk *and* talk? Or is it one or the other?'

Ramsay took the hint and carried on walking. "I don't see how it's done, the smuggling I mean. They have nowhere to offload the contraband other than at the slipway and Constable Storm says he's inspected their catch being offloaded and there was nothing but fish."

He continued turning the problem over in his mind as they walked on to the point and gazed out into the wide-open spaces of the North Sea.

8

ASSISTANT BEGINS INVESTIGATING

As she left Ramsay's guest house, Eliza considered her task. Would Percy or Percy's wife, Hilda, be her best hope? She wandered down the steep street into the heart of the village still wondering how she could 'accidentally' bump into either of them. She passed the police house as she walked and carefully scanned the building for signs of life. It was still early and there were none. On the positive side, however, there was no sign of police cars so the mob from Whitby and Scarborough were gone, or not yet arrived for the day. Should she take advantage of their being absent to talk her way into the Storm's house and start casually questioning them. She suspected this wouldn't work and carried on her way to the bottom of the street and the Ravenscar Fishing offices where she could ask her father for advice.

In the end, all Eliza's pondering was unneeded. She saw Constable Storm coming out of the office where her father was already at work.

"Hello, Constable Storm," Eliza hailed him as he seemed not to have noticed her presence.

"Oh, hello, Eliza," Storm replied. He appeared pre-occupied. "Going to see your dad?"

"I am. Were you?"

"Yes," Storm said, unhelpfully.

"More questions about that fateful last day," Eliza said, humorously.

"Yes," Storm said, still so preoccupied he hardly noticed Eliza had fallen into step with him.

"Like why no one saw old Harry going to the station or along the beach to the place his body was found?"

"Exactly," Storm responded. "Your father's office has a window that looks right along the beach. If he'd looked out, he surely would have seen Harry."

Eliza snorted. "Dad never looks up from those ledgers. It's why he's so stooped."

Storm nodded, his expression grim. "That's what he told me." He clearly didn't relish passing that back to his superiors.

"Have they determined when old Harry died?" Eliza asked. "Was it that day?"

"No, they haven't, and I couldn't tell you if they had," Storm said, suddenly coming out of the reverie and realizing who he was talking to.

Eliza nodded sympathetically. "I understand. It's only, when I think about it, if it was that day then Harry left the office around nine and was killed soon after. It sounds to me like he was going to do something that someone didn't want him to do. Investigate at the bank, maybe, or if he was using the tunnels as a place for secret papers, look through them."

"You shouldn't be thinking about this at all," Storm said.

"Oh, come on," Eliza cried. "Everyone in the village is thinking and talking about this — ever since the body was discovered."

"It's police business," Storm said, stiffly. "Anyway, you can't know what everyone is talking about."

"Not everyone, no, but everyone who came into our teashop is," Eliza replied. "They think with all those scientific tests you have nowadays, you should know to the hour when Harry died and that narrows it down, you see."

"The scientists can't give anything like that kind of precision," Storm said. "They can only give a range."

"Does the range include the day he disappeared?"

Storm nodded but said nothing.

"Then I'm betting he was killed only hours after he left the office, minutes maybe," Eliza said, excitedly, "and that means someone will have seen who followed Harry to the tunnel."

"Settle down, Eliza, lass. You're not police. Your opinion isn't driving this investigation."

"I should be police," Eliza said. "I could get more out of our fellow villagers in a day than you and those folks from Scarborough will."

"You wouldn't if you were the police," Storm said, gloomily. "People forget things when police ask."

Eliza nodded. "You're right. I'm better investigating on my own. Somebody must have seen Harry and his killer walking on the beach that day. I'll ask about."

"If the killer is here in the village, asking will get you murdered," Storm said. "You leave this to the police."

"Oh, I won't ask questions," Eliza said, airily, "I'll just chatter on like I usually do. And listen to the replies, of course. Nobody will think I'm investigating. See you." Eliza turned and made her way back to the slipway.

The time was approaching nine o'clock and the morning was a bright one. Was it a bright morning that day? She had to find out. Maybe no one saw anything because it was foggy. It often was in late summer. She stared along the beach. She could see Mrs. Turner with her two Scotties, and Mr. Wilson with his golden Labrador. A quiet day on the beach. As she turned, she saw a middle-aged couple in hiking gear studying a map and eating what looked like pasties from the nearby café that served the fishermen.

"It looks a nice day for your walk," Eliza said, smiling at the couple as they made their way past her heading for the sand.

"We hope so," the woman replied. "It wouldn't do to get stuck in the rain halfway and have the tide coming in."

"It wouldn't," Eliza agreed. "We had a man and his dog caught halfway recently. They found an old tunnel and a body."

The woman shuddered. "We read about that. In a way, it's why we're here. We've often looked over the bay, from the Ravenscar side, and thought it would be nice to walk the whole beach. When we saw it on the television news, we decided to do it."

Eliza was disappointed. "You've never walked it before then."

The man shook his head. "Today will change all that."

They walked down the slipway, onto the rocks, jumped down onto the sand, and were soon striding away south.

"I suppose it was too much to hope they walked the beach every day," Eliza muttered to herself as she headed back up New Street in search of Ramsay. She stopped, turned, and went to visit her father.

Eliza quietly opened the door into the Ravenscar Fishing building and peeked inside. Her father was, as she'd told Storm, hunched over the ledger in front of him.

"Dad," she called, "can I ask you a question?"

"What are you doing here?"

"My morning constitutional before I go and start setting tables," Eliza said. "What was the weather like that morning when Harry disappeared?"

"If you got up early, you'd know," her father replied sternly. "It was a foggy morning down here in the bay, but the sun came out by mid-morning. A nice day. Lots of holiday-makers on the beach in the afternoon."

"Thanks," Eliza said. "See you later, alligator." She closed the door grinning. Her father hated all those modern, trendy phrases.

* * *

ELIZA WAS WAITING at the entrance to the clifftop path when Ramsay and Bracken reached it, returning from their walk to Ness Point.

"Shouldn't you be at work?" Ramsay asked, as they grew nearer.

"You sound like my dad," Eliza said, grinning. "When I've told you what I learned, I'll go right there. We don't open until eleven at this time of year."

"What did you learn?" Ramsay asked.

Eliza rather breathlessly told him of her conversations with Storm and her father. She ended with a triumphant, "Well?"

Ramsay smiled. "Yes, you've done well. Clever idea of mine to recruit you as my assistant."

"What?" Eliza cried.

Ramsay laughed. "All right," he conceded, "you volunteered. It does help us see now how Harry could seemingly vanish and it does look as if he might have been killed that same day. Your father didn't mention an argument with his partner before Harry left but I think there must have been something of the sort."

"It may have been on the telephone," Eliza suggested. "Then Harry hung up and went off to find the evidence he needed. Armstrong, realizing Harry was onto him, hurried down from where he was staying and confronted Harry at the tunnel."

"Harry must have told him where it was, if that's the case," Ramsay said, "but you may be right. The dispute could have been quiet and on the phone. There's another possibility."

"What?"

"His argument was with his son, who drove to somewhere he could park and climb down to the tunnel. That way, no one would see him here in the village."

"We don't know where Harry's son lives," Eliza said. "He might be in London, for all we know."

"Or he might be nearby, keeping tabs on his inheritance," Ramsay countered.

"I'll ask everyone local who comes into the teashop today."

"And I'll find ex-Inspector Pritchard. He might give me the background on the local force here, if he's as innocent as he claimed," Ramsay said.

"And if he isn't?"

"I still may learn something," Ramsay said. "What people tell the police is often a clue to the good and bad, and both are kind of recommendation."

Eliza was puzzled. "Do you think it's wise to visit, Pritchard? If Baldock hears of it, it will confirm his suspicions of you."

"I know it's risky," Ramsay replied, "but he's one of the

few people here who can tell me what I want to know. I'll have to hope Baldock doesn't hear of my visits."

Eliza didn't look happier but said, "We should get together and exchange what we've learned tonight,"

"I agree," Ramsay said, "though not at The Seaview Hotel this time."

"Scrooge," Eliza said, grinning. "You could just buy me a Babycham at their bar. I have another dress I want to wear. I promise there are only the two dresses," she added with that winsome smile that lit up her face.

Ramsay groaned. "I'll pick you up at seven-thirty and we'll walk down together."

"No matter what anyone says, you are a gentleman," Eliza replied, walking away.

"Sorry, Bracken," Ramsay said. "You're keeping Mrs. Golightly company again tonight. I wish there were other guests staying. I feel like I'm lodging in someone's private house."

Bracken maintained a dignified silence.

"Are you fit for another long walk?" Ramsay asked.

Bracken jumped to his feet and thought: 'This is more like it.'

"We're going along the clifftops the other way this time, Bracken," Ramsay said. "I want to see if we can get down to the tunnel from a trail above."

9

RAMSAY AND BRACKEN INVESTIGATE

It was an hour's walk along narrow trails created by only a handful of feet. Fortunately, summer was gone and so were the insects Ramsay knew would have pounced on him from the tall grass and ferns on both sides of the path. Poor Bracken walked the whole way in shade, and it wasn't a warm day.

At a place he judged to be directly above the tunnel, Ramsay stopped and studied the steep slope down to the clifftop. The grasses and ferns were wet, and he could see himself slipping straight down the hillside and over the cliff. It wasn't a comfortable thought.

"We're going to be slow and steady for the next bit, Bracken," Ramsay said. "And I'm going to hold onto anything I can as we go."

Step by step, Ramsay made his way down, clinging onto ferns or bilberry bushes as he went. At the edge, he peered over the cliff and down to the beach. He wasn't directly over the entrance, as he'd imagined, but fifty feet past it. Slowly, he made his way back along the edge to where he knew the entrance to be.

"There's no way down here, Bracken," he said, looking along the edge to the north and south. "Maybe it's somewhere nearby. It wasn't the way we've just come so let's go on further this way."

Bracken, whose sure-footed pads had no difficulty on the wet vegetation was happy to continue and promptly set off, tugging Ramsay's right arm and giving Ramsay a minor heart attack.

"Not so fast, my friend," Ramsay said, as he too began moving cautiously along the cliff edge.

Finally, he found what he'd come for. A landslide, years ago, had brought down part of the cliff and there was a steep vegetation-covered ramp of rock and earth leading down to the sand below. Ramsay remembered seeing it on the fateful day, only it hadn't registered.

"It looks do-able," Ramsay said to Bracken, "by you, at least."

Bracken yawned. He couldn't see why they were waiting.

"I'll chance it, Bracken, but it's up to you to find the safest way down."

Ramsay covered the remaining distance along the clifftop and then studied the ramp. There was a three-foot drop and then solid earth. He sat on the wet turf and stretched out one leg until he felt his foot touch the ramp. It seemed solid enough, so he slid off the cliff and landed gently onto the ledge which was the highest point of the way down. Turning, he gathered up the now anxious Bracken in his arms and lowered him gently to the ramp.

"On we go," Ramsay said, as he gingerly took his first step. The ramp was even steeper than the hillside had been, and it was only ten feet wide at this point. He continued, crouching, gripping tightly to anything solid as he and Bracken slowly made their way to the beach. Soon he was halfway, the ramp was wider and the slope not so steep. If he fell now, he had hopes of surviving. It was a cold day but sweat beaded his brow as he continued. He looked for signs that others had passed this way but all he could see was litter among the low grasses and shrubs, and it could have been blown there at any time.

Ramsay jumped the last four feet to the sand and Bracken followed. "We made it," Ramsay said, "and if we can, a younger man can. And a younger man could make it down and back up again. We need to know where Harry's son is living."

They set off at a brisk pace heading for Robin Hood's Bay. "It's time I spoke to Constable Storm again," Ramsay told Bracken. "If he'll talk to me."

* * *

CONSTABLE STORM WAS at home having lunch, when Ramsay knocked on the police house door. The door opened, Storm saw who it was and said, urgently, "Come in. Don't let them see you." He practically hauled Ramsay through the doorway.

"It's nice to be made welcome," Ramsay said, with a grin, when the door was shut behind them.

"Not entirely welcome," Storm said, leading the way through the house to the kitchen at the back. "You can leave by that door," Storm said, pointing to a door leading out into a small garden, "if we have visitors."

"I only want to know where ex-Inspector Pritchard and Harry's son live now," Ramsay said, "then I'll be gone."

"Inspector Pritchard lives just outside the village on Station Road," Storm said. "He had to leave Whitby when it all happened."

"And Harry's son?"

"He went right away for a time," Storm said, "then came back. Local folk can't abide big cities and nine-to-five jobs, you see."

"And?"

"Oh, he lives over Ravenscar way, in a bungalow along School House Road. You can't miss it. It's the one right at the end where the road becomes nothing but a track."

"I see," Ramsay said, thoughtfully. "Both are within easy walking distance of the tunnel."

"Aye," Storm said. "Not quick though. An hour, at least for both."

Ramsay explained about his recent discovery of the ramp.

"It's hardly a discovery Mr. Ramsay," Storm said. "Lots of folks use it to get back and forth to the village, rather than going around the bay. Across the sands at low tide is much quicker."

"I didn't see much evidence of regular use on the ramp," Ramsay said, rather cross that his discovery was being pooh-poohed.

"You wouldn't. It's late in the season and wet underfoot. Folks here have more sense than to use it after summer is over."

"Have you Pritchard's address?" Ramsay asked, not willing to discuss the sense required to climb down steep slopes when it was wet underfoot.

Storm tore a page from a notepad and wrote it out.

"Thanks. We'll leave by the back way," Ramsay said, lifting the latch.

"Be sure to look before you step out onto the street," Storm said. "Baldock and his boys don't like me much and speaking to you would lead to unpleasantness."

"Why don't they like you?" Ramsay asked, pausing just outside the door.

"Inspector Pritchard and I worked together on a case about six years ago," Storm said, "before everything that happened blew up. I liked him and I don't believe he was in the pay of smugglers."

Ramsay nodded. "That's good to know. I like to hear both sides of a story. I liaised with him on a Newcastle smuggling case that we thought had a Whitby link. I couldn't believe what was said about him either."

Remembering his instructions, Ramsay and Bracken made sure no one was on the street before walking quickly out of the garden and into the street. As they made their way up, Ramsay said, "We can't walk to Ravenscar today, but we can call in on Station Road, after we have some tea in Eliza's teashop."

Bracken's disappointment was soon swept aside when Eliza, who quickly cleared them a small table near a window, brought him water and meat scraps, which he wolfed down greedily.

Eliza took her notepad from her shirt pocket, licked the pencil tip and asked Ramsay, "What would you like, sir?"

Ramsay smiled as he read from the menu, "A pot of tea and a selection of High Tea treats."

Eliza wrote down his order and said, softly, "I have news."

There were only two elderly couples in the teashop, and they looked deaf to Ramsay, so he answered in his normal voice, "So have I."

The quick glance one of the women gave him, told him that she, at least, wasn't deaf. He decided whispering would be better when Eliza returned.

Bracken was already looking hungrily around the room

when Eliza arrived back with a tray, saying, "High Tea for thee and 'low tea' for your companion." She put another plate of scraps on the floor that Bracken immediately pounced on.

With Bracken busy, Eliza sat on the chair opposite Ramsay. "Your old colleague Pritchard lives here in the village," she began.

"I know," Ramsay replied. "I spoke to Constable Storm."

"And I know where Harry's son lives as well," Eliza continued. "I can take you to both places."

"I know that as well. We may have to phone Harry's son," Ramsay replied. "It's too far to walk in the times you have available. I plan to visit Pritchard after my afternoon tea."

"I want to come too," Eliza cried, making both couples in the café look at her.

"It will be best if I make the initial contact," Ramsay said, quietly. "It might be uncomfortable at first and you being there would likely make it stay that way."

"I'm good with people," Eliza objected.

"I can see that," Ramsay said, "only this is different. He's an elderly man who was thrown out of a position he loved. Even my being there may be too much of a reminder. If he's important to the case, you'll meet him soon enough."

"Still..." Eliza pleaded.

Ramsay shook his head. "I'll make this initial contact while you continue here keeping the family business afloat. I fear your dad is right about his job and you'll all need this teashop to survive."

"Do you think Mr. Pritchard was wrongly dismissed?" Eliza asked.

"I don't know but I'm going there to give him a sympathetic hearing," Ramsay replied. "If he was wrongly accused, maybe those who are guilty are still active in the smuggling and police business."

Eliza said, "He's kept himself very much to himself since moving to the village. I didn't know who he was."

"He doesn't frequent your family teashop," Ramsay said, "but that isn't surprising for a single man."

"What's wrong with our teashop?" Eliza cried, indignantly.

Ramsay laughed. "Eliza, there are flowers and frills everywhere, including the crockery. A man may go in with his wife but not alone. People would begin to talk."

"I suppose," Eliza said, ruefully. "We are a bit feminine." She paused before asking, "What if he *is* the leader of smuggling in this region? Your visiting him will condemn you if he's ever arrested."

"It's a chance I have to take," Ramsay replied. "However, I'm not convinced he's the leader of a criminal gang. Not convinced yet, anyway."

Eliza nodded. "All right. But I want a full report of the interview when we meet tonight."

"Certainly, madam," Ramsay said, laughing. "Anything you say madam."

Eliza looked mutinous. "We're partners," she grumbled. "I should know what you know."

Ramsay nodded. "You will, when I know it. Now, after I finish my cuppa, I'm off. See you tonight."

10

RAMSAY CHECKS AN OLD CASE

RAMSAY FOUND THE BUNGALOW, an older home surrounded by a well-maintained garden and good fences. Pritchard might just be obsessive about his garden or keen to make approaching his house difficult for intruders.

"You may have to investigate his garden while we chat," Ramsay said to Bracken sitting at his feet. "*If* we chat, of course."

He rang the doorbell and waited. The opaque glass in the door showed a man approaching. Ramsay wondered if this entrance style was another way to ensure Pritchard knew who he was opening the door to.

The door opened and Ramsay said, with a welcoming smile, "Remember me, Len?"

Pritchard nodded. "I read your name in today's paper. I thought I'd get a visit sooner or later."

"Yes," Ramsay said, "I wish they'd said 'visitor' and not splashed my name all over the article. It'll make me even less popular with Inspector Baldock than I already am."

"Any enemy of his, is a friend of mine," Pritchard said,

grinning. "Come in. I'll pour us a drink. Whisky is still your tipple?"

"If it's Scotch," Ramsay said, as he followed Pritchard through the house to a room filled with afternoon sunshine.

"Is there any other kind?" Pritchard asked. "Take a seat and I'll get you a glass. I still drink the Glenfiddich you taught me to drink; I hope you haven't changed."

"I haven't changed in that or almost anything else," Ramsay replied, then deciding the direct way would be best, asked, "How is retirement suiting you?"

"It's dreadful," Pritchard said, bringing Ramsay a generously filled glass, "However, as they say about old age, it's better than the alternative."

"I was invalided out, against my wishes," Ramsay responded. "You were treated even worse, I hear."

Pritchard nodded. "You know what the bomber pilots used to say in the war, 'the flak is heaviest when you're over the target.' Well, I was clearly over the target only I didn't know it. By the time I did, I was out."

"You didn't stay in Whitby where you could keep watch?"

"I did for a while, but things happened; windows were broken, my garden shed spontaneously combusted, and so on. I thought it best to leave."

"You didn't travel far," Ramsay said. "Five or six miles at most."

"I'm from this part of the world, everyone I know lives within twenty miles of here. Where else could I go?" He laughed, and added, "Also, my pension doesn't cover gracious Riviera living."

"Are you still keeping watch?"

Pritchard shook his head. "No. When I decided to move, I decided to let it go. I'd have ended up with ulcers or a heart attack, if I didn't. Now I live for my garden and coach and rail tours of the country."

Ramsay was disappointed but did his best to hide it. "I wondered if you could give me background on what you were working on when it happened?"

"I can do that all right," Pritchard said. "The details are burned into my brain. I keep thinking, if only I'd got to them first. It's no use now. Too many years have passed."

"It's only three or four," Ramsay reminded him. "I'm sure the personnel haven't changed too much in that time."

Pritchard nodded but his expression became more serious. "Look, Tom, I understand why you're here and I appreciate you taking such an understanding approach, but it makes me suspicious. Why are you being so understanding?"

"Probably because my situation, while not nearly as unpleasant, has made me more open to seeing what I might have missed before. They didn't have to kick me out; we had men working at our station who'd also been injured in the line of duty. They were offered alternatives. I wasn't. Now as it happens, I'm enjoying being a free man so I'm not seeking revenge, but you see what I mean?"

"From what I hear you haven't stopped being a detective," Pritchard said, "so it may not have hit you yet. When it does, you'll be bitter, as I was. It wasn't the vandalism of my property that hurt, it was how the police, my ex-colleagues behaved that hurt. Their obvious pleasure at the attacks made me sober up quickly. Made me wonder if it wasn't them that carried out the vandalism, in fact"

"Moving to less painful subjects," Ramsay said. "We didn't find what I was looking for when I came to Whitby all those years ago. I remember you saying you wouldn't let it go. I presume, it's why they did what they did. Who was it you were closing in on when your colleagues set you up, if that's what happened?"

"I shouldn't need to say this to you, it *is what happened*."

Ramsay nodded. "When Inspector Baldock was threatening me with possible retribution for something I'd done before I'd even arrived here, he told me about you and when and why you were pushed out, I realized it must have been something like that."

"I think he's part of it."

Ramsay laughed. "That was exactly my thought when he was interviewing me."

"I'm serious. He's an unpleasant man even away from work. And he's always on the local smuggling cases but no one is ever arrested for them."

"Still, incompetence could explain his failures," Ramsay said. "People who know they're not good at their jobs are often aggressive toward people they see as a threat."

Pritchard shook his head. "There's more than that behind it. He wasn't the only one I thought might be involved. My old boss, he's dead now, was pally with Baldock and he too liked to be part of any smuggling investigations."

"How did he die? He can't have been so old."

"Car accident," Pritchard said. "Another reason I decided to move away and forget everything."

"A car accident right at the time you thought you were getting close, how coincidental."

"The accident checked out. There was no hint of anything criminal, only the timing it happened alarmed me. And, to what you just said, I didn't think I was getting close. It was only after that I realized I must have been, but at the time I was as frustrated by my lack of progress as I'd ever been."

"All right, who were the people you were watching when you thought you were getting nowhere?"

Pritchard sighed. "Tom, are you linking Harry's death to that smuggling case from years ago?"

"Not directly, Len," Ramsay replied. "Only, if the smugglers haven't been caught and there is still smuggling going on, wouldn't it seem likely the same characters are involved? After all, you and I are still here. Why not them?"

Pritchard nodded, though he seemed unconvinced. "The names I've mentioned, Baldock and my boss, Featherstone. Baldock was an up-and-coming youngster in Whitby then and very pally with Featherstone. To be honest, I wasn't certain I wasn't just suspicious of them because they kept leaving me out of the loop."

Ramsay smiled. "We all know those kinds of doubts."

"Not 'all of us.' Too many haven't the self-awareness to question their own motives," Pritchard commented.

Ramsay nodded. "Perhaps 'all' was a bit too broad a term. Was it just those two? What about boat owners and crews?"

"The Hornbeams in Whitby and Harry Peacock in Bay. Both seemed to do better than anyone else was doing, and I'm talking here of keeping their boats at sea and building their fleets. I don't know anything about their catches."

"Did you start watching Harry when you moved to Bay?"

Pritchard shook his head. "I told you. I came to my senses."

"Pity. I'd like to know more about our murder victim."

"The police's murder victim, Tom. Don't fall foul of Baldock; he's not a nice man to have as an enemy."

"He's already told me that," Ramsay replied, ruefully. "I let him get under my skin during the interview and gave him back what he gave me. I thought at the time his anger was suspiciously over-the-top if he was an innocent man."

Pritchard laughed, bitterly. "His anger is never far from the surface so you shouldn't read too much into that."

"Nevertheless, I need to solve this puzzle before he pins it on me," Ramsay responded. "I was hoping your knowledge might help me do that."

"My knowledge, such as it is, is at your service, Tom, but not me. I'm staying well out of it."

"Then fill up my empty glass, Len, and fill up my empty brain right after," Ramsay said, holding out the empty whisky glass. "And is it all right if my dog goes out into your garden? He likes to be outside."

"He can go out if he wants. I'll open the French windows," Pritchard said. "We could walk in the garden too, if you've a mind to."

Ramsay grinned. "I'll sit here a while longer. It's a good hike from my guest house to here."

"Are you sitting comfortably, Tom," Pritchard said, grinning, as he recited the opening lines from the BBC radio program *Listen with Mother*. "Then I'll begin."

Ramsay listened intently as Pritchard recounted what he'd learned of the smuggling operations and what he was doing to catch the smugglers in the act when he was suddenly thrown out of the force.

As he and Bracken stepped through Pritchard's garden gate and out into the lane, Ramsay saw Constable Storm standing motionless at the junction of Station and Whitby roads. Storm saw them and watched as they approached.

"Good afternoon, Constable," Ramsay greeted the man

brightly. Storm's expression suggested he had something serious to impart. "A better afternoon, weather-wise."

"Indeed, sir," Storm replied, portentously. He drew himself up straight and continued, "I have a message from Inspector Baldock."

"He's inviting me for tea?" Ramsay asked, grinning.

"No, sir. He's learned that you are making inquiries into the death of Harry Peacock and he's asked me to tell you to stop. If his case is harmed by your interference, he will prosecute you to the full extent of the law."

"He told me much the same thing the first time we met," Ramsay responded. "However, I'll take your caution into consideration, Constable. Thank you, and good day." Ramsay walked on with Bracken looking longingly back at Storm.

"It's no good, Bracken," Ramsay said. "You and I won't likely be invited back to the police house any time soon."

* * *

AS HE'D PROMISED, just before seven-thirty that evening Ramsay arrived at the door of Eliza's home and knocked. Bracken was once again left behind entertaining Mrs. Golightly. The older woman Ramsay recognized from the teashop answered the door.

"Hello, I'm Tom Ramsay," he said, smiling.

"I know who you are," the woman said. "You'd better come in for a minute. We had a small wardrobe issue that's just been sorted out. Elizabeth won't be long now."

"I'm sorry I don't know your name," Ramsay said. "Eliza just calls you 'mam.'"

"Doris," she replied. "Ah, I hear footsteps on the stairs."

A moment later, Eliza walked into the room in another

surprisingly chic dress. She giggled at Ramsay's evident surprise. "I told you there was another dress I had to wear."

Ramsay nodded. "Tell me, if an elderly fellow hadn't come into your life, where and when were you going to wear these dresses?"

"I'm always hoping a millionaire will drop into the teashop and fall madly in love with me," Eliza said, grinning. "I meant to be ready when he arrived, as you see."

"I do see," Ramsay said, offering his arm for Eliza to hold.

"Don't listen to a word she tells you, Mr. Ramsay," Doris said sternly. "Elizabeth's imagination runs away with her sometimes. We made those dresses from patterns and material I bought in Scarborough."

"Good night, mother," Eliza said grandly, as they left the cottage. "Don't wait up."

Doris shook her head and closed the door.

"Are you warm enough," Ramsay asked, as the cold night air surrounded them as they exited through the gate. "Have my jacket."

"My jacket is warm enough, thank you," Eliza replied, frostily.

"That tiny jacket covers nothing," Ramsay protested. "You'll freeze before we get to the hotel."

"I'm not spoiling the elegant lines of this outfit with your old man's jacket," Eliza said, "and that's final."

Eliza didn't die of hypothermia, as Ramsay had feared, though he wasn't surprised to see she was as happy to be inside as he was.

"On the way home, it will be dark," Ramsay said. "Then I expect you to wear my jacket however unsightly it is."

"Oh, it isn't unsightly on you," Eliza said. "I think it suits you perfectly."

"Someday," Ramsay replied, "someone will murder you."

Eliza laughed. "And you can catch them. Meanwhile, I'll have a Babycham, please." She perched herself on a barstool like a film star, leaving one leg elegantly stretched out under the fine cloth of her dress.

11

ESTABLISHING GROUND RULES

RAMSAY ORDERED the drinks and sat on the barstool next to Eliza. "Did you hear anything more from your clients today?" he asked.

Eliza was momentarily taken aback but recovered quickly. "No, my later 'clients' couldn't shed any new light on our puzzle. What about you?"

"My client of the afternoon was helpful," Ramsay said, as the barman handed him his whisky and Eliza her Babycham.

"What did he say?"

Ramsay sipped his drink until he saw the barman distracted by an order. Then he continued softly, "He thinks Baldock might be implicated in the smuggling."

Eliza snorted, completely ruining her chic image had anyone been watching. "Well, he would, wouldn't he?"

"Of course," Ramsay replied evenly, watching the barman from the corner of his eye. "I think we should move to that quiet corner over there," he added, gesturing with his whisky to a small table with two chairs in a window alcove.

When they were re-settled further from prying ears,

Ramsay answered Eliza's question, "I agree, he would point the finger away from himself. Except I worked with him, and he seemed one of the good guys to me."

"How long did you work with him?"

"About a month. Not long, I know," Ramsay replied. "But you can judge people in minutes, I find, and such judgments are rarely wrong."

"Has he been investigating all this time?"

"He says not," Ramsay replied. "However, I find that hard to believe, based on my own experience. People like us can't let go."

"It works both ways, though," Eliza said. "Maybe he stayed close to continue investigating or maybe he stayed close to continue running the local smuggling trade."

Ramsay nodded. "I thought that too. We need to know more about Mr. Pritchard, which is a job for you and your customers."

"You know," Eliza said, "if anyone is listening to our conversation, they're going to think I'm a prostitute. I've never realized until this minute how saying a woman has 'clients' or 'customers' could be misunderstood. I think sleuthing leads to thinking badly about everyone."

"Sadly, it does," Ramsay said. "And when you share your thoughts with people, which you occasionally have to do, they rarely forgive or forget."

"You mean I'll have to leave town when all this is over?"

"Not if you don't tell them what you're thinking," Ramsay said.

Eliza shivered. "And I thought the risk of being murdered was the worst that could happen."

"Being murdered would win you lots of friends and admirers," Ramsay agreed. "Being right never does, despite what happy endings you'll read in books or see on movies will tell you."

"Ah, the voice of experience," Eliza said, teasing him. "Have you considered it may be just you?"

"I see you will be murdered," Ramsay said sighing. "And I know how to cover my tracks."

Eliza stuck her tongue out at him, before saying, "What about Armstrong?"

"I plan to visit the Ravenscar Fishing offices tomorrow and interview him there," Ramsay replied.

"Will he speak to you, do you think?"

"People are always torn between talking and explaining themselves as innocent or not talking and raising the question of their guilt in the mind of the detective," Ramsay said.

"I'll remember that when I become Eliza Danesdale, the female Sherlock Holmes."

"Yesterday, you were Mata Hari," Ramsay reminded her.

"Yesterday, I was in disguise. Sherlock Holmes was always going about in disguise."

"And very unlikely it was too, in my mind," Ramsay replied.

"You don't like Sherlock Holmes?"

"I do like Sherlock Holmes stories. I just found the use of disguises made me less likely to believe the outcome. A bit like all those women pretending to be men, and vice versa, in Shakespeare's plays. Disguises are rarely effective at close quarters or for long periods of time."

"More from your experience?" Eliza asked.

Ramsay nodded. "Yes, sadly."

"What about one of Harry's crew members?" Eliza asked, changing the subject to one that was more comfortable for Ramsay.

"I have a couple of names to talk to and I plan on interviewing them tomorrow as well."

"I know most of them," Eliza said. "Why don't I interview some as well."

"Because you could be found washed up on a beach if you talk to the wrong one."

"They've known me since I was a toddler," Eliza protested. "They don't know I'm working with you."

"We meet in the teashop, and we've been here twice now," Ramsay said. "If they don't know now, they soon will. You watch your step around them. If they are smuggling, they have too much to lose to let you expose them."

Eliza frowned, her mind racing. "You may be right. Aren't you likely to end up dead on a beach somewhere too?"

"I'm trained to look after myself, you aren't," Ramsay said, firmly. "You do the gentler stuff; I'll talk to the dangerous ones."

Eliza's expression suggested she didn't agree with this directive, but she nodded. "All right, for now. But if they talk to me, I'm going to listen."

"Make sure they don't talk to you unless there's only one of them, you're nowhere near the boats, and you aren't being watched by others."

"All right, all right," Eliza retorted. "Who's your main suspect right now?"

"It's too early to say. The thing that always drives investigations is 'follow the money' and we have only one person that we know of who would benefit from Harry's death – Armstrong."

"We haven't seen or heard anything of Harry's will," Eliza said. "That might bring the son into the picture. What say you to us going together to interview him tomorrow afternoon? It's early closing in the village."

"We can take the train to Ravenscar and walk from there."

"Only if you're buying the train tickets," Eliza said firmly. "I thought we could cycle there. My dad will let you borrow his bike."

"How long to cycle there?"

"How fit are you?" Eliza asked. "It's all uphill, both ways."

Smiling at the old joke, Ramsay replied, "Fit enough," though he hadn't cycled for decades. "How long?"

"It takes us an hour to get to Ravenscar for cricket matches and dances," Eliza said.

"What time should I be at your house?"

"Two o'clock and don't be late," Eliza said. "It gets dark early now and the roads and tracks are uneven and narrow."

* * *

PROVING ELIZA'S POINT, they walked home in darkness; Ramsay was pleased Eliza consented to wearing his jacket. The evening air was cold, with a raw wind blowing in from the sea and heavy drops of intermittent rain sharply striking their faces.

"Winter is in the air tonight," Ramsay said, as Eliza cuddled into him.

"We must huddle together for warmth. That's what they taught us in Girl Guides."

Ramsay hugged her. "I'm not sure they meant on a five-minute walk from a bar to your home."

At the door, Eliza kissed his cheek. "Tomorrow at two," she whispered, turning away and returning his jacket.

"Don't be late." She unlocked the door and, with a brief wave, entered, closing the door behind her.

Feeling strangely bereft, Ramsay didn't move for a moment. Then, with a sigh, set off for the guest house. *Oh, to be young again.*

* * *

AFTER WALKING BRACKEN, and a leisurely breakfast, Ramsay made his way down to the slipway and the Ravenscar Fishing office, where Eliza's dad told him he was too early. Armstrong was never in the office before ten. Ramsay thanked him and he and Bracken went out to inspect the boats, most of which were on the water, some were tied up on buoys off the slipway and the larger ones in deeper channels under the cliff.

There were few people about. The crews would be sleeping after their night of fishing and the morning was too cold and blustery for idle sightseeing. The *Ravenscar Lady* boats were easily identifiable in their black livery with the silhouette of a raven on a white stripe that ran around the hull, immediately below the deck. The other boats had no company livery. They were simply varnished or painted roughly in nondescript colors, no doubt what was cheap when the owner was looking to maintain them.

Ramsay was beginning to think he'd have to get inside somewhere to wait, when he saw a heavy-set, bull of a man striding down New Street and clearly making for the offices. He crossed the small open area between the sea wall and the buildings to stand in the way of the man.

"Mr. Armstrong?" he asked, when the man was near enough to hear over the wind.

"Aye, who wants to know?"

"Tom Ramsay," Ramsay replied. "I'm the man who found your partner's body."

"So?" Armstrong asked, moving closer.

"You may know I'm an ex-police inspector," Ramsay said, establishing some credibility, "and I'd like to know a bit more about Harry."

"You'd best ask Inspector Baldock then," Armstrong replied, continuing to walk on to the office door.

"I hoped you might tell me more of the human side to Harry," Ramsay continued, walking alongside the man while Bracken sniffed at the man's ankles.

Armstrong opened the office door, turned to Ramsay and said, "I've nought to say. Good day to you." He entered the office, and slammed the door shut.

"Well, Bracken," Ramsay said, as they walked away. "What do you think that means? Innocent or guilty?"

Bracken, who was tired of standing in the wind and rain, didn't reply. He just tugged the leash toward home.

"I hope this clears up before two o'clock, Bracken," Ramsay said, as he hurried up the street. "I'd like to get something useful out of today and I don't want to cycle for two hours in this wind and rain."

Bracken suddenly veered off down a narrow alley and out into King Street before making his way up the street to a small cottage, where he sniffed the doorstep and sill.

"Ah, I see! Armstrong came from here, did he, Bracken," Ramsay asked. He grinned. "I wish I'd told you to do this fine piece of sleuthing, I'd be right pleased at my brilliance. I wondered why you were so interested in his socks and shoes."

Bracken's withering look told him it was where Armstrong came from and, yes, he generally was steps ahead of his friend who seemed to miss practically everything.

"But this isn't where he lives, or at least it's not the address I was given. I wonder who does live here?"

Having done his duty, Bracken was now eager to continue back to the guest house and Ramsay felt he was too.

* * *

As is so often the case with coastal regions, the weather changed abruptly — with the changing tide the locals would say — and the afternoon was sunny, though still with the stiff breeze that had chilled Ramsay and Bracken earlier that day. Consequently, just after two o'clock, Ramsay was mounted on Eliza's father's bike and, with Bracken trotting alongside, wobbling up the hill and out of Robin Hood's Bay, behind the fast-disappearing Eliza on her own bike.

With the climb out of the village over, they set off at a better pace along the moorland road to Ravenscar. As Eliza had predicted, there were what seemed to Ramsay some short downhill stretches followed by long uphill climbs. Ramsay considered tying Bracken's leash to the handlebars and having his dog pull him up.

Then they left the road and continued along a grassy track which finally brought them to another road and the cottage where Peacock's son was living. After parking their bikes beside the small porch, Ramsay knocked.

12

THE VICTIM'S ESTRANGED SON

THE DOOR OPENED AND A MIDDLE-AGED, bearded man asked, "What do you want?" Despite his age, he appeared more like a teenager to Ramsay, his appearance and clothes said 'beatnik' and 'unemployed' in Ramsay's mind.

"Hello, Arthur," Eliza said, brightly, "remember me?"

"Aye," Arthur replied, in a tone that didn't suggest he remembered her with any fondness. "What is it?"

Eliza jumped in quickly so Ramsay's too formal speech wouldn't have them dismissed without a hearing. "We want to talk about your dad."

"What about him?"

"Can we come in and talk?" Ramsay asked.

"Nay," Arthur said. "This is private property."

"This is ex-Inspector Ramsay, and he was the one who found your father's body," Eliza said quickly. "We're keen to ensure his killer is found and punished. I liked your dad."

Arthur nodded. For the first time he seemed to thaw a little. "He liked you, though he said you were a pest."

"He was right, I am a pest," Eliza declared. "And I intend

to pester the police into finding the murderer. Inspector Ramsay has agreed to help. Will you help?"

"Okay, what do you want to know?" Peacock's voice was even enough but his eyes betrayed his concern over Ramsay's presence.

"You and your dad fell out some years ago," Eliza said. "Why was that?"

"He wanted me to be a fisherman, I wanted to make records and manage 'Shades of Blue', our local pop group."

"Was that all?" Eliza probed.

Arthur's face betrayed his internal struggle. "It can't do any harm now, I suppose. There were things going on I didn't hold with," he answered, at last.

"Smuggling?"

Arthur nodded. "In a small way, nothing really bad. Just a case or two of foreign spirits but I could see the desire for more was growing in them all."

"Did it continue?" Ramsay asked.

"How should I know? I was out of it, and I never went back." His tone remained hostile in contrast to how he addressed Eliza.

"Did you know about the tunnel your father's body was found in?" Eliza asked, to recapture the rapport Ramsay's presence was in danger of breaking.

"Aye," Arthur said. "Others did too."

"Don't you think it odd then that no one searched it when they were looking for your dad?"

Arthur thought a while. "Mebbe not. I was in London trying to sign a new band and the others have left the village."

"When you returned, you didn't think of it?"

"Why should I? Dad and I haven't spoken in years and, if I had thought of it, I'd have assumed the tunnel would have been searched. I've been busy lately. My business isn't doing well. People only want Liverpool, London, or Manchester groups right now and I haven't got one."

"You're working on getting one?" Eliza asked, sympathetically.

His expression was glum. "Yes. I'm never off the phone, and if I am, it's 'cos I'm on a train to somewhere the groups hang out and that's nowhere near here."

"Why live here then?" Ramsay asked. "Wouldn't it be better to be in London?"

"Of course, but the entertainers I do manage are from the north and work the northern clubs. I can't drop them. They're what's paying my bills."

"I see. So, it isn't to keep your eye on your father's business?" Ramsay continued.

Arthur shrugged. "At the beginning, that was one reason for staying local. I thought Dad would come around to my way of thinking and ditch the booze smuggling." He laughed uneasily. "What a prig, I was then. A few bottles of booze horrified me and look at me now." He paused again. "Nowadays, it's not so much about the family business and more about keeping my grip on my local acts."

"Do you know what's in your father's will?" Eliza asked.

"I know what *was* in it," Arthur growled, "but I hear he made a new will when he took on a partner. I'm to meet with the lawyer tomorrow and learn what the changes were."

"Would you drop by the teashop and tell me after the meeting?" Eliza asked.

Arthur shook his head. "The lawyer is in Whitby. I'll be getting the train straight home to Ravenscar, not jumping off at Bay to tell you."

"Then can I phone you tomorrow night?" Eliza asked. "If Armstrong gets it all, that's a strong motive for murder."

Arthur nodded. "Okay. Do that." He gave Eliza his number and she carefully entered it into her notepad.

With this strand of the conversation ended, Ramsay returned to an earlier thread. "You said others knew about the tunnel," "Was that just children or did it include adults?'

Arthur considered. "I don't know about adults. I was thinking about me and my friends, who are now adults but moved away. My dad knew 'cos I told him when we found it."

"He didn't start using the tunnel as an office or to store things when you were around?" Eliza asked.

Arthur shook his head. "No. Not then."

"Is there anything you can think of that might help us?" Eliza continued.

"I don't think so."

"Well," Eliza said. "If you remember something, phone me at the teashop, please. It's in your interest to, you know. I just want justice for an old friend, but you have an inheritance to claim."

* * *

"Managing entertainers on the northern club circuit can't be very lucrative," Ramsay said, as he and Eliza returned to the road and prepared to mount their bikes. "Look at that garden."

"I expect he spends his money on other things," Eliza replied, "which is why he wouldn't let us in."

Ramsay laughed. "You have a suspicious mind."

"It's the company I keep," Eliza said. "Now are you going to get on that bike or just walk it home?"

Ramsay smiled ruefully. "To be frank, I'd dearly like to walk it to Ravenscar station and get the train home. I'm not sure I'll sit comfortably for weeks, if ever."

"I'd have expected an ex-inspector to have a car," Eliza retorted.

"I do have a car," Ramsay protested, gingerly settling himself on the bike seat. "But the train from Newcastle to Scarborough stops in Robin Hood's Bay and I thought sitting in a carriage watching the world flash by the window would be a pleasant start and end to my walking break, instead of driving myself."

"You should think ahead," Eliza said, as they cycled back along the road toward the moors. "That's what my parents tell me."

"I had no reason to believe I'd be investigating a murder," Ramsay said, eying the upcoming unpaved and irregular track with a jaundiced eye. He might have to walk that bit. "In fact, I wouldn't be, if I hadn't given Baldock my own equally plausible theory."

Eliza laughed, as they left the paved road and began bouncing over the uneven ground. "It will be best for us if Harry has cut Arthur out of the will, you know."

"You think he'll be more helpful?" Ramsay replied, before adding, "I'm pushing this bike until we get back to the paved road." He stopped and dismounted.

Eliza, seeing Ramsay stop, also dismounted and began walking, "I think he'll be angry enough to provide more than he did today."

"He wasn't very forthcoming, that's for sure," Ramsay said. "Though I'm not sure he would know more."

"One or two of Harry's crews are old Bay men and Arthur will know them," Eliza replied. "He'll have a good idea of what's been going on."

"My next job is to interview the two fishermen," Ramsay replied. "How do you suggest I do that? They're in bed by day and out at sea most nights."

"Try the *Ye Dolphin* pub early in the evening," Eliza said.

"That will be too public for interviewing," Ramsay mused aloud. "Do you have addresses?"

"I know where they live," Eliza said. "I'll show you when we get back."

Ramsay, pushing the bike up a small rise, got back on its seat at the paved road, and said, "Bracken led me to a cottage on King Street when Armstrong dismissed us. I'd like to show you. I want to know who lives there."

Eliza was also again seated. "The faster we get back, the sooner we can start interviewing." She set off with Ramsay and Bracken once again working hard to keep up. Eliza had joked the route was uphill both ways and Ramsay discovered that was true. The long uphills he'd struggled with when coming were now short downhills and the short downhills were now long uphills. If he didn't know it was his mind playing tricks, he'd have sworn witchcraft was involved.

Once back in the village, Ramsay returned the bike to Eliza's dad's garden shed with relief. Even walking at this point was painful and Eliza finding it amusing didn't improve Ramsay's mood.

"I'll start with the cottages on King Street," Eliza said, brightly, "because one of the men lives there as well as this mystery house you know about."

When Ramsay pointed out the house Bracken had followed the scent back to, Eliza said, "A widow lives here, a Mrs. Smith. You think she and Armstrong are having a fling?"

Ramsay shrugged. "Possibly."

Eliza nodded. "I haven't heard any gossip about her and Armstrong so they must be very discreet, which is almost impossible in a village as close packed as this, or there's an innocent explanation that people are aware of."

When they'd arrived back at Eliza's home, Ramsay asked, "What time will our two fishermen leave the house to get down to the harbor?"

"It depends but any time after ten should be good, though they may leave from the pub rather than their house," Eliza said, smiling.

"Isn't that dangerous?" Ramsay asked. "Drinking before going to sea, I mean."

"They know how much is safe," Eliza replied. "They've done it all their lives. I've had an idea, let's ask mam if she knows about Mrs. Smith."

Inside, they found Eliza's mother baking for the following day's stock.

"They say, Mrs. Smith is Armstrong's sister," she told them. "And she's certainly from the North-East so she likely is."

Ramsay nodded, though he was disappointed. An affair could have created possibilities for motives or rifts between people, all conducive to solving cases. *Still, claiming to be brother and sister would be a good cover for an affair.*

"I should be going," Ramsay said. "Bracken and I need our tea and your teashop is closed."

"I'll make us tea," Eliza said. "Stay and we can talk about tonight."

"Tonight?" her mother asked, suspiciously.

Eliza laughed. "Inspector Ramsay wants to interview some of the fishermen. He hopes to meet one or two tonight when they're preparing to sail. He won't know which ones are safe to talk to unless I point them out. We need to plan for that." She held the kettle under a tap and filled it.

"Don't you get involved in any talks with those folk," her mother replied. "They're a rough lot on them boats."

"I'll stay hidden, I promise," Eliza said. "That's what I need to tell my sleuthing partner, how we can make this work." She spooned out tea leaves from a caddy into a teapot decorated with roses.

"Sit down in the living room, Tom," Eliza's mother said. "Eliza will bring the tea through in a minute."

13

A LOYAL FISHERMAN

Guessing this was a pretext to get him out of the room, Ramsay did as she suggested, and he wasn't surprised to hear the whispered, agitated conversation in the kitchen confirming his supposition. He didn't always pick up on such polite social gambits. This time he had, and he felt rather proud.

"Here we are," Eliza said, as she entered the room with a large, heavily laden tray. "Mam says after all that cycling, you'll need feeding up." She took two bowls from the tray, one of water and one of meat scraps, placing them on the floor next to Bracken who thought: 'Oh yes, definitely after my afternoon of trotting, I need feeding up.'

Ramsay poured the tea and handed Eliza a cup. "Hey," Eliza said, grinning, "we don't let guests work in our house. Mam and Dad would not approve."

"We're partners," Ramsay said, "and your parents aren't with us."

"Armstrong really wouldn't speak to you?" Eliza asked, taking a scone from the tiered plates of pastries and preparing to butter it.

"Not a word," Ramsay replied. "But I don't think we should read too much into it. He doesn't strike me as a chatty sort of fellow."

Eliza laughed. "That he's not. He's a man of few words and even fewer that are pleasant."

"Not like old Harry?" Ramsay suggested.

"Not like him at all," Eliza agreed. "Harry was a cantankerous soul but generally a talkative and fair man, if you didn't get on the wrong side of him. Armstrong has a streak of unpleasantness in him a mile wide."

"Or is it just he doesn't like you?"

Eliza grinned. "It's true, he doesn't, but he doesn't like anyone else either, so far as we can see. Unless it's his sister, of course," she added, mischievously.

"How do you suggest we watch tonight without you being seen?"

"Where New Street and King Street join..."

"Right at the slipway?" Ramsay offered.

"Yes. There are some nooks and crannies a 'slip of a girl' like me could hide in, while a mature man might stand outside — blocking a passerby's view — and within whispering distance. We can go now and scout it out."

Ramsay groaned. "I need feeding up before venturing out again."

Eliza's expression was immediately solicitous. "I understand. An elderly man like yourself..."

"I'm in the prime of life," Ramsay protested.

"Oh, certainly. An elderly man in the prime of his life would find two hours exercise a lot, I'm sure," Eliza said. "Perhaps after your nap we could go?"

"Our partnership could be dissolved, you know."

"Then you'd never know which of all the men heading down to the boats was Thornton Duck."

"It might be a price worth paying," Ramsay growled, "but, for now, we'll finish our tea and reconnoiter those nooks and crannies you suggest."

* * *

Eliza was right. Between the sheds and buildings beside the slipway were small gaps where, in the dark, someone could hide. Ramsay looked about the open space and said, "If he's coming from the *Dolphin*, he will appear on this side and, if from his house on that. I'll stand right here tonight," he decided. "Now, which is the best crevice for you to hide in?"

After making sure no one was watching, Eliza slid into the two possible openings, one after the other. "I won't see him until it will be too late," she complained. "So, neither of these two works."

"To see him arriving," Ramsay said, "you'd need to be among the boats on the seawall. That way you're looking up both streets."

"Then you need to be over there too, or I can't alert you," Eliza said, "and we don't know which of these boats may go out tonight."

"I think these small boats only go out in daylight," Ramsay said, thoughtfully. "That's what I've seen so far, anyway."

Eliza crossed to the boats and sauntered from boat to boat, examining them closely. "Come, look," she whispered.

Ramsay followed her to an older boat that looked in need of paint.

"This one hasn't been out for some time," Eliza said. "There's litter pushed down under the tarpaulin. I could hide inside, peeking out, and you could be lounging against it, watching Bracken investigating scents or marking his territory."

Ramsay looked around the open area and up the two streets, before saying, "It'll be a cold wait."

"We'll dress warm," Eliza retorted. "Stop being so soft."

"Ten o'clock?"

"That should be time enough," Eliza replied. "It will be dark enough for me to get into the boat without being seen and early enough to catch him if he sets out for the boat early. He is one of the most experienced men in the crews; he may be the one who starts getting the boat ready for the voyage."

"It would be perfect if that were so," Ramsay said. "I could talk to him tonight and not try to arrange for a meeting tomorrow. I want to make time tomorrow for the other one, John Robinson."

"You'll pick me up as you pass my house on your way down here?" Eliza asked, suspiciously.

Ramsay smiled. "I will. Now Bracken and I must get back to the guest house or Mrs. Golightly will be upset. She likes meals and guests to be punctual."

They walked back up the hill and parted at Eliza's home. "See you later, alligator," she sang as Ramsay walked on.

"In a while, crocodile," Ramsay responded, mildly pleased that he knew something about the newspeak of the age.

* * *

WHEN RAMSAY ARRIVED at the Danesdale cottage door that evening, Eliza was already exiting it. "I was watching at the window," she told him. The wind blew her hair across her face. She took a knitted woolen hat from her pocket and, gathering up her hair, hid it all in the hat, which she pulled down over her ears.

"Do you have gloves?" Ramsay asked.

"Yes," Eliza said, with an exasperated sigh, "and I've a clean handkerchief. Oh, and clean undies, in case I'm taken to the hospital."

Ramsay laughed. "All right. I'll stop fussing."

"Good. Now let's go before my dad decides he wants to come and protect me."

After days without a reminder of his family, that gave him such a severe heartache, he gasped. *I didn't protect my children when they needed me.*

"Too cold for you?" Eliza asked.

"The wind took my breath away for a moment," Ramsay replied. *And realistically, can I protect Eliza if anything goes wrong tonight?*

Eliza tucked her hand in his arm, and they hurried down the street, heads down against the wind that was in their faces. At the slipway, the wind was driving a powerful swell and waves against the seawall. Spray flew over the wall and splattered on the open ground and the parked boats.

"Cold *and* wet," Ramsay said, ruefully. "I'm glad I left Bracken at home."

"Keep watch, while I climb into the boat," Eliza said. She pulled the tarpaulin aside, opening a gap wide enough for her to climb through. "Ugh! The sea-foam is making everything slimy." She hitched herself up, sat on the side and swung her legs into the boat. A moment later and all Ramsay could see were her eyes gleaming in the darkness.

An hour passed and Ramsay's feet were frozen by the time he heard Eliza whisper, "He's coming down New Street right now."

Ramsay had already noted the man — well wrapped

against the October night, striding down the hill — and set off at once to meet him in a darker area between the streetlights.

"Thornton Duck?" Ramsay asked quietly as they neared each other.

"Who wants to know?"

"Tom Ramsay. I'm the man who found Harry Peacock's body."

Duck didn't pause in his stride and Ramsay was forced to fall in with him. "I wanted to talk about Harry Peacock and events leading up to his death," Ramsay continued.

"Talk to the police, they should be able to answer any questions you have," Duck said.

"I don't want to involve them," Ramsay said. They were at the slipway now and Duck still wasn't stopping. "I'm interested because I think I can do a better job than they will and will keep secrets that need to be kept."

Duck didn't reply. He began dragging a small boat parked with the others down to the sea.

"Can we talk?" Ramsay asked. "There's no one about to overhear."

The sea swell rose up the slipway and the boat Duck was holding floated on it. He leapt nimbly inside and using an oar, pushed the boat away from the land.

"I've nothing to say to you or anyone," Duck called back to Ramsay, as he maneuvered the boat to face the waves and the boats moored farther out, before rowing powerfully away.

Ramsay marveled that anyone would set out in such a small craft, or that, having done so, could prevent it being swept against the rocks. He realized he really didn't understand the sea or fishermen. He watched until he saw Duck climb aboard one of the Ravenscar Fishing boats and then whispered, "You can come out now. He's in the fishing boat and there's no one on the street."

Eliza climbed stiffly out. "You'd think it would be warm with that heavy tarpaulin on top," she grumbled, rubbing her hands and arms to warm them.

"We shouldn't wait here," Ramsay said. "The others will be coming soon."

Eliza linked her arm in his and pressed closely to him. "We'll look like a courting couple," she explained.

"You won't get any heat from me," Ramsay said, grinning. "I'm frozen through." They walked a few more steps before Eliza stopped, reached up, and kissed him on the lips. Ramsay jumped, as though he'd had an electric shock.

"Warmer now?" she asked.

Once he'd overcome his surprise, Ramsay said, "Much, but I don't think we should overdo our disguise." He set off walking again, confused and concerned.

"Disguises need to be maintained, if they're to work," Eliza replied, smiling up at him. She took her arm out from his and put it around his waist, hugging him tight.

"Only until we reach your home," Ramsay said, putting his arm around her, "or even before. Your parents would be horrified to see this."

"They'd like you better as my boyfriend than a lot of others," Eliza said, chuckling.

Ramsay sighed. "We have only John Robinson, the fisherman from the opposing camp to interview. Where might I meet him?"

"He works on a farm during the day," Eliza said, "so I expect the pub in the evening after work."

"Tomorrow night, you and I are going on a pub crawl, only not together. You need to find a companion to go with."

"Why can't I go with you?"

"Because officially you aren't helping me in any way with my enquiries. Remember?"

"All right," Eliza replied, grudgingly giving him the point. "But once you've talked to him, we can meet and share information. Right?"

"You will have talked to Arthur Peacock by then so yes, we must."

"And what will you be doing?" Eliza demanded.

"I'm going to phone one of my old colleagues," Ramsay said. "I've been putting it off because I've leaned on him quite a bit in the past few months and I'm not sure if he'll welcome my call."

"That's it?"

"And waylay Armstrong again," Ramsay said, unwrapping his arm from her. "Here we are at your door. Goodnight. We'll talk again tomorrow."

"Won't you come in? Warm yourself by the fire?"

Ramsay shook his head, then paused. "Maybe I will for a few minutes. Your dad can tell me about Armstrong's mood after I accosted him in the street."

Eliza laughed. "You really are the last of the great romantics, aren't you?"

14

THE VICTIM'S BUSINESS PARTNER

Eliza's parents were seated either side of the fireplace, father reading and mother knitting, with the radio playing light classics in the background when the two sleuths entered the room.

"We're freezing," Eliza told them from the door. "Inspector Ramsay and I are having a hot drink. Would you like one?"

"We've had our cocoa, thanks," Eliza's mother said, laying aside her knitting and rising from her chair. "You two get by the fire. I'll make the tea."

Rather embarrassed, Ramsay followed Eliza into the living room, where she stood directly in front of the fire taking all the heat. He sat on a dining table chair and envied her.

"What have you been doing to get so cold?" her father asked.

"We were waiting for Thornton Duck to come down to the harbor," Eliza replied. "It's cold enough for snow out there."

"Then you might want to share some of the heat with your guest," her father said.

Eliza laughed. "He told me he was warm enough so he can wait."

"Mr. Danesdale," Ramsay began before Eliza could add any other hints about the evening, "did Armstrong tell you I'd approached him yesterday?"

Eliza's father nodded and a rare smile creased his face. "He was right put out about it."

"He didn't say anything incriminating, in his anger?"

"Not he. He's too sharp for anything of that sort, sadly."

"We've been told tomorrow is when the will is to be read," Ramsay continued. "You may know your fate sooner than you think."

"I'm sure I know it already," Danesdale said. "Still, it will be good to have the matter settled one way or the other. It's the waiting that's hard to bear."

Ramsay nodded his agreement. "I can imagine it would. While we wait, have you any other ideas where we might look for an answer as to who murdered Harry?"

"For instance, dad," Eliza interjected quickly. "We asked you about a disagreement between Harry and Armstrong right before Harry's disappearance. Were there any maybe a week or a month before?"

"There were some, but you'd expect that. They were both blunt speaking, hot-tempered men."

"Do you know what they were about?"

"They weren't about fishing."

"Did Armstrong want Harry to sell some boats to pay off the loan, perhaps?" Ramsay asked.

"Oh no," Danesdale replied. "Harry was keen to expand the fleet. Armstrong wanted to do something different with the catch."

"Then you've nothing to worry about, surely," Ramsay said.

"Expand the fleet," Danesdale responded, "reduce the workforce is what I got from comments they said at other times."

Eliza's mother arrived carrying a tray laden with tea and pastries. "You best eat something to warm you up," she handed Ramsay a small plate. "You'll likely not feel much of the fire with Elizabeth standing there."

"I'm moving," Eliza said, crossing the room to the table and taking a plate. "I'm starving cold and starving hungry." She took two slices of *parkin* from the tray and sat across the table from Ramsay.

"Move closer to the fire, Inspector," Eliza's mother said. "While you have the chance."

Ramsay smiled. "The room is beautifully warm, thanks. I don't need to get chilblains by toasting myself."

Eliza's father suddenly said, "Armstrong is worried about the will, I think? He told me he was going to hear what was in it tomorrow and wouldn't be in. His expression wasn't as happy as I'd expect if he was sure everything was coming to him."

"Here's hoping Arthur Peacock gets the business then," Ramsay replied.

Eliza's father shook his head. "It can only be fifty percent at most because Armstrong loaned the money on him being given fifty percent of the business."

"Even if Arthur only gets half, it's surely better than Armstrong having everything his own way, Dad." Eliza said.

"You know Arthur Peacock," her father retorted sarcastically. "He'd sell his own mother. He and Armstrong may have arguments, but it won't be about cutting costs and increasing profits."

Ramsay let the talk run on for a time before saying, "I must get back or Bracken will make Mrs. Golightly take him for a walk and that will never do."

He was escorted to the door by Eliza and her mother, which, Ramsay thought, stopped Eliza playing any more foolish games. *At least, I hope they are games. With Eliza only nineteen and me fifty-five, I'm nearly old enough to be her grandfather.*

* * *

THE FOLLOWING MORNING, before breakfast, Ramsay and Bracken made a phone call to Inspector Morrison's home.

"You promised you'd ask no more favors," Morrison said, when he heard it was Ramsay and what he wanted.

"I know," Ramsay said, "but it's happened again and there's a Sam Armstrong from Newcastle here too. There can't be any criminals left in the city. I'm finding them wherever I go."

"If this Armstrong is a criminal," Morrison pointed out, "you would know about him. You've only been gone six months."

"Then you won't be breaking any rules telling me what a fine upright citizen Armstrong is," Ramsay said encouragingly.

"I'll ask around," Morrison replied, equally discouragingly. "Now I must go to work, and you should go back to retirement."

"One more thing," Ramsay cried, as he imagined Morrison slamming down the handset, "find out what you can about an Inspector Len Pritchard at Whitby."

Morrison sighed. "What's this about?"

"I worked with him briefly about five years ago on that

smuggling case, remember?" Ramsay asked. When Morrison said he remembered the smuggling case, Ramsay continued, "He was pushed out of the force sometime after that. I've heard his side of the story, now I'd like to know the other side."

"What's this really about, Tom?" Morrison asked, suspiciously.

Ramsay explained about his meeting with Baldock and the man's hostility, and ended by saying, "I believe him when he says he'll be happy to pin something on me."

"Your 'missing girl' stunt made a lot of people angry here as well, Tom," Morrison told him. "That wasn't well done."

"I understand but the girl's safety came first in my mind," Ramsay responded. "You must see that."

"I trust you," Morrison said, chuckling. "Not everyone worked with you as long as I did so they see you as a rogue male causing havoc."

"If you trust me, and thanks for that, please dig out what you can for me before I'm locked up somewhere and they've thrown away the key."

Morrison laughed. "It would serve you right. However, I'll look into it, but it's outside our area. It'll take some time."

Ramsay replied, "I understand. Get the Armstrong background first and the Pritchard information later."

"I'll see what I can do," Morrison said. "Now let me get on with *my* work."

Ramsay thanked him and hung up the phone. "He's one of the good ones, Bracken. I always said so." They set out on a brisk walk along the clifftops, which allowed Bracken to sniff out rabbits and Ramsay to study the boats unloading at the sea wall. "How do they do it, Bracken? If it isn't in the fish, and there isn't anywhere for them to drop contraband off before they get here, how is it done?"

As he'd learned Armstrong wasn't going into the office today, but was catching the train to Whitby, Ramsay decided to spend the day at the station, trainspotting. He wasn't entirely sure how or what one did in this peculiarly passive pastime, so he took his camera, a notepad and pencil, and enough dog treats to keep Bracken happy as the hours slowly slipped by.

Ramsay was glad he'd chosen to start early because Armstrong strode onto the station platform as Ramsay was settling himself in for a long day's wait. He couldn't believe his luck and sprang up from the bench he'd been sitting on.

"Mr. Armstrong," Ramsay said. "We meet again. I'd very much like to hear from you about what was happening in Harry Peacock's life before he died."

"Why? This is a police matter, as I've already told you."

"I know, I just can't get the policeman out of me, I suppose. I feel I must do something for the dead man; it's just the way I am."

Armstrong looked at his watch. "My train will be here in four minutes."

"Off to Whitby for the day?" Ramsay asked.

"Obviously," Armstrong said, shortly.

"Then I'll be brief. Was Harry worried about anything or anyone, do you know?"

"I don't believe Harry Peacock was the kind of man to be worried by anything or anyone," Armstrong replied.

"You and he didn't fall out over anything?"

Armstrong nodded his expression grim. "This is why I didn't want to talk with you. I know very well where you want to place the blame."

"I only want to know the events leading up to his death,"

Ramsay said. "After all, if you and Harry argued, someone may have overheard. I can't imagine your discussion would have been quiet."

"We had disagreements about how the business should be run. Now I had half of it, I expected him to take notice of my concerns. He thought I should be a 'silent' partner and leave the running of it to him."

"Do you know anything about fishing?"

"No, but I do know about business," Armstrong replied. His expression brightened as he saw the train approaching the station. "Now, if there's nothing else?"

"Who do you think might have killed him?" Ramsay asked.

"I was introduced to Harry by a mutual friend. She suggested I might be interested in providing Harry a loan," Armstrong said, "for a price of course." He was almost shouting now as the train ground to a halt with the squealing of iron wheels on iron rails, hissing steam, and shouting driver and stationmaster. "I have no idea who Harry might have upset before that time. And have you thought about his son? He's a shifty customer if ever I saw one."

Ramsay thanked him, as Armstrong opened a carriage door and climbed in. The door slammed shut and Armstrong sat at the farther side of the carriage to signal the conversation was over.

"What do you think, Bracken?" Ramsay asked, as they walked out of the station onto Station Road. "He makes a good point about others who may have wanted to harm Harry."

Bracken thought: 'We should follow Station Road out of the village and into the countryside where I could at least see sheep, even if I never get to herd them.'

"You're right," Ramsay said, as Bracken tugged him along. "It was a long boring wait and you do deserve a treat for being so patient.

Bracken stopped dead and dutifully sat while the promised treat was produced and handed over. When a second wasn't offered, he set off once again for the open country.

* * *

Ramsay and Bracken were back at the guest house in time for lunch. They were welcomed at the door by Mrs. Golightly, who added, "There was a phone call for you, Mr. Ramsay, from an Inspector Morrison. He asked you to phone him back at home tonight."

"I'll do that, thanks for telling me," Ramsay said, as he climbed the stairs to his room. "I'll freshen up and join you in a moment."

"I'll feed Bracken," Mrs. Golightly replied, stroking Bracken who hadn't followed Ramsay and was waiting patiently to be shown where his lunch was. "You poor thing," Mrs. Golightly said, leading the way to the kitchen. "The way he walks you all over the country is criminal."

Bracken paused eating long enough to give her his best downtrodden dog expression: 'I hope she'll look at this face and keep the excellent meals coming. I'm not sure I'll ever be able to go back to canned dog food.'

"Eliza called in to remind you to visit the teashop later," Mrs. Golightly told Ramsay, as he entered the dining room. "I hope she isn't becoming too familiar," she added, warningly.

"Not at all," Ramsay said. "She's just at that age where they still have the energy of children and have also developed the stamina of grown people. I like having someone young around, don't you?"

"Not really," she responded tartly. "They're so sure of everything and you can't tell them anything. I find them wearing. However, if she isn't bothering you then I expect it's all right."

"Her mother is in the teashop too, remember," Ramsay said. "What mischief can she do there?" Even as he spoke, he felt a flutter of anxiety inside. *What mischief indeed.*

15

THE DISLOYAL FISHERMAN

Ramsay and Bracken entered the teashop with minutes to spare for 'High Tea', five o'clock. He was relieved to see the café was almost empty, and a few customers preparing to depart. He chose a window seat away from the others and waited for Eliza to appear, which she did with a tray for an elderly couple sitting near the door.

After dispensing crockery, cutlery, a teapot, and jug of hot water to the couple, she came across to Ramsay.

"What can I get you, sir," she asked, emphasizing the 'sir' with a mischievous grin.

"High Tea, please, and some water for Bracken," Ramsay said, smiling.

"Coming right up," Eliza said, hurrying away in a manner that rather unnerved Ramsay. She was back a moment later with a water bowl and a plate of meat, which she placed carefully at Bracken's feet before stroking his head. "Yours won't be long," she told Ramsay, and again walked away with an alarming sway of her hips that borrowed more from Marilyn Monroe than Yorkshire. The word 'mischief' swam through Ramsay's mind, accusingly.

Eliza was back with the sandwiches and cakes, which she placed on the table while whispering, "It was fifty-fifty. Arthur got Harry's half of the business. Armstrong has invited him to the office tomorrow morning to discuss the future."

"Your dad may be safe, then," Ramsay said, quietly.

"Pigs might fly," Eliza muttered, as she returned to the kitchen for his tea. Ramsay was relieved she walked more like herself this time.

"I'm taking my break," Eliza announced as she placed the pot, hot water jug, milk, and cups on the table before sitting down beside him. "It's been busy here today."

"Your mam won't mind being left to manage the place on her own?" Ramsay asked, smiling.

Eliza pulled a face at him. "She knows I'll serve anyone who comes in, break or not. What she doesn't like so much is you coming here involving me in murders."

"You explained about your volunteering, I hope?" Ramsay asked. He felt uneasy at this outright statement of something he'd guessed at.

"I'm a grown-up and I'll do as I want," Eliza replied. "They're both such timid creatures, my parents. They wouldn't say boo to a goose."

"According to the law, you're not an adult until you're twenty-one," Ramsay reminded her, "and they're your parents. They're entitled to be concerned."

"Old people are hopeless," Eliza said. "One day we young people will run things and fuss about everything *you* do to make life interesting. See how you like it then!"

Ramsay laughed. "That happens naturally with age. You don't need a change in the law for your turn in the cycle of life."

"Can't come soon enough. Now, did you meet Armstrong," she added, quietly.

As they nibbled Ramsay's sandwiches, he told her of his meeting with Armstrong. "I think he has a point," Ramsay said, as he finished. "If Harry was doing something illegal, we should be looking there or at Arthur."

"We don't know he was doing anything illegal," Eliza responded. "Percy Storm couldn't see anything illegal, anyway. Not that that would normally weigh much with me," she added, sarcastically.

"I need to speak to John Robinson, the fisherman who stopped working for Harry," Ramsay said. "We must find him tonight. Have you arranged a friend to share the evening with?"

"Yes," Eliza replied. "I haven't yet thought of a way of ditching her when the time comes, though."

"We'll start at seven," Ramsay said. "Where?"

"*Ye Dolphin* first, then on from there. The village has very few drinking spots, so he'll be easy to find."

"He won't be in the hotel bars then?"

Eliza laughed. "No and you'll see why."

* * *

AFTER THE EVENING MEAL, Ramsay and Bracken went out for their walk, which meant Ramsay could phone Morrison at the local phone box without being overheard by his landlady. "What have you got for me?" Ramsay asked, after the briefest of salutations.

"Nothing you'll find useful," Morrison replied. "As I pointed out when we spoke earlier, you and I haven't heard of Mr. Armstrong because he's never been part of any criminal investigation. We couldn't even find a civil case with his name attached to it."

"Does anyone know anything about him? Anything?"

"Not that we know of. I asked around and he doesn't have friends, though most people spoke highly of his business acumen," Morrison answered. "He doesn't have family I can find, not here anyway. He has a sister in Yorkshire; where you're staying, I understand."

"Bother," Ramsay said. "I was hoping to hear he didn't have a sister."

Morrison laughed. "Not everyone in the world is a criminal. You know of his sister then?"

Ramsay explained, adding, "My guess is she's the one who told him about Harry needing cash. I wondered how that happened."

"If you need any more information about honest citizens," Morrison said, "call on someone else. I've wasted a day's worth of police time investigating harmless innocent people. There are rules about that, you know."

Ramsay apologized and thanked him for his help, and then asked, "And Pritchard? You won't forget him, will you?"

Ramsay thought he could feel Morrison's frustration even through the phone line; however, he was pleasantly surprised when Morrison assured him that he hadn't forgotten and the 'wheels were in motion', which Ramsay understood to mean Morrison had asked for files to be provided. He asked after Morrison's family, and, on hearing everything was well, hung up. "Bracken, we should have gone to Berwick or Blackpool for our walking trip. Anywhere far from here. Baldock will have me in jail before I've even begun, at this rate."

Bracken's look suggested: 'I'm beginning to think this might be a good thing.'

"We'll walk," Ramsay told him. "Then I'll get you back to Mrs. Golightly and I can go pub crawling."

* * *

*Y*E *D*OLPHIN WAS quiet when Ramsay walked in and looked about for Eliza. She was nowhere to be seen so he ordered a pint at the bar and took up a position where he could survey the whole room.

A group of men entered and ordered at the bar, but they looked like young men starting their evening, rather than disgruntled workers drowning their sorrows.

At this time, Eliza and her friend entered the bar, and the young men immediately took note. Eliza's friend ordered at the end of the bar furthest from the men and carried their drinks to a table at the side of the room opposite where Ramsay was sitting. Eliza gave him no sign of recognition, which he was relieved about. But his relief lasted all of two minutes, right up until she removed her coat revealing a mini skirt that, in Ramsay's mind, was positively indecent. He knew these things were all the rage right now, only he hadn't seen any in the places he frequented. It grew worse. She sat facing him and slowly crossed her legs. *Mischief,* he thought, despairingly. *More mischief.*

Time passed, and Ramsay sipped his pint slowly. This would be a long night. He watched the room and Eliza, who was chatting to her companion and studiously ignoring him. Men came in and out of the bar but Eliza gave him no indication Robinson was among them.

Then the door opened, and a man dressed in farm working clothes entered; he looked out-of-place. Ramsay quickly looked at Eliza who was staring directly at him. Their eyes locked and Ramsay felt a jolt inside like he'd brushed against an electric fence. Feelings were creeping into his safe world again and they all made him uncomfortable.

Eliza's gaze moved from Ramsay to the newcomer, who was making his way to the empty end of the bar. Ramsay followed Eliza's gaze. He looked back to her and raised his eyebrows in a question. She nodded, so slightly, he'd have missed it if he hadn't been watching for it. She turned back to her friend and Ramsay rose from his seat and walked to intercept the newcomer.

"John Robinson?"

"Aye. And you are?" Robinson replied.

"I'm Tom Ramsay. I found Harry Peacock's body and I wanted to talk to you about Harry and Ravenscar Fishing."

"I've talked till I'm blue in the face about that, but no one listens."

"I will," Ramsay said. "If you'll let me."

"It'll cost you a pint," Robinson replied. "Best bitter."

Ramsay caught the barman's attention and ordered a pint and a Scotch. When they were served, he led Robinson back to the table where his first drink was waiting.

They sat and Ramsay let Robinson take a long, slow sip before he began, "You worked for Harry Peacock once, I understand."

Robinson nodded. "Straight from school but I was never trusted."

"Why do you say that?"

"I was never on Harry's boat," Robinson said. "Ten years I was with them and never once on *Lady 1*."

"Why was that do you think?" Ramsay asked, when it was clear Robinson wasn't about to continue. This could be a long interview.

"I asked questions and was looking to get a better deal for the lads," Robinson replied. "Harry didn't like that."

"Were you a union man?"

Robinson laughed, bitterly. "Nay, man. I don't hold with that stuff. I just felt we weren't sharing the sales equally. Harry's crew seemed to get more. Harry said it was cos they caught more but I didn't see it."

"Yet he kept you on?"

"I was a good worker, he knew that. Others thought the same way I did, but they had families to support and kept their heads down and their mouths shut."

"When did you suspect there was more to this unequal sharing of wages?" Ramsay asked.

"When Harry bought *Ravenscar Lady 3*. The crew he hired weren't local men, except one, and nor was the skipper. To successfully fish out there, you have to know the waters and the behavior of the fish, how they move with the seasons and the time of night."

"The crew of *Lady 3* were also better paid, I imagine," Ramsay ventured.

Robinson nodded. "It seemed like it. Then only a few months later, he bought a bigger, more modern boat and moved himself and his crew to it. Hiring some local men to crew *Lady 1*. By now, I was right suspicious and told others so."

"But it was just the wages you thought suspicious?"

"Nay. I'd been keeping careful watch for weeks and I knew by now something wasn't right. Some nights, Harry's boat would sail farther out after assigning our fishing spots, and they'd arrive back much later in the early hours of next morning."

"Well, they would, wouldn't they, if they went out further?" Ramsay asked.

"Of course, but they must have gone almost to Holland to explain the time -- and they didn't. I watched the boat. They went a long way, five miles maybe, but the boat's lights went out, they didn't sink down over the horizon."

"You believe they met another boat?"

"I can't think of any other reason they would be out there. Our boats weren't trawlers meant for deep-sea fishing, not even the new one Harry bought," Robinson replied.

"I've thought about this a lot since I found the body," Ramsay said. "If it was smuggling, how do they get the contraband ashore? Did you find the answer to that?"

Robinson shook his head. "That's why no one believes me. I can't answer that."

"I heard there are tunnels under Robin Hood's Bay that smugglers used in the old days. Do they exist? Could Harry have found them?"

Robinson laughed. "If there were tunnels, they'd be open to the public at a shilling a guided tour. Nah. There are no tunnels."

"Yet I found Harry's body in one."

"That tunnel was part of the old Alum mine, not in the village, and nought to do with smuggling," Robinson said.

"I know. Only, if there was one there no one knew about, can't there be others?"

"Still doesn't explain how the goods could get from a fishing boat at sea into this imaginary tunnel on land," Robinson replied.

"You never saw them stop up close to the cliff at Ness Point, for instance?" Ramsay asked.

"No but like I said they came in long after the rest of us," Robinson replied.

"Would it be light by then?"

Robinson shook his head. "Maybe at midsummer but not generally. We're talking about four in the morning."

Ramsay had a sudden thought. "You said earlier 'some nights' Harry's boat went farther out. How often was this? Daily? Weekly?"

"Nay, nothing like that," Robinson replied. "It wasn't regular, like. It was just once in a while."

Ramsay considered this thoughtfully. It made sense, he thought. After all, contraband wouldn't be shipping to a schedule like regular goods, only when it was available. It seemed to draw an end to the conversation, so he continued, "I've asked everything I've thought of. Is there anything you remember we haven't talked about?"

Robinson shook his head and Ramsay thanked him for his assistance, adding, "Weren't you afraid Harry would have you silenced for speaking out?"

"I wasn't," Robinson said, "but this new man may be different. He's not one of us."

"Then we never spoke," Ramsay said, finishing his drink and putting on his coat.

Robinson laughed. "Everyone in here tonight knows we did but they also know no one has proved anything so far and I don't expect you will either."

Ramsay left the pub, nodding to Eliza as he left. She took the hint and, minutes later, joined him outside.

"I'll get rid of Connie and meet you at the guest house," she told him, before he could speak.

"Mrs. Golightly wouldn't accept you up in my room alone with me," Ramsay said, "not even with Bracken to guard you."

"Then where?"

"I'll be at The Seaview Hotel. Join me when you can,"

Ramsay replied, before adding, "and don't offend Connie to do that."

"Oh, Connie won't mind," Eliza said, confidently dismissing her companion's feelings without scruple.

"Don't burn any bridges," Ramsay said. "This case won't last forever."

"Okay, okay, I get the message. See you soon." Eliza returned to the pub while Ramsay made his way down to the seawall and The Seaview Hotel.

16

THE VICTIM'S HOUSE

AFTER AN HOUR, Ramsay assumed Eliza must have done as he'd asked because he'd finished two glasses of Glenfiddich, and she still hadn't joined him. Reviewing what he'd learned since he started, he decided it was either Armstrong or someone he'd never heard of related to Harry's criminal enterprises. What particularly bothered him was Robinson hadn't provided a plausible explanation for how the goods, if they existed, were taken from the boats to shore. One question that came to mind as he waited was, where did Harry live? Eliza would know.

It was almost closing time when she appeared, once again in her silk-like dress. Ramsay couldn't believe it was silk, but it looked like it. Probably, one of those new man-made fibers he heard so much about.

"You changed," Ramsay said, smiling.

"I haven't many opportunities to wear nice clothes and I'm not passing on any," Eliza said, perching on a barstool beside him.

"It's emptying out," Ramsay said, "and we can't talk here.

I'll get your drink. You grab that table over there." He pointed to the small table they'd used previously.

"Our table," Eliza said, grinning. "You really are a romantic."

"What are you having?"

"Campari," Eliza said, before adding, "I hope I like it."

Ramsay joined her with their drinks and settled onto the chair facing.

"Well?" Eliza demanded, before sipping her drink and pulling a face.

"It's bought," Ramsay said. "So, you're drinking it."

"I expect it's an acquired taste," Eliza replied, still grimacing. "I just have to keep drinking until I do like it. Now tell me!"

Ramsay recounted Robinson's information and then said, "What did you learn from Arthur?"

"I told you the most important parts," she replied. "He gets his dad's house, his dad's bank account, and half the business. My guess, is he'll have sniffed, smoked, or injected the bank account before the week is out."

"Did he tell you that or have you taken a dislike to him?"

"He said 'it's party time' at some point. I think he'd already started celebrating when I phoned," Eliza said. "I can see Armstrong having the lot in a month."

"That reminds me," Ramsay said, "where did Harry live?"

"On a farm on Ness Point. Didn't I tell you?"

"No but that's what I was hoping you'd say," Ramsay replied. "Now I just need to work out how he got the goods from the sea up those cliffs to his farm."

"He couldn't. Not without being seen."

Ramsay nodded, glumly. "I know."

"It has to be Armstrong," Eliza said, "or Arthur and I

don't believe it was Arthur because he was really worried about the will the other day. I'm sure he didn't know he'd do so well out of it."

"He must have assumed he'd get something and maybe that was enough," Ramsay said, shaking his head. "Like you, I think Armstrong but there's always Mr. X."

"I must have missed him," Eliza said, smiling. "Who is he?"

"Someone with a motive we don't know about, most likely a motive concerning the criminal activities."

"Then you still haven't ruled out your old colleague Pritchard?"

"Him or someone else? One of Harry's crew perhaps," Ramsay said. "Maybe it was an argument about something we don't know about, and it got heated."

"And this somebody just happened to have a heavy metal bar handy? And knew about Harry's tunnel hideout?"

"I know, I know," Ramsay protested, "but it is possible, particularly if it was a crew member. They could have watched Harry for years and known all about it. Maybe, they felt their share wasn't big enough."

"If we're opening it up to all possibilities," Eliza said, "others in the village could have watched him too and had their own scores to settle."

"There's no radar here at the village, is there?" Ramsay asked, off topic.

"Not here no. Why?"

"What if the goods were loaded onto a small boat and brought into Harry's hideout only when it was full tide?"

"It couldn't be in daytime," Eliza said. "Practically everyone in the village walks on or looks along the beach every day."

"I see small boats sitting just inside the bay most of the day," Ramsay said.

"Crab potting boats," Eliza said, nodding.

"Then maybe they off-load to a boat that goes crabbing all day and bring the goods in on a nighttime full tide," Ramsay mused.

Eliza shook her head. "Then it couldn't be very big, or the goods would be seen by everyone. There's no hold or cabin on those boats."

Ramsay nodded, despondently. "Even from the clifftops, I'd have seen a boat filled with crates."

"Maybe there is no smuggling," Eliza said. "We've only got disgruntled men who think there is and local legends that gave them the idea. Anyway, look how small the village is. No one could afford to buy booze every day and I've never seen a big transport vehicle hauling anything away, let alone contraband."

"How do the fish go out?"

"On the early morning milk train," Eliza replied. "And the train's guard would notice if the boxes didn't include fish. You can be sure of that."

"Maybe you're right," Ramsay said. "There's no smuggling and Armstrong just wants to sell the boats to make a profit. Nothing illegal in it. Except, someone killed Harry."

"As you suggested, a personal score to settle or an argument that got out of hand."

Ramsay suddenly noticed the hotel staff silently watching them. "I think they want to clean up and close up."

They finished their drinks and exited the hotel, Ramsay offering apologies to the staff as he left. Outside, the night was clear. Lights of the Raven Hall hotel across the bay and farms on the hillside twinkled in the darkness. "Frost tonight, I think," Ramsay said, buttoning his coat.

"Another night of huddling for warmth," Eliza said, stepping closer and linking arms.

"For a northern girl, you seem to feel the cold a lot," Ramsay replied, smiling. He hugged her arm tightly and found he enjoyed that sensation too. They began walking up the hill where, in shadowy spaces, other couples too were keeping out the night chill.

"I'm a sensitive flower," Eliza said, "but only when you're around." She smiled and kissed his cheek. "Now, Inspector, what are our jobs for tomorrow."

"There'll be nobody at Harry's farm," Ramsay said, shakily. "Bracken and I will investigate there."

"While I wait on tables gleaning snippets from customers, I suppose."

"Or phone Arthur Peacock again and see if he can say what exactly it was made him think his father was a smuggler," Ramsay replied.

"If he's befuddled enough," Eliza agreed, nodding, "he might say something useful. I must say, Inspector, I don't think we're making enough progress to keep you from being the scapegoat for Harry's death."

Harry nodded. He too had thought this, and he lived in dread Baldock would be pounding on the guest house door sometime soon. The warning sent through Constable Storm had been harmless enough, but only because Storm wasn't the man to effectively relay such a message.

"What about Baldock as the prime suspect," Eliza asked. "Have we forgotten him?"

"He hasn't appeared in any of the statements we've heard," Ramsay replied. "He could be Mr. X, of course, as well as anyone else."

"Pritchard thought he was," Eliza said, "and I don't like Baldock. That's good enough for me."

"Do you know him?"

Eliza shook her head. "No but he threatened to implicate you and that makes him public enemy number one in my book."

"Your loyalty is touching."

"Oh, I'll visit you in prison, have no fear," Eliza said, lightly, "and keep investigating to clear your name. I'm not the quitting kind."

Ramsay shook his head, pleased but rather self-conscious. "I'll be out on the headland at seven in the morning," he told her, as they reached Eliza's gate. "If you can get up for then, care to show me Harry's farm before you go to work."

"I'll be there," Eliza replied, grinning and kissing him lightly on the lips. "See you bright and early," she whispered as she walked to the door. "Goodnight."

This is becoming awkward, Ramsay thought, as he walked back to the guest house. *I know she's only teasing me, but others won't. 'May-December romances' aren't as common in real life as they are in fiction and people can be disagreeable. And if she isn't teasing, what will I tell Bracken?*

* * *

"Good morning," Ramsay said, as he and Bracken stepped out from the guest house door to find Eliza waiting for them.

"It's freezing," Eliza said, glaring at him.

"We'll soon warm up, Bracken likes to maintain a fast pace wherever he goes," Ramsay said, his arm outstretched as Bracken strained against the leash.

"At least the grass is frosty instead of wet," Eliza

remarked, as they entered the path, leaving the street behind.

"Your rubber boots will keep your feet dry," Ramsay replied, unsympathetically. "Now, how far to Harry's house?"

"Not far. That's it there." Eliza pointed to an old stone house and rundown outbuildings less than a quarter of a mile away.

"Harry wasn't a farmer, I deduce," Ramsay commented, seeing the state of the farm.

Eliza shook her head. "He liked the view over the bay to Ravenscar, which is where he grew up and started fishing from. Everybody said he was mad when he began because the waters around the scar are so rough."

"Even from here I can see that," Ramsay replied. He stopped and studied the path and the rough ground that would lead them to Harry's farm. "There's no sign of a track so he didn't come to the edge of the cliffs and haul his contraband up by hand."

They set off across the grassy tussocks, myrtle and bilberry bushes, Ramsay wishing he too had a pair of rubber boots as his feet and ankles grew wetter. Bracken was delighted; he raced across the ground chasing scent after scent, each ending disappointingly at a rabbit burrow where he couldn't go.

At the farm, Ramsay inspected the outbuildings first. They were almost totally derelict and held nothing of interest. The house was locked.

"I imagine Arthur will sell it," Eliza said, as they examined the windows for a possible way in.

"As Arthur's neither a farmer nor a fisherman," Ramsay agreed. "I imagine you're right."

"Poor dad," Eliza said. "Arthur will sell everything to

Armstrong who'll sell the boats and lay all the crews off. Harry may have been an angry old man, but he kept a lot of people in work."

At the back of the house, they found an old coal cellar. Ramsay tugged at the handles and the doors moved.

"Breaking and entering is against the law in this country," Eliza reminded him.

"I expect Baldock and his men will have searched the place, anyway," Ramsay said, letting go of the handles. He turned to look back at the cliff edge. "Could a tunnel go from here to the cliff?"

"There's no entrance that can be seen from the beach," Eliza said.

"Could it be underwater? And could a diver guide the goods into the tunnel and place the goods on a shelf above the water inside the cave for people coming down from the house to collect?"

"I don't know," Eliza said. "Do you think it's possible?"

Ruefully, Ramsay shook his head. "I'm growing desperate to find any smuggling — that's the truth of it. Grasping at straws, basically."

"Have you considered them dropping the goods off at Ravenscar?"

"Yes, but even if that is possible in that rough water over there, how would they get them up that cliff," he pointed to the towering headland across the bay, "without being seen?"

Eliza agreed, adding, "There must be something. If it isn't smuggling, what is it?"

Ramsay laughed, before saying, in a stage sinister voice, "All will be revealed."

17

A NEW SUSPECT

"There's no evidence of smuggling here," Eliza said, slipping her arm through his and turning them both away from the house.

"One last look in that barn building," Ramsay said, leading her to the only one of the outbuildings that still had a roof. "We'll check the floor for trapdoors."

"If the police have been here, they will have found it," Eliza pointed out.

"Hah!" Ramsay exclaimed. "Not if they don't believe in what they're searching for."

The floor yielded no trapdoors to their gaze but, Ramsay thought, *there are signs something has certainly been stored here.*

"Harry was no farmer," Ramsay said, musing aloud, "and yet he bought and lived in a farmhouse where he could see the sea. It can't be a coincidence. It must mean something."

"It means he got the place cheap when the old farmer died and the land was sold to neighboring farms," Eliza said. "I remember him saying that."

"Is that all it was?" Ramsay wondered aloud. Bracken tugging at the leash which took Ramsay by surprise. "What is it?" he asked, allowing himself to be dragged to a pile of rubbish piled near the door. Bracken went around the refuse, growling fiercely.

A rat shot out from the heap and out the door, Bracken desperate to follow. "No, Bracken," Ramsay told him, pulling hard to stop the eager dog. "Focus on why we're here." As he spoke, he saw the corner of a sheet of paper among the refuse. He pulled it out of the heap. It was only a torn off corner, but Ramsay recognized it as being like the papers he'd seen near Harry's body. He showed and explained the find to Eliza.

"So what?" Eliza said. "It only shows Harry had these documents in his possession, not that they or the goods were stored here."

Ramsay pulled at the rubbish until the pile was spread out across the floor. There was nothing else that seemed related to smuggling.

"We should go," Eliza said, bored. "This is another waste of time. We haven't found anything to help us at all. This whole investigation is just fairy stories and all leading to dead ends."

Ramsay nodded his agreement, too disappointed and puzzled at his inability to find important evidence. He suspected Baldock was ahead of him, and the police had found anything that was relevant.

"It has to be Armstrong," Eliza said, returning to their earlier discussions. "We should concentrate on him."

"If we knew exactly when Harry died," Ramsay replied, "we could, but we don't."

"I'm going to ask everyone if they saw him any time from August the fourteenth to the sixteenth, the days you were told he could have died," Eliza said, stubbornly. "Someone will know. They always do in a village."

"Certainly, the smuggling angle isn't turning up any leads," Ramsay agreed. "Arthur said he was away on business. We need to confirm that, and I know someone who might help us there."

"Constable Storm?"

Ramsay nodded. "Exactly. If they haven't already checked, he could make some discreet enquiries."

"If Baldock finds out Percy has helped us again, he'll lose his job," Eliza reminded him. "You told me he'd already sent Storm to warn you off. Even a Percy Storm would understand he was in Baldock's sights, as well."

Ramsay shrugged "That's up to the constable. He can always say no."

* * *

Constable Storm, however, was happy to tell him the police had confirmed Arthur Peacock was far away from Ravenscar and Robin Hood's Bay at the time they believed Harry was murdered.

"He couldn't have secretly come back one day?"

Storm shook his head. "No. He was talking to a lot of pop star hopefuls all that week."

"Did you look into the possibility he had someone else murder his father while his alibi was rock solid?" Ramsay asked.

"We did and it seems unlikely," Storm replied. "He hasn't the money, for one thing. He's practically bankrupt."

"A strong motive, then," Ramsay mused aloud. "Only, no opportunity and he wasn't nearby to carry it out. It seems I must mark him down as 'unlikely' on my list."

"We have," Storm said. "Now, if there's nothing else Inspector, I should walk my beat. The villagers like to know the police are awake."

"Oh," Ramsay said, acting surprised, "before you go, did the medical people narrow down the time of death?"

"That information is being withheld," Storm said, seriously.

"But it was in the range of dates you gave me earlier, say August the fourteenth to sixteenth?" Ramsay asked.

"Right in the middle, as it happens," Storm said, nodding.

"Well, that should help Inspector Baldock a lot," Ramsay responded. *And me too.* As he walked, his question to Storm about Arthur having an accomplice popped back into his mind. Armstrong could also have had an accomplice. A disgruntled member of the crew or a skipper, perhaps? Eliza's father might know.

Ramsay set off down the hill. "Sooner or later, we'll learn something useful, Bracken," Ramsay said, as they walked, "and today might be the day."

Bracken sneezed, or was it a disbelieving snort?

Mr. Danesdale was at his desk, as he always was when they visited, when Ramsay and Bracken entered. The sight of him hunched over ledgers depressed Ramsay. *Imagine spending your life that way.*

"Good morning," Danesdale said, in his ponderous, tired voice.

"Good morning," Ramsay replied. "I have another question. Are we alone?"

Danesdale nodded, and said, "For now."

"When we last spoke, I asked if Armstrong and Harry had argued before Harry was killed. Did you see Armstrong and one of the fishermen, or maybe a skipper, talking together just before Harry was killed?"

"As Mr. Armstrong became more involved with the business, he began talking to the skippers, why?" Danesdale asked.

Ramsay was now leaning against Danesdale's desk and asked, quietly, "Any particular skipper?"

Equally quietly, Danesdale considered before replying. "The new one, Vernon Caldbeck mostly, I'd say. You think he killed Harry on Armstrong's orders?"

"It's just a thought," Ramsay said. "I'm not suggesting it happened, only that it could have happened."

"Would either of them have known about Harry's hideout?" Danesdale asked. "I mean, I didn't, and I've lived here most of my life."

"One or the other of them could have watched Harry's movements over the preceding days and found it that way. If they were planning a takeover of the company, they'd prepare and plan accordingly."

"I suppose," Danesdale replied. "But surely, they wouldn't need to kill Harry. Armstrong had fifty percent ownership of the business and that man Caldbeck had been doing whatever that boat was doing for some time. They could have blackmailed Harry into giving them what they wanted by threatening to go to the police with what they knew."

"Do you think Harry was the kind of man to accept blackmail calmly and rationally?"

Danesdale grinned and shook his head. "That's true. He'd be more likely to throw the man out with a boot up the backside. Not a subtle man, our Harry."

"And Caldbeck is likely not the kind of man who takes

no for an answer either. There'd likely be a fight and, maybe accidentally, Harry was killed."

Danesdale nodded. "Let me show you something." He crossed the floor to a filing cabinet and opened the top drawer, removed a ledger and returned to his desk before flicking through the pages. "Here," he said, turning the ledger to Ramsay and pointing at a sizeable cash withdrawal.

"To Armstrong," Ramsay read aloud, "for business expenses. Did he explain?"

"Only that he'd incurred these expenses while negotiating possible new outlets for our fish, where we'd get a better price than we're getting from our current buyer. He was going to provide receipts for these expenses, and he hasn't."

"Have you reminded him?"

"No," Danesdale replied. "To be honest, it had slipped my mind with all that has been happening. Your questions reminded me."

"Were there more payments?"

Danesdale nodded. "Wait." He drew another ledger from the filing cabinet and leafed through the pages. "Here," he cried, pointing. "One payment before and one after Harry's death."

"The police need to be told," Ramsay said. "I can phone them, if you'd rather not. I take that back. It would be best for you if you've suddenly remembered this and then you'll have called them right away."

Danesdale's expression was even more solemn than usual. "They'll say I withheld evidence."

"You'd forgotten. Today you were checking something and saw the payments. Put together a story you can live with and phone them."

"I'll tell Percy," Danesdale said. "He can tell that Inspector."

"Do whatever makes you comfortable but don't mention I was here," Ramsay said. "Baldock doesn't like me, and he'll be angry to find I had anything to do with this discovery. It must be yours and only yours. Do you understand?"

Danesdale picked up the phone and dialed the number for the police house. Ramsay waited until he was sure Eliza's dad told Constable Storm of his discovery before waving goodbye and quickly leaving the office. Outside, a thin drizzle was beginning to fall, little more than a 'sea-fret' but bidding to become harder soon.

"You and I need to be well away from here before Percy Storm arrives, Bracken," Ramsay said, "or he'll guess we had a hand in it." They began hurrying toward New Street when Ramsay saw Armstrong on King Street. Ramsay changed direction immediately.

"Here's our villain, Bracken," Ramsay said, quietly. "Act nonchalant."

"Mr. Armstrong," Ramsay called, as Armstrong knocked on the nearby cottage door. "Visiting your sister?"

Armstrong paused and turned to face Ramsay. "I am. What's that to you?"

"Do you visit her a lot?" Ramsay asked, approaching Armstrong.

"Again, I ask, what's that to do with you?"

"I wondered," Ramsay said, "if you'd visited on the day Harry Peacock was killed?"

"I've already told the police I did, and Mona has confirmed that to be true," Armstrong said. "There. Will that do you?"

"All day?"

"Of course, not all day," Armstrong replied, testily. "Only

most of it and I was meeting other people when I wasn't here. My sister lives alone. I live alone. We've always been close. Now, if you don't mind, I'd like to get out of this rain."

He knocked again on the door, which opened, and he stepped quickly inside leaving Ramsay and Bracken to make their way down to the slipway. Bracken still hoping for a run in the country, Ramsay deep in thought. Both had their wishes thwarted by a sudden downpour that drove everything from their heads but finding shelter.

18

SUSPECTS IN CUSTODY

RAMSAY AND BRACKEN found their first welcoming shelter at the Danesdale's teashop. They rushed in, sodden and eagerly searching for warmth.

Eliza laughed when she saw them walk in. "Have you two been swimming?"

Bracken shook himself and water flew from his coat, splashing the door and doormat. Ramsay hung his coat on a hanger and said, "We've been interviewing. I hope you have too." He could speak freely because the shop was empty. The morning break customers were gone, and the lunch crowd hadn't yet arrived.

"I asked customers questions," Eliza replied. "I didn't get any useful replies. No one I spoke to can remember seeing him those days. It was two months ago, as they all reminded me."

Ramsay grinned. "A large, hot pot of tea, please. We had better luck than you did."

"I'll get the tea and we'll talk," Eliza said, hurrying of into the kitchen, returning a moment later with water and scraps for Bracken.

"How is it Bracken is always served before me," Ramsay complained.

"Because Bracken is nice and you're always so glum." Bracken gave her a broad smile in response to her stroking his head.

"My tea will be getting cold," Ramsay said, breaking up the small mutual petting party going on at his feet.

Eliza returned with the tea and two cups and saucers. "Now," she asked, laying the tray on the table and pouring the tea before adding more hot water to the pot, "what did you learn?"

Ramsay explained.

As Eliza listened her expression grew somber. "Poor Dad. Baldock will drag him over the coals for this memory lapse."

Ramsay nodded. "I'm afraid so. I only hope he'll stick to his story and not blurt out I had anything to do with it. That really would send Baldock over the edge."

"You think it was the new skipper, Armstrong paid off?"

"His name's Vernon Caldbeck, I've just learned, and he is the most likely person," Ramsay replied. "He was brought here to be the skipper of that one boat and has no ties to Harry or the village. He's also the one who oversees whatever it is they're bringing in."

"I was wondering about diamonds," Eliza said. "They'd fit in Caldbeck's pocket, and no one would know they were there. And Amsterdam, the city of diamonds, is straight over the horizon."

"I'd thought that too," Ramsay said, "but, as far as I know, diamonds aren't an item worth smuggling in Europe. After all, London is a big diamond cutting and selling city, and they don't have any trouble getting a supply of them."

"Perhaps they're stolen diamonds or something," Eliza

said. "I'm just trying to think of goods they could bring in without anyone noticing."

Ramsay nodded. "I understand. I've been doing the same. I'd thought of drugs but, again, there's a problem. Drugs don't come to us from Europe, not in any quantities anyway."

"Maybe they're starting to," Eliza suggested. "Anyway, what's next?"

"I plan to sit here until Bracken and I are dry and warm," Ramsay said. "I hope that, within a very short time, I'll see a police car racing past here on its way to the police house."

Eliza laughed. "I want to see that too."

THEY HAD some time to wait. Ramsay had drunk two pots of tea and eaten a lot of hot buttered toast before the sound of a fast moving, approaching, car made him crane his eyes to the window. He frantically waved to Eliza who was putting together a tray behind the counter. She hurried over just in time to see two black police cars race by on their way down to the Ravenscar Fishing office, one with a grim Inspector Baldock in the rear seat and the other filled with officers.

"Poor dad," Eliza said again. "I warned mam of what was likely to happen. I'll just go and tell her it's happening." She hurried off into the kitchen before returning to serve the two couples waiting for their lunch. With that done, she returned to Ramsay's table. "Armstrong will fire him for sure now."

"I fear so," Ramsay said. "But if Armstrong is held in custody, Arthur Peacock may need your dad to keep the business operating."

"Will he be kept in custody though?"

"Baldock strikes me as the sort of man who would keep

him in to unnerve him and make him more ready to talk," Ramsay said. "We'll know soon enough." He returned to watching from the window.

"Shouldn't you be returning to Mrs. Golightly for lunch?" Eliza asked.

Ramsay shook his head. "The arrangement I made was I'd only have lunch if I returned for lunch. I'd expected to be walking most days, you see."

"Then I should bring you a lunch menu," Eliza said, walking to the counter and returning with the menu.

Ramsay and Bracken had finished lunch before they heard a car's engine straining up the hill.

"This will be them, Bracken," Ramsay said. Bracken leapt onto the chair at the window and watched with Ramsay. Eliza soon joined them.

"It's madness to let cars go down that hill," Ramsay said, as the grinding of gears told them a car climbing the hill was coming nearer. "It's much too steep."

"The police should buy better cars," Eliza said.

The black rover passed in front of the window with Armstrong and a man Ramsay guessed was Caldbeck in the back seat. Baldock was watching them moodily from the front.

"There's not much to this police work, is there?" Eliza said. "A doddery old man remembers something he should have known days before and it's done."

"Armstrong may have perfectly good explanations for those two payments," Ramsay replied, "and he could be back before the day is out."

Eliza snorted. "Hah! I'm guessing he hasn't or Baldock wouldn't have hauled him away with the other one."

"Armstrong may just be waiting until he can have a lawyer present before explaining. Those two may be the murderers but there's a lot of ground to be covered before the police have a case against them."

"You didn't put my dad in danger for the fun of it, did you?" Eliza asked, suspiciously.

"I wouldn't do that," Ramsay replied. "I do think we have the answer; Armstrong had motive, means and opportunity. I'm just warning you not to get too comfortable too soon. Villains are slippery customers and always have another story to tell."

"So, we continue tomorrow?" Eliza asked. "What can I do?"

"Keep grilling the customers and I'll re-visit Percy Storm and my old colleague, Len Pritchard."

"This isn't fair," Eliza grumbled. "You question all the interesting people while I interview dotty old dears."

Ramsay laughed. "Both of us are interviewing potential witnesses. I doubt I'll get anything more from my two than you get from your twenty." He did, however, hope to hear something useful, particularly if Pritchard knew Armstrong was being held by the police.

Even as he was speaking, Ramsay saw Constable Storm making his rounds of the village. Quickly bidding Eliza farewell, Ramsay and Bracken left and intercepted the policeman.

"Good afternoon, Constable," Ramsay said. "Inspector Baldock seems to have taken a suspect into custody. Is that true?"

"It was very public, wasn't it," Storm replied. "Two suspects are being held for questioning. I've no doubt the case is over, and it was my doing that made it happen," he added, rather smugly.

"I hope then you get some credit," Ramsay said. "I know how these things go; you see."

"Aye, you're right there," Storm replied. "Still, I'm not looking for promotion out of the village. I like it here. It's my home and always has been."

"What has he on these two?" Ramsay asked. "I know inspector Baldock would happily include me in his list of suspects so I'd like to hear he can't."

Storm laughed. "Aye, he's set against you, right enough. But the evidence that came to light today can't involve you so you should be safe."

"Are inquiries continuing?" Ramsay asked. "Or is he confident he has his man?"

"They're continuing," Storm replied, "so you're not out of the woods yet."

"Is the arrest about the murder or the smuggling?" Ramsay asked, keeping the conversation going as they walked. He wanted as much from Storm as he could get before the constable realized he may be saying too much to a member of the public.

"There's no arrest, Mr. Ramsay. The questions being asked of the suspects are about the murder but there's no doubt as the interviews continue, the smuggling will come into it."

"You never caught them smuggling, I think you said," Ramsay probed.

"That's right," Storm answered. "It's possible they were tipped off on the days I inspected the boats as they unloaded."

"In a small community like this, it's easily done," Ramsay agreed, sympathetically, before adding, "You know, I've looked at the bay up and down, north to south, and every other way and I can't see how anyone could land contraband goods. It makes me wonder if the smuggling story isn't a cover for something else."

Storm nodded. "I decided in the end it was just unhappy people who'd fallen out with Harry Peacock spreading tales because I couldn't see how it could be done either. In the end, I stopped looking."

"That makes me feel better," Ramsay said. "If a local man with years of experience doesn't think it's happening, I'll give it a rest too. I thought it was just me not knowing the sea and boats."

"The murder will likely turn out to be personal," Storm said. "Or business related. Fishing's a cut-throat world nowadays."

Ramsay laughed. "Right from the start, everyone told me Harry was an unpleasant old man. I just didn't want to believe that's all it was. If the murder is wrapped up, I need to consider how to use the rest of my holiday. The weather isn't always good for walking. Can you suggest some places?"

"There's Whitby Abbey and the 199 steps where Dracula landed and climbed up to the church," Storm replied, "but likely you've seen them. Scarborough Castle is popular with visitors, not that there's much left to see. Oliver Cromwell's men saw to that." He paused, then said, "If you want to see a modern wonder, and a dramatic sight at that, there's the Early Warning Station at Fylingdales."

"A modern radar station doesn't sound very appealing," Ramsay said, grimacing. "I thought we had enough of that stuff in the war."

"Normally, I would agree with you," Storm said, "even though I'm in the Territorial Army and enjoy the war games we do as exercises up there. No, what makes this so popular with visitors is the dramatic location, right on top of the high moor and their design. They're like three giant golf balls, same color too, and they fairly dominate the countryside around. I imagine it's how a Norman castle looked to the locals when they were first built."

"Just as oppressive, you mean," Ramsay said, grinning. "I'll keep it in mind. Does the territorial army exercise with the Fylingdales site guards?"

Storm laughed. "Not exactly, but we do practice defending it and, as a policeman, I've helped keep the Ban the Bomb protesters from climbing the fences and doing the men and equipment in there some minor mischief."

"I imagine the army staff in there would make short work of any student radicals."

"They're Royal Air Force personnel," Storm said, "but I reckon the result would be the same."

"Not local men then?"

Storm shook his head. "No, like I say, air force, so drawn from all over the country."

"They must live locally, I imagine," Ramsay mused.

A momentary expression of doubt crossed Storm's face before he replied, "I couldn't say, sir."

Seeing he'd gone beyond even the garrulous Storm's lack of discretion, Ramsay smiled and said, "Of course not. Quite right. Anyway, thanks for setting my mind at rest on the murder case, constable. I'll bid you good day and let you get on with your patrol." As he walked away, he considered why Storm's expression should change from its usual stolid simplicity when asked if the men lived locally.

19

AN EX-POLICEMAN'S EVIDENCE

Ramsay and Bracken headed back up the hill toward open space and out of the almost claustrophobic, tightly packed village. It was also the road to where Pritchard lived.

"You know, Bracken," Ramsay said, when he was sure there was no one to overhear him, "I can't help feeling many of our investigations back in the day came to nothing because of a Constable Storm character in the local force."

Bracken didn't care about a past he had no part in and continued straining at the leash, pulling Ramsay ever quicker to the open country and his favorite things, sheep and rabbits.

It was a bright afternoon now and the autumn leaves shimmered in the breeze as they walked the narrow lane from the station toward Fylingthorpe. Pritchard's house seemed asleep as they passed on their way and Ramsay decided Pritchard was out. As their walk drew farther and farther afield, Ramsay checked his watch regularly. He wanted to catch his old colleague and interview him today. When he judged the time right, he tugged Bracken's leash and said, "Time for the next interview."

Pritchard was in his garden, deadheading roses, when they arrived. "Hello, Len," Ramsay shouted, crossing the lane to speak to him. "I wondered if we'd see you on our walk."

"Tom," Pritchard replied, smiling. "This is a nice surprise. Come in. You'll want a cup of tea, I imagine, after your constitutional stroll."

"I don't want to bother you," Ramsay said — lied — "but you're right. Refreshment would be very welcome. Bracken is a fine companion, only he's still young and needs lots of exercise."

"He can run around in my back garden while we talk," Pritchard said, opening the gate to let them enter. "I like to keep the roses looking nice," he continued as they entered the house. "They look so sad when there are too many dead blooms on the bushes. Do you have a garden, Tom?'

"I do but it's not a patch on yours," Ramsay replied. "I haven't your green thumb."

"Fertilizer and work are the only secret I have," Pritchard laughed, as he plugged in the electric kettle. "And lots of free time."

"We both have that," Ramsay replied, letting Bracken off the leash and holding open the door for him to go out.

"Now what was it you really came for?" Pritchard asked.

Ramsay decided not to protest his innocence and said, "Baldock took Armstrong and one of the skippers into Scarborough headquarters. Did you hear?"

Pritchard shook his head. "I don't encourage gossip. You think he has the wrong man or men?"

"Not necessarily," Ramsay replied. "I hope Baldock has the right people because he was threatening me at the start of it all. I'd like to be sure I'm not suddenly roped into a murder charge in some way."

"I don't see how I can help?"

"I wondered if you'd thought any more about the smuggling racket and Baldock's possible involvement?"

Pritchard shook his head. "I never think about it anymore."

"Did you ever suspect smuggling through the village here?"

"Not really," Pritchard replied. "The kind we were looking at needs a big port, not a fishing village. How could they land enough contraband from a fishing boat to make the risk worthwhile?"

"That's the conclusion I've come to as well," Ramsay said. "It's just talk."

"So far as the big stuff goes, yes," Pritchard said. "Smaller items, maybe."

"I thought of diamonds and drugs," Ramsay said. "What are your thoughts?"

"How about industrial secrets?" Pritchard suggested. "They could be in film or photos. They wouldn't need much space."

"You think companies in our country would be part of something like that?" Ramsay asked. "Paying people to steal industrial secrets?"

"We keep hearing how we're falling behind industrially," Pritchard said. "Maybe stealing the plans of other people's products is the way forward, if we can no longer develop our own. Germany and Holland are just over the water there and they're both big in chemicals. Much of our own chemical industry is just up the coast on Teesside."

"You make a good point," Ramsay said slowly, "and I never thought of that. Thanks." His mind went back to the documents on the floor of the tunnel. Bills of lading, he'd thought, but maybe they were more than that. Maybe a cover for whatever was being brought in?

"I presume it was a falling out among thieves that led to the murder," Pritchard said.

Ramsay grinned. "For someone who isn't interested in crime anymore, you've thought about it a lot."

"I'm interested in the murder, not the smuggling."

"Though they're likely related," Ramsay said, "wouldn't you think? Where there's illicit money being made, people become greedy and suspicious. My feeling is they'd agree on the business but fall out on how the loot is being shared."

"You know," Pritchard said, thoughtfully, "they didn't question me about Harry Peacock's murder. No reason to, I suppose, but I do have a piece of information I could have shared."

"Then you should take it to the police, Len. You know that."

"It's likely nothing," Pritchard said. "Just something I saw."

"What did you see?"

"Armstrong and Harry Peacock arguing," Pritchard said. "Not just arguing. A real shouting match, threats and everything. Though they weren't really shouting because it was too close to where other people might hear. Each looked like they could kill the other. I'm not easily scared, well, you can't be after years in the force, but I wouldn't have stepped between them."

"When was this?"

Pritchard continued, "It was around two weeks before Harry went missing. I can't narrow it down better than that right now. If I can find the receipts of my shopping that day, I'll know and I'll phone you."

Ramsay considered this. Armstrong had a blazing row

with Harry two weeks before Harry went missing and he drew out a large sum of money from the company funds only ten days *before* Harry went missing. And another, a week *after* Harry went missing. Why the wait from getting the money to Harry's death? Ramsay's mind ran on. Of course, they needed Harry in his tunnel and fog in the bay. Simple. In his mind, the murder case was over.

"Len," Ramsay said, "you have to phone and tell Baldock. What you've just told me strengthens his case immensely."

"I don't see how," Pritchard said. "Armstrong and Harry were two short-fused men having a quarrel. They probably had them often."

"They did but what you witnessed sounds of a different kind altogether and the timing is telling, wouldn't you say?"

Pritchard nodded. "Very well, I'll phone him now. Stay while I call. He may have questions you could answer better than me."

"No! Don't tell him I'm here or that it was talking to me that jogged your memory," Ramsay said, quickly. "He'll decide I'm framing Armstrong and I'll be arrested."

Pritchard laughed. "You might at that. Very well, I'll say I heard about the arrest, and it reminded me of what I saw and heard."

"He'll want those receipts."

"I'll look for them, but they weren't for important items," Pritchard responded, "so I imagine they're long gone." He reached for the phone book and found the number of the police offices in Scarborough. He dialed and asked for Inspector Baldock.

It took some minutes before Ramsay heard Pritchard say, "It's Len Pritchard. I've just heard you have Armstrong in custody in connection to Harry Peacock's murder and I witnessed something you should know about."

Baldock's reply very clearly upset Pritchard.

"Look," Pritchard growled. "I'm telling you this because I believe it's the right thing to do. Not to deflect suspicion from me. Do you want to know or not?"

Baldock must have agreed he did for Pritchard described the argument he'd seen and the approximate time, as he'd told Ramsay.

"I understand it isn't proof of murder," Pritchard replied testily in answer to a question from Baldock, "it's just circumstantial. However, I thought you should know."

Pritchard listened for a moment before saying, "Yes, I would testify in court to what I've just said, and I'll make a statement at the police house here in the village today or tomorrow."

After some further discussion, Pritchard hung up the phone. "That man is a pig, and I don't mean it the way the public means it."

"I couldn't agree more," Ramsay said. "Anyway, thanks for providing your evidence, Len, even if it was to someone who hates us both. It took him a while to get to the truth, but I do think Baldock now has the killers in custody, and I can relax."

"Don't bank on it," Pritchard said, shaking his head. "If he has it in for you, you won't be safe until you go home."

"You could be right, only I'd like to sort out the smuggling angle if I can." Ramsay bade Pritchard farewell, collected Bracken who was worrying a stick to death, and they left. Bracken triumphantly carrying the stick as his trophy. Ramsay, deep in thought, made his way to the teashop where Eliza and her mother were closing but Eliza's mother went off to make him tea and bring Bracken water.

20

A NEW CLUE

Eliza couldn't sit to talk because of the closing work, which made Ramsay smile because it made her so furious. Her whole demeanor spoke of her frustration.

By the time Ramsay and Bracken had finished, the room was cleaned and tidied to Mrs. Danesdale's satisfaction and Eliza was able to install herself in the chair opposite Ramsay.

"Well?" she demanded.

"Well, yourself," Ramsay said, enjoying teasing her for a change. "What have you learned?"

"Nothing!"

"I had a good day," Ramsay replied, before relenting and telling her what he'd learned.

"Why didn't we think of industrial secrets?" Eliza grumbled. "I heard a play on the radio about it only a week or so ago."

"That's probably why Pritchard thought of it," Ramsay said.

"And the fisticuffs in the backstreet," Eliza exclaimed. "I

wish I'd seen that. I wonder who would win?" Her face took on a thoughtful expression as she tried to decide.

"It wasn't quite fisticuffs," Ramsay said, "though it's possible it did come to that at some time. Or maybe Armstrong decided he should get rid of Harry before that happened."

"Yes, I see that. He realized where this would end and got his retaliation in first," Eliza agreed, nodding. "What now?"

"You keep interviewing the customers," Ramsay said. "Bracken and I are going to revisit Harry's house. I want to find more of those papers I saw at the tunnel, and we found a piece of at his farm, now I have a better idea of what they might be."

"Wait until evening and I'll come too," Eliza pleaded.

Ramsay shook his head. "I won't have you involved with breaking and entering. You're too young to have a criminal record."

"Then can we break into the tunnel tonight after dark?"

Ramsay was about to say no when he stopped. "What time is the tide this afternoon or evening?"

"Wait," Eliza cried. She sprang to her feet. "We have the tide tables."

Ramsay was about to ask why but she was gone, returning only a minute later with the pamphlet. "Customers often ask us, you see, if they're thinking of walking along the beach to Ravenscar."

"High tide tonight will be midnight!" She crowed triumphantly. "It's going out now and will start returning around six. If we're at the tunnel before then, we've plenty of time to search and be back before the beach is covered."

"It will likely be boarded up," Ramsay said, thinking what he might take with them for leverage.

"You're an old man," Eliza said, grinning, "find yourself a solid walking stick."

"I doubt a stick would do it," Ramsay said, ignoring her jibe at his age. He was in the prime of life and these days, he felt it. "Metal is what we need."

"I'll leave here early to change," Eliza said. "Dad has a crowbar in his shed. I'll bring that."

"I'll meet you outside your home at five," Ramsay told her. "I can hide the crowbar down my pantleg."

With that agreed, Ramsay paid his bill and left the teashop, telling Bracken, "We're walking on the clifftops again. No chasing rabbits. It's too dangerous."

It was a blustery afternoon, gusts of winds shivered the grass and bushes, sending leaves flying, all of which pleased Ramsay. Few people would walk along the edge of a hundred-foot drop with the wind shifting about.

When they reached the place they'd crossed to Harry's farm last time, Ramsay looked carefully around and, seeing no one, set off across the rough ground. He'd been afraid there may be a police presence or even that Arthur Peacock may be at the farm but, when they arrived, there was no one.

"Now, Bracken, you stand guard," Ramsay said, as he sized up a kitchen window at the back of the house. Bracken looked puzzled so Ramsay repeated his command. "Sit and bark at any strangers."

Sliding the blade of his penknife between the window and frame, he lifted the latch and swung it open. Its hinges groaned as he forced it wide enough for him to climb inside, which he did with some difficulty. "I need to get all of me fitter, Bracken," he muttered to his dog who was watching him with a serious, disapproving stare, "not just my legs."

Ramsay quickly examined the rooms and their contents on the ground floor. An old desk and filing cabinet in one had his heart racing but they were empty. "Baldock's men," Ramsay muttered grumpily.

Upstairs he had similar success until he peered into a wardrobe. The clothes were still in place, and he searched the pockets. Nothing. He pushed them aside and saw a sheet of paper fallen in a corner at the back. Carefully, he lifted it to the light. A list of fish prices at nearby ports. Could it be a code? It seemed unlikely. He stowed it away in a pocket and continued searching the room, before doing the same in the other bedroom.

Returning downstairs, he examined the kitchen. A corkboard on the wall had once held paper, he could see, for the corners of sheets were still held by pins. *Baldock again*, he thought, almost angrily.

A low growl stopped his thoughts and he rushed to the window. Bracken was on his feet, his hackles raised. Ramsay climbed out of the window and pushed it shut. The latch was too stiff to reset; he hoped no one would notice.

With Bracken at his heels, he made his way quickly to the corner of the house nearest the clifftop path. Now he could hear a vehicle approaching and he ruffled Bracken's head. "Well done," he whispered.

The vehicle stopped at the front of the house and a car door slammed. He heard the front door being opened and gave whoever it was a minute to go inside.

"This way, Bracken," Ramsay said, walking quickly back to the path and on toward Ness Point.

"That was too close for comfort," Ramsay told Bracken. "You did well. You understand more than most people I know." He'd never trained Bracken in guard duty, and he'd rather expected Bracken to bark when he hadn't brought him through the window and into the house.

"Don't go too far," Ramsay said, as Bracken set off

following an interesting scent. "I want to see who was visiting the farm."

As they returned from their walk, he saw a police car driving away from Harry's farm. "I wonder what they were looking for," Ramsay said softly. "Something Armstrong has told them about? Here's hoping it isn't the sheet of paper I've taken. If it is, I'm in trouble."

He removed the paper from his pocket and studied it as he walked.

"If this is a code, Bracken," Ramsay said after a careful reading of the page, "I don't understand it."

Bracken's expression suggested: 'that's was the whole point about codes. Isn't it?'

"You're right. It wouldn't be much of a code if a random person could pick it up and decipher it in minutes," Ramsay agreed. "Only, I have seen many coded messages and sometimes you can spot it's a code. There's something about the arrangement of the words or sentences, you see."

Bracken wasn't persuaded and set off following another scent while Ramsay puzzled out the list of ports, fish and prices. He stopped.

"Bracken," he called, "we're going back to the house." Ramsay had suddenly realized Armstrong may have told the police that Harry had a place where he kept precious items secure. Had the police found Harry's hidden safe?

They rushed back to the house and once again Ramsay climbed inside leaving Bracken outside. He was right. In the bedroom where he'd found the sheet of paper, the wardrobe was pulled aside, and a small compartment exposed. It was empty.

"Bother!" Ramsay said. "I should have thought of that."

He left by the window in deep thought. *What did they*

find? What led to its discovery? Was it from Armstrong or Caldbeck? And if so, how did they know about it?

"I missed something important there, Bracken," Ramsay said, sadly. "What was it?"

Bracken didn't answer. There were too many scents to consider before thinking about irrelevant details.

* * *

The teashop was closed when Ramsay and Bracken returned to the village. Eliza was probably changing for her night of crime scene investigation. Ramsay briefly wondered what she'd wear.

"We'll visit them before we go home, Bracken," Ramsay said. "Maybe Mr. Danesdale can confirm this price list is commonly used."

It was Eliza who opened the door when he knocked.

"Find anything?" Eliza whispered, as she let him in.

"Did you?" Ramsay responded.

"No. It's hopeless asking old people about one day two months ago. They can't remember yesterday."

"I found this," Ramsay said, handing her the sheet of paper. "Does it mean anything to you?"

Eliza scanned it quickly. "I've never seen anything like it. I don't remember dad having anything like this either."

"Would your dad know if this is a regular fishing industry document?"

Mr. Danesdale, however, confirmed Eliza's assessment. He hadn't seen the price list presented in this way. He showed Ramsay what the official documents looked like.

"Someone transposed them from the official documents to this list," Ramsay said. "Any ideas why that might be?"

"Maybe they thought fishermen could understand it

better this way," Danesdale responded, "or maybe they were copies for some other purpose."

Ramsay frowned. "But what other purpose, that's what I don't understand."

"I'm afraid I can't help you, Mr. Ramsay," Danesdale said. "We use the industry documents only."

Ramsay thanked him and left. He and Bracken wandered back up the hill to his guest house where he'd await the evening's adventures. The wait was painfully long, and it was a great relief when he saw the clock reach four forty-five and he could put on his coat, hat and gloves. Bracken, when he found he was to be left behind once again, was as angry as Ramsay feared he would be.

Eliza too was on time. She joined him at the gate before hustling him away from the view from her home's windows. When she was sure they were out of sight, Eliza handed him the iron bar she'd taken from the shed. He slid it down his trouser leg where the cold metal made him shiver.

"To the tunnel," Eliza whispered, "and the final piece of the puzzle."

"We hope," Ramsay said, gloomily, as they linked arms and strode quickly down the hill to the beach in the growing darkness.

21

SUSPECTS RELEASED!

With the tide not long out and rain showers in the afternoon, the rocks between the slipway and the sand were treacherous that evening and they were thankful for the powerful flashlight Ramsay had brought with him to light their way. The pungent smell of recently exposed seaweed accompanied them until they stepped down onto the sand, which was still firm from all the water. Now they were able to pick up the pace.

When they reached the point he'd climbed down days before, seen now as a dark bulk against the sky, Ramsay said, pointing, "If we're cut off by the tide, this is our escape route."

"In the dark it won't be easy," Eliza said, staring at the steep landslide.

"It's all we have," Ramsay said.

"Then the sooner we get into the tunnel, the sooner we'll be finished, and on our way back to the village."

They hurried on and arrived at the door minutes later. Handing the torch to Eliza, Ramsay retrieved the crowbar from his pantleg and began feeling at the edge of the door's edge to find a place to start. When he found one, he slid the bar into the gap and pushed. The door groaned but remained in place. He wriggled it further in and, using his whole body, leaned hard on the crowbar. For a moment, it seemed the door was going to win. Ramsay threw his weight even harder against it. A loud c-r-a-ck echoed out from the cavern and the door sprang open an inch. Handing the bar to Eliza, he pulled the door open enough for them to slip through.

The first thing Ramsay noted was the police had thoroughly emptied the tunnel. The floor was clear of the papers and rubble that had been there when he'd found the cave. Ramsay and Eliza examined the floor as they moved further into the cavern.

"Where was Harry's body?" Eliza asked.

Ramsay took her to the spot, still marked by a stain on the floor. "And the papers were all over the floor here," he added, sweeping the beam around them.

They examined the fallen roof that closed the tunnel, making it into a cave. It too had been well searched, evidenced by the rocks that had been thrown aside, exposing their un-weathered undersides.

"Was there anything written on the walls?" Eliza asked.

"Last time I was here I had no light, so I don't know," Ramsay replied. "Let's look."

"Was there a desk or chair?" Eliza asked. "If Harry was using this place, you'd expect both, wouldn't you?"

"There wasn't," Ramsay replied. "I don't think he was using it like an office, more like a storeroom, I'd say."

"If they were smuggling in something small, they wouldn't need a storeroom."

"I thought 'storeroom' because of the papers, which I thought were bills of lading. Now we've changed our theory, the purpose of this hideout becomes more mysterious," Ramsay said. "Maybe it held a small safe to store money and product?"

"And the killer took it with them?"

"Why not? It might have been the most efficient way to carry the loot," Ramsay replied.

"A very small safe, then," Eliza said, sarcastically.

"It may not have been a 'safe' in the usual meaning of the word," Ramsay said. "A briefcase or suitcase. Something Harry didn't want found if his house was burgled, or if your dad or Armstrong went rummaging around in his office."

"Risky, though," Eliza said, as their inspection of the walls revealed no new evidence. "Leaving something as valuable as it was to be stumbled upon by any hiker looking for shelter."

"Not if the door was well fastened and the loot was only being stored here for a short period of time," Ramsay said. "We don't know that he came here regularly. It may have been only the once."

"You think something big had been handed over, money or the shipment, and he needed a quick hiding place to sort it out?"

"Something like that," Ramsay replied. "All of this is just conjecture. We don't know what happened, or why it happened, or why it happened here. To be honest, we don't know much at all. Still, Baldock may get it out of Armstrong and his accomplice, which will save me racking my brains over it all night."

"If the killer did take it away," Eliza said, "there's no reason for us to stay, is there?" Now she'd seen the tunnel, it no longer held any attraction. It was cold, wet, smelled of long years of decay and, worse, the sound of waves lapping on the beach was growing ever so noticeably louder. The tide had turned, and it was coming in.

Ramsay sighed. He'd hoped something might have been left by the forensics crew but there was nothing. He swept the torch's beam around the space slowly, hoping something they'd missed might appear. Nothing did. "Let's go, or we might have wet feet before we get back to the village."

* * *

THEY WERE BACK LONG before the tide had reached the rocks so, with dry feet, they set off up New Street. As they approached *Ye Dolphin*, Eliza said, "I'm frozen. A brandy would warm me up."

"So would getting home and a nice coal fire," Ramsay said, severely.

"We might meet Robinson or Duck in there," Eliza replied. "Now we have new ideas on what they might be smuggling, we might get more out of them."

"Mr. Robinson never got near any smuggling, and Mr. Duck denies there being any smuggling," Ramsay reminded her.

"Ah, but..." Eliza began.

"No interviewing," Ramsay said, then relented. "Though a brandy may be considered medicinal."

"It's in all stories with survivors of cold," Eliza agreed. "I feel we would be wrong not to have some. Our health may be at risk."

"Do you like brandy?" Ramsay asked, amused.

"It doesn't matter if I like it or not," Eliza said, stepping into the doorway. "It's medicine, right?"

Ramsay agreed it was and ordered two brandies from

the bar. When he'd paid, they took a seat well away from the bar and the few customers leaning against it.

"I need more information about Len Pritchard," Ramsay said, after they'd both sipped their drink. "Can you start asking about him?"

"Tricky," Eliza replied. "People don't like to be seen gossiping about neighbors in public. Other people is all right, not neighbors."

Ramsay understood what she meant. "Then don't ask about him, ask who has seen him and what he does."

Eliza nodded. "I'll find a way. It's not bad, brandy. Better than Campari, anyway."

"Don't get a taste for it, unless you plan to smuggle it in from France," Ramsay replied. "It costs an arm and a leg."

"If it's medicine, and I'm now sure it is because I feel warmer already, it should be tax-free. The government needs to be told this."

Ramsay, not sure she was entirely serious, said, "You can protest later. After we've finished this case."

"What are you going to do?"

Smiling, Ramsay replied, "The same. I can't rule out Len right now and I'd like to. It's not comfortable knowing I worked with someone who was suspected of working for the other side."

"There's no smoke without fire," Eliza reminded him.

"Exactly. I need to eliminate him from my inquiries about smuggling," Ramsay agreed, "and at this moment, I'm not sure."

Eliza said, "He did suggest industrial secrets to you. Or do you think that also is a red herring?"

"The people we're dealing with are familiar with herrings," Ramsay said, chuckling, "so why not some red ones."

Eliza groaned. "Until now, I never fully understood what they meant about puns being the lowest form of humor."

"Sorry to pain you," Ramsay said, smiling. "Now, if you don't want to hear more, you get me a picture of Len Pritchard's life in the village by tomorrow night. I think we'll find there's a lot to be gained from that."

"You'll come into the café at lunchtime to debrief?" Eliza asked.

"I'll be there. Now drink up and let's get home," Ramsay said.

"What's the rush," Eliza replied. "It's early. We have hours before closing time."

Ramsay laughed. "Are you sure? You don't have friends you should be with?"

"I've known my friends since I was a toddler. I want to hear about the wider world. Tell me about big city policing. Was it dangerous?"

Ramsay was taken aback. He'd never been asked this by someone without an ulterior motive. "You can't call Newcastle a big city," he replied, hoping to deflect her from what promised to be an embarrassing monologue on his part.

"It's bigger than anywhere I've ever been," Eliza told him. "Stop trying to change the subject."

Ramsay laughed. "All right. To answer your last question first, it isn't dangerous ninety-nine percent of the time."

"Then why did you retire early?"

"The other one percent of the time," Ramsay said, and told her of the incident and being invalided out.

"I shouldn't have made you cycle all that way," Eliza said, alarmed. "I didn't know."

"I'm perfectly well," Ramsay replied. "It's just the police doctors who didn't think so."

"Still, we have to be careful with you," Eliza replied. "I'll do all the strenuous stuff from now on. You take it easy."

Ramsay said no and moved onto the more everyday police duties that were dull and safe.

Eliza nodded, when he'd finished speaking. "I can imagine. I've only been doing this investigation a week or so and it's mind numbingly boring. If we don't have a chase or a shoot-out soon, I'll go mad."

"Be careful what you wish for," Ramsay said, seriously. "Remember, this is rural England, not 'gangland' London. A quiet investigation and arrest are what we do best."

"Like I said, boring. I'll see if Arthur Peacock can get me a singing spot in a pop band."

Ramsay frowned. "You won't be surprised to learn I think that's a terrible idea. That isn't the life for anybody, let alone a decent young woman like you."

"It would be a lot more exciting than what I see ahead," Eliza cried. "That's why you must take me along as your partner."

This was what Ramsay feared. "I'm just a retired man who has stumbled across two mysteries, one after another." He thought Eliza may know about the Lake District kidnapping case but she couldn't know about the pet thefts and three cases would seriously undermine his argument "The law of averages says there won't be another one."

"One of our customers yesterday asked if you'd look into a mystery that's puzzling them, after we finish with this one," Eliza said. "They're a lovely old couple and they need help. We could start there."

Now Ramsay was alarmed. "They should go to the police or, if it isn't criminal, hire a private detective."

"You're a private detective and people trust you," Eliza

responded. "I'll introduce you when you're next both in the café together."

Ramsay could see himself under Baldock's hovering paw for weeks to come. He had to stop this. "I'll talk to them but only to tell them to go to the police."

Eliza beamed. "I'll tell them you'll listen to their story. Now, another brandy would be nice, please."

Later, they walked up the hill where Ramsay was about to leave her when the door flew open and Eliza's father burst out, "They've let Armstrong go. He wants to speak to me in the office first thing in the morning. I'm done for!"

"Maybe we should all be there," Ramsay replied, "and Arthur Peacock as well."

"I'll call Arthur now," Eliza said, pushing past her father in the doorway and snatching the teashop keys from a hook.

"We'll come with you," Ramsay said. "Arthur might need some persuading to face an angry Armstrong."

22

AN ANGRY PARTNER

Waiting in the Ravenscar Fishing office next morning was excruciating, even for Ramsay. He couldn't imagine how Mr. Danesdale felt.

To break the silence that had crept over them, and lighten the moment, Ramsay said, "It will be like one of those wrestling matches on television, only much less funny."

"Do you watch wrestling on TV?" Eliza asked, shocked to find he did anything normal people did.

"Well, no. I don't have a television set," Ramsay admitted. "I've seen it on TV sets in shop windows."

There was a brief silence as the three digested this insight Ramsay had shared. As Eliza was perched on the edge of her father's desk, Ramsay sat in the guest chair. Bracken lay on the floor beside him wearing a gloomy expression. It looked like they were stuck here for some time.

"Do you know when they might appear?" Ramsay asked.

Both Eliza and her father shook their heads. "Early, is what they both said."

"Have you a good story ready for Armstrong?" Ramsay asked Danesdale, who shook his head.

"What is there to say? I told the police about those two payments and that's why he's been held and questioned."

Danesdale's usual solemn expression was grimmer than Ramsay had ever seen it. His face was positively white with worry.

"Tell him the police sent men to check the books and they found it," Ramsay replied.

"Well, they did," Eliza's father said, glumly, showing them a receipt on police notepaper. "But only after I told them about it. They came with Baldock."

"Show Armstrong that. He likely doesn't know when Baldock decided to take him in for questioning," Ramsay responded.

Danesdale shook his head. "I won't be convincing."

"If the police had been doing their job properly," Ramsay added. "That's exactly what would have happened. I think Baldock would be pleased to have you cover for his lack of process."

Before Danesdale could answer, the door opened, and Arthur Peacock entered the office. He looked surprised to see the three waiting for him.

"Good morning, Arthur," Danesdale said. "You know these two, I think," he added, gesturing to his two companions.

Peacock nodded at Ramsay and Eliza, before saying, "I don't think you two should be here though."

"I'm here because I have more questions of Mr. Armstrong," Ramsay said.

"And I'm here because I'm a witness if this gets ugly," Eliza stated belligerently.

Peacock was clearly taken aback at this. Though

whether it was Armstrong's imminent arrival or the thought of answering more questions couldn't be established. "More questions that I'm not obliged to answer."

"Very true," Ramsay said, "though why you wouldn't answer them, I'll leave to Inspector Baldock to consider."

"Are you working for him?"

Ramsay smiled. "Not exactly. However, I do give him all the information I gather. He thinks I have something to do with the smuggling you see, so it's in my best interests to make sure he gets the right answer."

"Not my problem, Mr. Ex-policeman," Peacock said. Before he could say anymore, the door burst open, and Armstrong strode in.

"You're fired," he screamed at Eliza's father. "You shopped me to the coppers."

Eliza's father flinched and hesitated before saying, "I did no such thing."

"Then how did they know about the loans I took out?" Armstrong yelled. Now he was almost nose to nose with Eliza's father. Ramsay rose from his chair and even Peacock stepped forward.

To Ramsay's amazement, Eliza's father replied calmly, "The police sent three men here to go through the company's books. I imagine that's how they knew."

Armstrong hesitated, before saying, "Can you prove that?'

"Certainly, I can," Eliza's father replied. Hands shaking, he lifted a sheet of paper from the top of his In Tray and handed it to Armstrong. "As you see, they've given us a receipt for the ledgers they took away."

"R-i-ght," Armstrong said, slowly. "Well, I'm back now. Clear these people out of your office and come into mine. We've some catching up to do."

"Our office," Peacock said, steadily, "I think you mean."

"What talents can you bring to the business?" Armstrong said. "You can't fish and you've no clue about managing anything but teenagers, which you do by plying them with drugs."

Peacock flushed red with anger and his reply was almost a snarl. "Whatever talents I may or may not have, this business is fifty percent mine until you buy me out."

"Buy you out?" Armstrong roared; his temper suddenly re-awakened. "Are you mad? The best thing we can do here is sell the lot and split the proceeds down the middle."

This infuriated Eliza. "And what about the village, the villagers, the fishermen? There's nothing here if the fishing industry goes."

"Then they can buy us out," Armstrong yelled back. "Let them try running a business for a change, instead of moaning about how others do it."

"Where would they get the money?" Eliza shot back, glaring at him.

"The bank, where everyone goes to get loans," Armstrong retorted. "Now get out of here, you and that washed-up has-been policeman. This is private property and you're trespassing."

"They're here at my invitation," Peacock said. "Mr. Ramsay has some questions about smuggling and murder he'd like answering."

"I've answered all the questions I'm going to for this lifetime," Armstrong said. "The real police couldn't pin anything on me, and I don't plan to let this washed-up has-been try as well."

"Hey," Ramsay cried. "I'm not trying to pin anything on anyone. I just want to get the truth."

"R-i-g-ht," Armstrong replied, with a sneer.

"If you hope to sell this business," Ramsay began, "for a substantial sum, you're going to need the smuggling rumors quashed. Nobody will buy if there's even a hint of wrongdoing."

Armstrong considered this for a moment before grudgingly agreeing. "That's a point."

"It's the same with the murder," Peacock said. "You didn't do it and I didn't, but potential buyers won't just take our word. That needs to be closed out too."

Armstrong ran his hand across his mouth and face. "Very well. We'll talk, then you go. This business needs some direction for the coming days." His words were conciliatory but his whole stance was aggressive. His hands were clenched in fists, his body trembled with barely suppressed energy, or maybe rage.

"You were able to convince the police the withdrawals you made from the company funds weren't payoffs, I take it?" Ramsay asked. Maybe goading him a little would reveal more than the neutral stance he'd tried up until now.

"I did and what it was for is my business, not yours."

"Your alibi for the time of Harry's death has been accepted?" Ramsay asked.

"What is this?" Armstrong said. "These are questions for Baldock, not me. How would I know if he's accepted them or not?"

Ramsay suggested. "They released you?"

"They also told me not to leave town as they may have further questions," Armstrong replied. "They released me because they couldn't hold me any longer without evidence, or the confession they were hoping to browbeat out of me."

"When you loaned Harry the money to buy his new boat, did you have the company looked into?" Ramsay asked. "I'm sure a canny businessman like yourself wouldn't have bought into this if you thought it was a criminal enterprise."

"I did the usual paperwork checks," Armstrong admitted. "They showed everything to be above board. A steady business, which I thought good enough to take a share in. I wanted to move down here to be near my sister. This seemed a way to have some excitement as well."

"It must have been a shock when you arrived to find all the rumors going around about smuggling?" Ramsay asked.

Armstrong nodded and seemed to relax. "I asked my sister why she hadn't mentioned this when she'd told me about Harry needing funds."

"What did she say?" Eliza broke in quickly.

"That it was nonsense. Harry had assured her if there was any smuggling, it wasn't on his boats. She was friendly with Harry, you know."

Eliza looked shocked but said nothing, letting Ramsay continue.

"I assume Harry told you the same?"

"He did and I believed him," Armstrong replied. "Particularly when I saw Constable Storm inspect a catch being unloaded and he assured me he often did inspect the catches. It made me feel a lot better, though still uneasy the rumors weren't dying away."

Ramsay continued. "What did you and Harry argue about then?"

"I've told you all this before, the business," Armstrong replied. When he saw Ramsay was waiting for more, he added, "Harry's focus was on the fishing. I wanted us to look closer at the sales side. I saw opportunities for growth in processed products."

"You'll need to explain that to me," Arthur interjected. "Where exactly would this processing take place?"

"Later, later," Armstrong said, waving the question away. "Right now, I want to clear up any remaining doubts Mr. Ramsay has so I can get on with my life."

"The skipper who Baldock was questioning," Ramsay asked. "Do you know him well enough to trust he isn't a smuggler?"

"I didn't know him at all until Harry disappeared," Armstrong replied. "Up until then, Harry managed the boats and crews. And to your point, all I know about him is he's the skipper of *Ravenscar Lady 4* and catches his fair share. Why do you think badly of him?"

"He's a rough looking sort," Eliza interjected. "More than the others, I mean."

"We can't all be Cary Grant," Armstrong retorted. "He's a fisherman, not a prospective husband."

"Eliza's point is he stands out from the others and not in a good way," Ramsay interjected. "That makes people suspicious."

"It's nonsense," Armstrong replied. "Now, if you don't mind, Mr. Peacock, Mr. Danesdale and I have business matters to discuss." His gaze included Ramsay and Eliza, who took the hint and reluctantly left.

"At least Dad seems safe for now," Eliza said, as they made their way up the hill.

Ramsay agreed, saying, "I hope your father takes notes. I want to know everything that's said in that office this morning."

"I have to help mam open the teashop soon," Eliza lamented. "What are you going to do to move us forward?"

"My old colleague back in Newcastle should have something for me by now," Ramsay replied. "I'll hear what he has to say and decide after that."

23

IS HIS OLD COLLEAGUE GUILTY?

When Eliza was indoors, Ramsay and Bracken once again set out along the clifftop path while Ramsay marked the time until he thought Morrison would be at his desk. By nine o'clock, they were at the phone box and calling Newcastle City Police.

Ramsay had guessed right. *Thank heavens for regular office hours and the consistency people brought to them.*

"I was going to call you today," Morrison said, when he heard Ramsay's voice. "Your friend Pritchard left under quite a cloud it seems."

A sudden squall outside the phone box had Bracken pressing against the door, which Ramsay opened to let him inside, while saying, "I understood that from people down here. Pritchard says he was framed."

"They all do," Morrison replied. "Anyway, the people down there became certain that he was at best leaking operational details to the smugglers and, at worst, was part of the gang."

Bracken didn't like being in the cramped phone box and his constant wriggling to be free threatened to knock

Ramsay over. "What was it made them suspicious? Did Pritchard spend more than he earned, for instance?"

"No. It was the way the smugglers always knew when the raids were to happen," Morrison said. "In the end, they told Pritchard, and only Pritchard, there was to be a raid. The men taking part in the raid weren't told until the last minute. When they stopped the boats, they were still clean."

Ramsay didn't like the sound of this, too many obvious issues. "That's weak. The person who told Pritchard could be the leak, and so could anyone on the committee who planned this trap."

"Of course," Morrison replied, "only they were all senior officers with years of experience and solid reputations. To most, it looked conclusive."

Ramsay grunted in disbelief. "It's also possible that there was no contraband coming in that day or night and the police had been given false information. The smugglers own trap being sprung on Pritchard who was getting too close."

"Your objections are sound," Morrison agreed. "Only the people down there at that time were sure they'd proved him to be the smugglers' inside man. They pushed him out to grass."

"Have they had more success since Pritchard left?" Ramsay demanded.

Morrison laughed. "They've arrested some small-time smugglers; the big stuff seems to have moved to a different port."

"Does it say in the file what is being smuggled?"

"The usual stuff, booze, cigarettes, and the like," Morrison replied. "All the items our government has placed high taxes on."

"Nothing like drugs, or diamonds, or industrial or state secrets?" Ramsay asked.

Morrison laughed. "There's no mention of them. Anyway, diamonds would go straight into London and be cut in days to make them unrecognizable, and drugs come to us courtesy of our cousins in the west. Industrial secrets possibly. After all, there's a lot of industry in Yorkshire and Durham that may be looking for a helping hand."

"I thought that, but I also think they'd go through Middlesborough or Hull," Ramsay said. "That's where the products leave from, and the raw materials come into."

Morrison agreed. "It wouldn't be a small place like Whitby."

Or Robin Hood's Bay, Ramsay thought. *Hmm, my old colleague Pritchard is looking more guilty the deeper I dig into the story.*

"What will you do now?" Morrison asked.

Ramsay replied, "Assume Pritchard is guilty, follow the evidence and hopefully prove him innocent."

"What evidence?" Morrison asked.

Ramsay paused. "I thought you might give me the names of those senior officers and I'll find one of them to interview."

"Fat chance," Morrison said. "Ask your friend Pritchard."

Ramsay thanked him for his help and hung up. He pushed open the heavy phone box door. "Come on Bracken. This sleety rain and wind will wash me clean after listening to that sordid tale. What a bunch they must have been in Whitby five years ago."

They didn't walk far; the wind and rain were even worse out on the clifftop.

"We'll visit our friend Len, Bracken," Ramsay said, turning into Station Road and away from the guest house. Bracken didn't look amused.

Fortunately for them both, Pritchard was at home, and they were invited inside quickly.

"It must be bad to bring you out on a morning like this," Pritchard said, as Ramsay took off his coat and Bracken shook his dry.

Ramsay laughed grimly. "Dogs have to be walked no matter what the weather is."

"I suppose," Pritchard replied, leading them through into the sitting room. "I'll put on the kettle. You'll welcome a hot tea, I'm sure. What would Bracken like?"

After all the domestic arrangements were done, Pritchard returned to his earlier question. When Ramsay explained, he responded, "I mentioned Featherstone, he was my boss at the time, the others were the Chief Constable, Matthews was his name, and the Super, Lackenby. He's since gone abroad, retired I understand."

Ramsay grimaced. "If he's gone abroad, he's my chief suspect, but I'll have to make do with Matthews. Where will I find him?"

Pritchard grinned. "When I heard Lackenby had retired abroad, that was my reaction too. But, from what I heard, it wasn't to Spain or South America, or anywhere we have no extradition treaty. His son had emigrated to New Zealand and Lackenby and his wife wanted to spend time with their grandchildren."

"I'm still suspicious," Ramsay replied, "but that's all we can be."

"Matthews wasn't a local man," Pritchard said. "He went down south to be nearer his family, I heard."

"Then who else could fill me in on what was happening in the Whitby police station at the time?'

Pritchard hesitated. "I can tell you who I questioned but that won't help you overcome your doubts about me because he and I know each other well. We were on the same cricket team for years and now we're on the same bowling team."

"You're right," Ramsay said. "I need someone neutral, or even hostile, if I'm to fully exonerate you in my own mind."

"I'm glad you said 'fully'," Pritchard replied. "At least you're giving me the benefit of your doubt."

Ramsay said, grimly, "I want to nail these smugglers, Len, as much as I did all those years ago. I'm sure we've identified the murderers, even if Baldock couldn't get enough to hold them this time, now I want the smugglers. They've been making fools of us for too long."

"If you want to speak to someone hostile, ask Baldock," Pritchard continued. "He'll know someone, other than himself, I mean."

"I hate giving him any ammunition against you and me but I'll phone him on my way back to the guest house," Ramsay replied. "I want to hear both sides of this story. I know what I think, I just need to feel sure."

Pritchard frowned. "Let me remind you of what I witnessed so you have both sides clear in your mind."

"By all means, remind me."

"I'd led several raids on boats returning to port that we'd been tipped off were carrying contraband. Every one of those raids turned up nothing. We suspected there was someone in our station leaking information."

Ramsay smiled. "Understandably."

"The Chief Constable and the station Superintendent called me into a meeting one afternoon, just the three of us," Pritchard went on. "They told me they had good information of a special shipment arriving that evening, and I was to lead the search of the boat when it docked. I was to pick my team but not tell the men what boat or when the raid would take place until the minute we left the station."

"You must have been concerned about this, Len? After all, if there was nothing on board it was your word against two senior officers."

Pritchard nodded. His face was white with tension just telling the story. "I carried out the plan to the letter. There were a number of boats coming in and we kept out of sight until the one we wanted tied up. There was no time for them to have unloaded anything and they didn't unload to another boat on the way in. I watched for that carefully, as you can imagine."

"Your search found nothing?"

Pritchard nodded. "Correct. Either we'd been fed false information, or my two bosses had set me up. I chose to believe it was the first, until I was suspended, and an inquiry started."

"You were able to count on your men confirming you hadn't told them of the target, I imagine," Ramsay said.

Pritchard laughed sardonically. "You can be sure of it. The inquiry concluded that them not knowing proved it could only have been me who leaked the information to the smugglers."

"But how?"

"I'd a cricket match that evening and I'd called the team captain to tell him I couldn't be there," Pritchard responded. "They learned of it, well, I told them, and they interviewed the captain. He confirmed that's what we talked about, but their view was he was an old friend and had been told to give me an alibi or, more likely, he was in on it too. My contact among the smugglers, if you like. He wasn't invited to speak to the inquiry, of course."

"Were you?"

Pritchard shook his head. "I was called into the station to hear the inquiry's findings and offered a way out – take early retirement and say nothing to anyone."

"And here we are," Ramsay said, quietly. Pritchard's story had so many similarities to his own early retirement decision. It invoked considerable sympathy on Ramsay's part. "Is there anything else you've thought of before I go into the lion's den asking for help?"

"Nothing, other than thirty years of exemplary service and even some medals along the way," Pritchard replied. "That didn't count much to them, I don't expect it to count much now."

Ramsay thought for a moment, before asking, "Do you take expensive vacations? Or collect Old Masters?"

Pritchard laughed. "Tom, I don't even have a car. Day trips on buses to nearby beauty spots are my summer holidays. And I've no family that I'm planning to leave a fortune in my will. If I'd been the smugglers' inside man, I was really bad at selling myself."

"They would argue you were being blackmailed into doing it, rather than for cash," Ramsay said, thoughtfully. "I'd best be off, Len. This is rotten for both of us, but I want all the criminals locked up at the end of it, smugglers and murderers, and we haven't achieved either yet."

Ramsay and Bracken walked back to the phone box in a somber mood. He knew only too well how easy it was to blacken someone's name and implicate them in wrongdoing. He saw no good for Len Pritchard coming from his investigation, only more grief. Nevertheless, Ramsay phoned Scarborough police and asked for Baldock.

Baldock, when he answered the phone, wasn't in the mood to be sidetracked in his investigation by irrelevant questions from long ago. He told Ramsay so, forcefully.

Ramsay responded mildly, "Just a name of someone local who can give me the lowdown on Pritchard's involvement in smuggling."

"Didn't Constable Storm relay my message the other day?" Baldock demanded.

Ramsay responded, "He did and I'm not interfering with your murder investigation."

"If the murder has anything to do with smuggling, you are," Baldock yelled, making Ramsay sharply pull the handset away from his ear.

"We don't know that it does," Ramsay continued, when there was a brief silence. "After all, I'm told by everyone I meet there is no smuggling."

"Then what are you investigating?" Baldock, shouted triumphantly.

"The old case I was on with Len Pritchard," Ramsay said, "and I'm not investigating, only researching. Did Len Pritchard scuttle my investigation years ago? I'd like to know."

"It's water under the bridge now," Baldock replied, more calmly. "No one cares. No one who was there then is there now."

"But they may still be around to talk to," Ramsay said.

Baldock groaned. "Okay, okay. I give up. Talk to Chris Cloughton over at Whitby. I'll phone him and tell him what it's about. Give me an hour."

He gave Ramsay a phone number and was about to hang up when Ramsay shouted, "Wait."

"What now?"

Ramsay said, "I'll talk to your man Cloughton but you need to talk to Inspector Morrison up in Newcastle. He was my old detective sergeant back in the day and he can give you background on me. You can trust him. He'll give a fair appraisal."

"If you say so," Baldock replied. "Now get lost and I'll get back to real work."

Bracken by now was thoroughly unhappy about his morning so far and gave Ramsay a look that told him so.

Ramsay stroked him, saying, "The weather is better. We'll take the clifftop path for an hour."

24

THE EVIDENCE AGAINST HIS OLD COLLEAGUE

It was just past the hour when Ramsay and Bracken returned to the phone box and Ramsay called the number he was given. It took a moment before he was put through to Inspector Cloughton and he introduced himself.

"Baldock called," Cloughton said, neutrally. "He told me you want to know why we were so sure it was Pritchard leaking information to the other side. Though what business that is of yours, I don't yet see."

Ramsay explained about working with Pritchard years before and now, staying in the neighborhood, he learned of Pritchard's dismissal. He explained about the murder and its possible linkage to smuggling.

"You're retired, I understand," Cloughton interjected, cutting Ramsay off in mid-sentence.

Ramsay decided to play his possible sympathy card. "Invalided out after a shooting. Only to fall into this mess."

Cloughton snorted. "And one in the Lake District a few months ago where you had us all running around looking for kidnapped teenagers you were sheltering, as I recall."

Ramsay ground his teeth in frustration. Did Cloughton

really recall? Or had Baldock primed him to be unhelpful? "This one is more personal for me and the force, I think. That's why I'm looking to understand the background. I want to help clear away these questions that have been hanging fire these past years. Inspector Baldock thought you could provide the information I need to understand Pritchard's role in it all."

"So, Baldock said," Cloughton responded, "and, as I told him, he could have explained it as well as I can,"

Ramsay chuckled. "Didn't he tell you he suspects me of having a hand in what's been going on? We got off on the wrong foot, Inspector Baldock and I. He thought the information would come better from a neutral source, I guess."

Cloughton was silent for a moment, before saying, "Very well. Here's what I know. I was the local union representative at that time and was invited onto the inquiry team to see fair play, if you like. Inspector Pritchard wasn't in the union, of course, but it was felt I would have the interests of the accused at heart. And I did, at first."

"What you learned persuaded you otherwise?" Ramsay suggested.

"I'd always admired Inspector Pritchard," Cloughton continued. "Looked up to him when I first joined Whitby. My disappointment when I learned he'd been an informant for years was more than I could bear. He broke my heart, Mr. Ramsay. I don't mind admitting it."

"What was the evidence that did that for you?"

Cloughton replied, "We had an informant we trusted. He'd always given good information to his point of contact. None of us knew who he was, only that he always came through when we needed him."

"And he told his police contact that Pritchard was corrupt?" Ramsay asked.

Cloughton laughed derisively. "More than that. When he'd first told his police handler, he wasn't believed. That's how highly Pritchard was viewed in the station. The informant became angry and offered to set up Pritchard. That's what was done. The informant arranged to meet Pritchard at a temporary empty house and a tape recorder was installed in an adjacent room. It was exciting stuff; I can tell you."

"Playing spies, you mean?"

Cloughton agreed. "That and some of us had never seen a tape recorder, they were so new then. Anyway, the meeting was held and taped. The tape was processed and played back to the Chief Constable and the Superintendent first. Then when the inquiry was set up, we heard the relevant parts of the conversation."

"You were sure it was Pritchard speaking?" Ramsay asked.

"Absolutely! The recording was so good, so clear, there was never any doubt. From that moment on, Pritchard was nothing to me. As I said, he wasn't in the union so I had no reason to advocate for him and I wouldn't have wanted to, even if he was."

"There were witnesses who watched Pritchard go into and leave the house?"

Cloughton laughed. "Of course. This was done by the book. No one wanted to get this wrong. He was held in such high regard, you see."

Ramsay asked, "Where is that police contact now?"

"He became one of the 'Ten Pound Poms', you'll remember the program that helped Britons to move to Australia after the war, so somewhere down there," Cloughton replied.

Ramsay mused aloud, hoping for a sharp reaction,

"Everybody close to this has moved far away or died. Doesn't that strike you as odd?" He was to be disappointed.

"Not really. Time passes, people die, and people move on. It isn't unusual at all," Cloughton replied.

"Did the informant move on as well?"

Cloughton snorted. "After that interview, his handler never heard from him again. It's the usual way for traitors in any criminal organization, isn't it?"

"Often it is, yes," Ramsay replied thoughtfully. "I imagine his disappearance reinforced the notion that Pritchard was the smugglers' inside man?"

There was a pause before Cloughton responded, "It did for most of us. Pritchard silencing, or having silenced, the one man who could testify against him and getting away with it because we had no firm evidence, is part of why we're all so bitter about how we'd been betrayed."

"I can understand how you feel," Ramsay said. "With Pritchard gone, did you have any success in the smuggling case?"

After a long silence that Ramsay thought suggested embarrassment, but may have just been Cloughton considering how to answer.

Finally, Cloughton said, "No. We'd removed Pritchard, but he'd removed our informant. There have been some small successes. We think the big shipments go elsewhere now."

"That's a result too," Ramsay replied. "Shutting down one port of entry, I mean."

"Not the result we wanted, though," Cloughton admitted.

"Thanks for this," Ramsay said. "I can only imagine what it's cost you to talk about it. Before I leave you to get on with your day, is there anything else I should know?"

Again Cloughton hesitated before saying, "Smuggling into Whitby seemed to go quiet when Pritchard left the area and the rumors of smuggling into Robin Hood's Bay grew from the moment he moved there. It's likely a coincidence or just plain malice on someone's part, only it is so and there's no smoke without fire, they say."

Ramsay thanked him and rang off. "What do I make of that, Bracken?" Ramsay asked as he exited the phone box.

As Bracken hadn't heard the conversation, he gave Ramsay a quizzical, questioning look that appeared to say: 'Excuse me, I need to be caught up on the facts.'

"I'll tell you as we walk," Ramsay said, setting off toward their now favorite stroll along the cliff top path. He outlined aloud, what he'd been told. It seemed to confirm that Pritchard was one of the smugglers, if not the prime driver in it all.

"But I ask you, Bracken. Would the head of an international smuggling ring live so close to his crime and have so little to show for his efforts."

Bracken gave him to understand such a man would not.

Ramsay continued, "And if he was just their inside man, why is he still alive? He's no use to them as a retired man and he's a walking, talking time bomb under their feet if he suddenly gets an attack of conscience."

Bracken had scented a rabbit and no longer cared about retired policemen, smugglers, or baffling puzzles. There were, after all, more important things in life.

Ramsay walked to the point and back in gloom. He liked Len Pritchard and had hoped he'd be easily exonerated. It seemed, if he was to be exonerated, it wouldn't easily be done. He arrived at the teashop wondering if he shouldn't just return home and read about the case when it appeared in some future newspaper.

Eliza, smiling broadly when he entered, said, "Cheer up, it might never happen,"

Ramsay returned her smile. It was wonderful having all that youthful energy to lift his spirits. "Have you had a good morning sleuthing?" he asked.

"I have," Eliza said, hurrying away in answer to a customer's raised hand signaling a need for attention. "I'll tell you when it's quiet."

Ramsay took his usual seat. It seemed to be always free for him at lunchtime. Did that mean he was now accepted as one of the lunch time crowd? As someone who'd lived alone for so many years, he felt strangely happy about the possibility.

"We might have to wait a moment, Bracken," Ramsay said, as Bracken seemed eager to go behind the counter in search of his usually delivered treats. He wasn't accustomed to being kept waiting.

And he wasn't this time either, as Eliza emerged from the kitchen with a full tray, she gave him a beaming smile and a wink. Bracken's face broke out into a matching smile as Eliza placed a bowl of scraps, and one of water, in front of him.

"You need to be careful, Bracken," Ramsay said, severely. "I think that girl has set her sights on you."

Bracken took no notice; jealousy was such a mean emotion and one unworthy of his friend.

"What can I get you, sir?" Eliza said, accentuating the 'sir' in a way that disturbed Ramsay every time she took his order. *Would the other customers think she was only teasing him? He hoped so, though he no longer believed it himself.*

Ramsay ordered a ham and pease pudding sandwich with a pot of tea. Eliza hurried off before he could add, 'and information.'

She returned moments later with his tea and hot water before rushing across the room to serve an elderly couple who'd just entered. Ramsay recognized them and noted their table had been free as well.

He'd returned to his favorite occupation of gazing out of the window across the open land to the sea while he sat at this table. Somewhere out there, the answer to this puzzle lay waiting to be discovered. He, however, didn't intend to go to sea to find it. He'd find it on land or not at all.

"Your sandwich, sir," Eliza said, and added, more quietly, "I've something interesting to tell you about you know who." She left immediately to clear dishes so a group of four elderly people could sit down.

"It can't be as devastating as what we learned, Bracken," Ramsay muttered.

Bracken, who'd finished his scraps, had the good manners to take an interest in his friend's words but as there were no more forthcoming, he lay down and napped.

25

MORE EVIDENCE AGAINST

When the lunch rush was over, Eliza sat across from Ramsay and began, "Old Mrs. Henderson...," seeing Ramsay's blank expression, pointed across the room and added, "she sits at that table every day at ten o'clock. You must have seen her."

"I'm more of a lunchtime regular," Ramsay said sorrowfully.

Eliza shrugged. "Anyway, she saw Pritchard and Harry arguing fiercely and more than once. She lives in the cottage with the climbing rose over the door. You'll remember seeing it, I'm sure."

Ramsay nodded, though he had no idea where the cottage was. He assumed it must be down near the slipway for Mrs. Henderson to witness arguments more than once.

"She thought Pritchard was telling Peacock he must do something, and old Harry was having none of it. It looks like he is involved with them after all."

Ramsay couldn't help but think she was right, and the local police were right too. He recounted what he'd learned.

"That settles it for me," Eliza said. "I can't believe he's

walking about free when there's so much evidence against him."

Ramsay replied, "We must be careful here. The police didn't think they had enough of a case and Mrs. Henderson overhearing a quarrel, or quarrels, isn't enough to make it certain, would be my guess."

"Then we need to find the evidence because nobody else is looking for it," Eliza cried. "And I'm not sure now we did identify the murderers. If an informant can be disappeared, then why not an underling whose forgotten his place?"

Ramsay grinned at the idea of the Harry Peacock he'd had described to him being an 'underling'. "We'll see what else Mrs. Henderson knows and if her neighbors also heard or saw anything. Your dad might know something as well. I'll start there after lunch, and we'll visit Mrs. Henderson when you finish work."

Eliza nodded enthusiastically. "I think we're finally getting somewhere."

"I hope it's only on the smuggling side of the investigation," Ramsay responded. "I'd hate to think Armstrong and that thug were innocent."

Eliza laughed. "I haven't forgotten about them. You're right. They might be released now but they must remain the murderers or dad won't have a job."

"Your dad may even disappear too, one day," Ramsay added. "Those kinds of people rarely forget who shopped them."

Eliza shuddered. "I never thought of that. Maybe we should leave Pritchard for another day. And concentrate on getting Armstrong and that man locked up."

Ramsay had thought of that too and dismissed it. Justice must be served; however hard it was on those caught in the crossfire. Being caught in a real crossfire hadn't changed his mind on that.

"I told Baldock we'll only look for evidence about smuggling and let him sort out the murders," Ramsay told her.

"Hmm, didn't you say your interest was finding Harry's murderer?"

"And I helped do that," Ramsay protested. "Now I want to finish the job. If we stop the smuggling, we'll stop the criminality that it breeds."

WITH LUNCH OVER, Ramsay and Bracken walked down to the Ravenscar Fishing office where he found Eliza's father as always, scribbling in a ledger. A Facit calculator on the desk beside him.

"Aren't the sums coming out right today?" Ramsay asked, as he approached the man who'd hardly looked up as Ramsay opened the office door and crossed the floor to his side.

"It's the month end numbers," Danesdale said in reply, assuming everyone would understand what that meant in the accounting world.

"I have another question," Ramsay said, flopping down in the guest chair at Danesdale's desk and looping Bracken's leash around the back.

"What now," Danesdale said, wearily.

"Did you ever see or hear Len Pritchard here in the office?"

"Yes, he came here a few times," Danesdale said. "We all knew each other from school, you know."

"His visits weren't like policeman and suspected smuggler then?"

Danesdale shook his head slowly, remembering. "I

didn't get that impression, no. Though they did seem to have words occasionally. I heard them arguing in the street outside the office more than once."

"You didn't hear what was being said?"

"If I did," Danesdale replied, "it wasn't something very memorable."

"Did Pritchard have an interest in the business?"

"No, not officially, anyway," Danesdale replied. "When Harry was short of cash, it's possible Len Pritchard helped, I suppose. Maybe that's what they argued about. Harry was always better at borrowing than repaying."

"You also knew Harry from before working here?"

"I said, we went to school together," Danesdale replied. "Len Pritchard too. I thought everyone knew that."

Ramsay sighed. The number of times over the years when, after days of painstaking work, evidence would come to light only to have one of the first witnesses they'd interviewed say 'well, I could have told you that. I thought everyone knew' was galling.

"I'm not from this area," Ramsay reminded him.

"No, of course you aren't," Danesdale said, nodding thoughtfully. "I took it for granted others you spoke to would have told you, I suppose."

"Is there anything else you know that an incomer like me might not know?" Ramsay asked.

"I don't think so," Danesdale said, slowly. "But I don't know what you don't know, do I?"

"Were Harry and Len friends?" Ramsay suggested.

"At school? Not really."

"What about after, when they were young men?" Ramsay asked, despairingly trying to drag something useful from this interview. He remembered someone saying

'Danesdale was a nice man but...' and he finally fully understood what they'd meant.

"Definitely not," Danesdale replied. "Harry married the girl Pritchard was in love with. Len didn't take it well and moved to Whitby right after. The excuse he gave for moving was to be nearer his work, but everyone knew the real reason."

"I can see how that would cause a rift," Ramsay said.

"They were different characters as well," Danesdale said, seeming now to get into his stride. "Len was always so upright and honest. Harry was a bit of a scoundrel. Not exactly criminal, you know, just sailed close to the wind, as they say hereabouts."

"Makes me wonder why any woman would choose Harry over Len," Ramsay remarked.

"Harry was more fun," Danesdale said, sadly, "even I could see that."

"Could they have collaborated in a smuggling operation?" Ramsay asked.

Danesdale frowned. "These rumors of smuggling have everyone chasing their tails. I've worked here for years, and I know nothing about any smuggling beyond the odd bottle of schnapps, brandy, or vodka."

"So, you think not?" Ramsay persisted.

Danesdale, normally so still he seemed asleep, was visibly agitated by this question. "Harry and Len could have collaborated but so could many others."

"You think they'd patched up the quarrel from their youth enough to cooperate?" Ramsay asked.

Still squirming in his chair, Danesdale replied, "I would say so, yes. They generally talked together like old friends when Len came here."

"Did they include you in their conversations?" Ramsay continued, desperate to keep Danesdale talking.

"Sometimes," Danesdale said, "not always. I was the year below them at school you see."

"That does make a difference," Ramsay agreed. "You see what I'm driving at. A fisherman with boats that could bring in contraband and a police inspector who could ensure the police were looking elsewhere when the boats docked make quite a team."

Danesdale's hands were almost a blur of agitated twitches by now. "I do see that, but I don't believe it. It isn't in Len Pritchard's character."

"People change," Ramsay said. "They become bitter at being passed over or think they're entitled to more than they're getting. There are many reasons. Couldn't Pritchard have fallen into this way of thinking?"

Danesdale was horrified at this, and cried, "How should I know if something like that happened to him? He lived in Whitby and rarely came back here until after his father and mother died."

"When was that?" Ramsay demanded. *Was that the trigger?*

Danesdale considered. He was less agitated at a simple question of fact like this. "His father, years before but his mother only eight years ago. She's buried at St. Thomas's church on Station Road, if you want to confirm that."

"I will," Ramsay replied. "And he lives just across the street."

Danesdale looked puzzled. "Not directly across the street," he said, seriously.

Ramsay smiled. *Accountants did like to have things just so in their lives and conversation.*

"Quite so," Ramsay agreed, "Just very close. Maybe that's why he came back here to live?"

Danesdale nodded. "That and knowing so many people here. He also has an uncle, aunt, nephews and nieces here."

"After he retired," Ramsay agreed, nodding. "It's what he told me too. You know he left the police force under a cloud of suspicion; I suppose?"

Danesdale became quietly agitated again. "Suspicion is a terrible thing. If they had proof, they should have arrested him, not leaving him hanging out to dry like that. It's wicked. People shunned him at first, you know."

"I didn't," Ramsay said. "How awful. Did you and Harry have doubts?"

Danesdale shook his head. "None. We both knew the kind of man he is. Harry said to me one day 'No wonder those Whitby coppers haven't caught anyone, if they're that bad at judging characters.' And he was right."

Ramsay continued probing. "You can see though why someone like me, who doesn't know Mr. Pritchard well, should find it mildly suspicious that, after leaving the police because he was thought to be the smugglers inside man, he takes up right away in his new home with a man who owns a fleet of fishing boats?"

Danesdale's expression became even more bleak that it had been. "After Harry's wife died, which was ten years or more ago, they'd become friends again. Their shared grief brought them together and when Len returned to the village, he and Harry saw more of each other. It was nothing more than that."

"I think I understand Len Pritchard better now," Ramsay said. "Thanks for that. I heard he argued with Harry, and it made me wonder if I was doing the right thing in visiting him. I don't want to give Inspector Baldock wrong ideas about me."

"I'm glad I could help clear Len's name," Danesdale said. He was less agitated now.

"Did you get the sense Len was asking Harry about smuggling?" Ramsay asked. "Maybe Len hoped to clear his own name."

Danesdale's agitation began again. "I've told you. I don't know what caused the arguments, but they weren't serious. Len would visit again, and Harry welcomed him every time. They didn't cause a rift."

"You didn't think that odd?"

Danesdale shook his head a little too vigorously to be convincing. "They were old friends and one-time rivals. They argued without falling out. It isn't uncommon, especially where men like Harry are involved."

"You would discount the possibility Len was giving Harry orders, would you?"

Danesdale laughed nervously. "Even if Len had given him orders, Harry wouldn't have followed them. He wasn't that sort of man."

"Perhaps 'orders' was too strong a word," Ramsay said, "maybe suggestions or guidance, possibly."

"No. Nothing like that. Now I must get on. I want these books finished by tonight," Danesdale said. "Good day to you." He turned back to his ledger and refused to say more.

Ramsay bade him goodbye and, with Bracken, left the office. "What was your opinion of all that, Bracken?" He looked down at Bracken whose expression said: 'He wasn't telling the truth.'

"I agree," Ramsay replied to Bracken's silent statement. "Here's hoping Mrs. Henderson or a neighbor of hers heard something relevant. Too many people around here are surprisingly hard of hearing."

26

APPROACHING THE POLICE AGAIN

Mrs. Henderson was not inclined to help, when Ramsay, Eliza, and Bracken knocked on her door that evening. She peered at them from the part way opened door and asked what they wanted. Eliza explained and introduced Ramsay, who asked her about the events she'd told Eliza about.

"I heard a row, looked out of my window and saw Len Pritchard arguing with Harry Peacock as they walked up the street," she said, in answer to Ramsay's question.

"Did you hear what they were arguing about?" Ramsay asked.

She shook her head. "At my age, the hearing isn't what it was."

"Did you tell the police any of this?"

Mrs. Henderson snorted derisively. "My Ron wouldn't like me talking to the police."

Correctly guessing 'Ron' was her late husband, Ramsay asked why Ron was against the police.

"Ron said fishermen risk their lives out at sea every day to put food on their own family's table and the tables of hundreds of others. Police sit in offices all day, only coming out to try and trip up honest fishermen and arrest them for nothing. He didn't hold with them, and I agree with him."

Mrs. Robinson was about to close the door when Eliza said, desperate to keep her talking, "We're trying to make sure Harry's killer is put away for a long time, Mrs. Henderson. Surely Ron would have agreed with that."

Mrs. Henderson paused, before saying, "Aye, he would. Harry were a good man."

"You thought him a good man, Mrs. Henderson," Ramsay said. "There's many who didn't like him."

"Harry was a real man," she replied, "there's many who don't like real men. Even if that weren't so, he kept a dozen men or more employed here when there's nought else for folks to do. He was worth more than all his critics together."

"I see that," Ramsay said, "which is why we're so keen to find his killer."

"The police have them, don't they?"

"They had to let them go," Eliza interjected before Ramsay took all the conversation, "and they don't know that Len Pritchard argued with Harry, do they?"

Mrs. Henderson replied, "Don't they? I wouldn't know what they know. If Percy Storm's involved, everyone will know what they know but I don't listen to gossip."

"Would any of your neighbors have heard the rows?" Ramsay asked. "Maybe their hearing is better than yours."

Mrs. Henderson laughed. "Hazel next door did. Ask her." She gestured to their left before shutting the door with a solid thump that spoke of grave displeasure.

"Oh dear," Eliza said, as they walked the few feet to the door of the next cottage, "I hope I haven't lost mam a valuable customer."

Hazel was hardly more forthcoming. The police hadn't asked her anything about rows in the street and she hadn't volunteered the information. It was the police's job to find out things, not have decent folk do their work for them.

Ramsay gritted his teeth at this before asking, "Did you hear what the row was about?"

"Which one?"

Ramsay bit his lip before saying gently, "Any one of the rows you heard."

"I think Len Pritchard wanted to go out with Harry when he was out fishing. Harry said he didn't want any amateurs on a working boat at night. Len would end up overboard and there'd be no end of questions to be answered."

"Len didn't accept that answer?" Ramsay asked. "To me, it seems an eminently reasonable reason for Harry to refuse."

"Me as well," Hazel replied, "but Pritchard didn't. He seemed to think Harry should take him for some reason. I heard they were old schoolmates but really…"

"Yes, really…" Eliza said. "It couldn't have been about smuggling, could it?"

Hazel laughed. "Not that old wives' tale again. I don't know why he wanted to go and I'm not guessing either. You'd have the police round here demanding I put it in writing."

"Can you remember what Len said?" Ramsay asked. "You remember what Harry said."

Hazel chuckled. "When Harry's blood was up the whole village heard what he had to say. Len not so much."

"Then you don't?" Ramsay pressed her.

"Nay, I don't. I think he was asking to go on the boat because Harry's answer seemed to suggest it. That's all."

"Is there anything else that comes to mind?" Eliza asked, hoping for something new.

Hazel considered for a moment, and then said, "As Harry was walking away, Len shouted something to him. I didn't understand what he meant but it sounded like, 'I want to see for myself what goes on out there.' It couldn't have been fishing he meant because there's nobody interested in that."

Ramsay laughed. "Very true. Thanks for talking to us, Hazel. I hope you won't mind if we come back if we have new questions."

Hazel grudgingly agreed and Ramsay and Eliza walked away in contemplative silence until Eliza said, "He was still investigating smuggling, do you think?"

"I'm torn between hoping that's what he was doing and wondering if he was concerned that his smuggling operation wasn't running as well as it should. Did something go wrong with a shipment, and he wanted to understand why?" Ramsay replied.

"I didn't think of that," Eliza said. "If he was checking on his smuggling operation, does that mean Harry was blocking him because he was the one who had made it go wrong? Was Harry trying to take over Len Pritchard's operation?"

Ramsay too had been considering these possibilities and he didn't like the answers he came up with. It was all too neat. Pritchard is forced from Whitby and smuggling in Whitby appears to have moved elsewhere. Pritchard moves to Robin Hood's Bay and smuggling rumors begin. Pritchard is seen arguing with Harry Peacock and Peacock is killed. It looked like a solid case, only his experience told him to distrust what seemed to be real. They were often covers hiding the truth. He explained his misgivings to Eliza.

Eliza was unimpressed. "You just don't want to believe someone you know and like is the villain of the piece. I, on the other hand, hardly know him so I can see what's going on clearly."

Ramsay laughed. "I've thought that too."

"Then tell Baldock what we've learned and wrap this up right now," Eliza cried. "What more do we need?'

"Evidence would be nice," Ramsay replied.

"We aren't going to find evidence though, are we," Eliza said. "Nothing was written down in these conversations. There are only witnesses."

"When we learn what was being smuggled, we'll find the evidence we need."

"No one has found any evidence of smuggling, have they?" Eliza said. "Whatever this is about, and it isn't conventional smuggling, Pritchard is at the head of it."

Ramsay was too deep in thought to respond; indeed, he'd hardly heard what Eliza had said. He mused aloud, "How does a police inspector in a small port like Whitby stumble upon a product that pays so well that people risk jail to transport it for him? And what is so small and that valuable?"

"We probably know that," Eliza replied. "Industrial secrets."

Ramsay shook his head. "Len Pritchard was the one who suggested that to us. He'd hardly do that if that was what he was smuggling."

"He had to say something to maintain his cover as the 'wronged smuggling investigator,'" Eliza replied sharply. "As we know, it was from a BBC radio play only weeks before. You'd soon discover that if you didn't already know, and you'd dismiss his suggestion as too convenient. I imagine he had a good laugh after you'd gone, putting you off the scent like that."

Ramsay didn't reply immediately as he went through all the possibilities in his mind. They'd reached *Ye Dolphin* when his mind was brought back to his surroundings by Eliza saying, "We should talk more over a drink."

Days before, Ramsay would have said no. Tonight, however, he realized he too needed company beyond his landlady and his faithful Bracken.

"We should," he replied, and held the door for her to enter.

Inside was already buzzing with conversation and the cheerful clinking of glassware. He ordered himself a Scotch and Eliza a brandy. When the drinks arrived, they retired to a small table away from the crowd at the bar.

"You're an expensive drinker," Eliza began, as they settled themselves. "Most men drink beer."

"Back home, when I was young, they'd say I was a cheap drinker. Grown men drank what they called a 'boilermaker', which was a whisky and a pint of beer," Ramsay responded. "I economize by leaving out the beer."

"Are you going to tell Baldock what we've found?" Eliza demanded.

"He would dismiss it because it came from me," Ramsay replied, "which may be a useful strategy to gain time for more of our investigation. I could tell Constable Storm and have him pass it on. That way it might be acted on quickly."

Eliza snorted angrily. "And Percy Storm would get all the credit."

"Well, I don't want the credit," Ramsay said. "It will encourage more people to seek out my help and I want to be retired."

"You don't, you know," Eliza told him. "Your eyes, your

face, light up when a new piece of evidence is found. Accept it. It's your destiny, your fate, to use your skills helping others this way."

Ramsay chuckled. "My skills, such as they are, come down to perseverance and an open mind. Anyone can do it."

"If anyone can do it, why don't they?"

"They've better things to do with their lives, I imagine," Ramsay retorted.

"Then there's the need for you," Eliza countered. "You have the skills, the time, and the inclination. You must carry on when this is over, and you have to take me along with you. I'm your people person. That's my skill."

Ramsay couldn't help but agree with her on that last part. Should he ever be mad enough to do this even part-time, he'd need someone like Eliza to learn the things people would never tell an old policeman like him.

"I'll make you a pledge," he declared, at last. "If I do decide to take this up as a second career, I'll hire you as my assistant."

Eliza eyed him warily, sensing there was a 'but' in there somewhere. "Promise?"

"I promise. But I don't intend to do anymore investigating after this is over."

Eliza almost sighed with relief. She'd been afraid his 'but' would involve her parents or her going to college, or some other such nonsense; she knew the ways of older people all too well. His resistance to the path she was certain he was on, was just talk. She held out her hand, "It's a deal."

Laughing, Ramsay shook her hand. "You'd be better off getting the train to Scarborough every day and attending college. There are lots of new careers out there for young people. Things we never dreamed of when I left school."

Eliza smiled, pleased she'd guessed where his mind would take him. Old people were so predictable, it was tiresome. She'd rather expected better from him. She continued holding his hand, tightening her grip when she felt his own grip loosen. "We're real partners now. Don't forget it."

Ramsay was so embarrassed; he couldn't find words to say.

27

STILL NOTHING DEFINITE

AT THE GATE to her home, they stopped. Eliza faced Ramsay and said, "Don't forget, tomorrow you're telling Percy Storm what we've learned."

Her earnest expression communicated her concern to Ramsay, and he agreed he would. He doubted it would help. They needed real evidence, or a confession for that.

With her point carried, Eliza kissed him lightly on the cheek and said goodnight. Ramsay walked home slowly, his mind in turmoil. Did she see him as a kind old uncle, or something more? He was realistic enough to know he was no catch, as the saying went, but he was growing afraid she was leading up to a step that would ruin their friendship at best, and her life at worst. He couldn't let that last possibility happen.

Bracken and Mrs. Golightly welcomed him home with expressions almost as grave as his own. "Has something happened?"

"Not here," Mrs. Golightly replied, frostily. "What about you?"

"We learned a lot from the two witnesses we interviewed," Ramsay said, stroking Bracken's head, which remained as stiff as a board. He wasn't going to sell his soul lightly.

"They must have been long interviews."

Ramsay chose his words carefully. "They were and they gave us a lot to think about. We stopped in for a drink to discuss what we'd learned and think on next steps."

"Ah," Mrs. Golightly said, solemnly. "What came of all this thinking, may I ask?"

Ramsay laughed. "Of course, you may. I'm going to tell Constable Storm what we've learned in the morning. I've no doubt you would have heard by lunchtime anyway."

"Heard what exactly?"

"Two witnesses heard Len Pritchard and Harry Peacock arguing in the days before Harry died."

Mrs. Golightly frowned. "That's what you learned? Half the village argued with Harry Peacock on any given day without murdering him. It's hardly earthshaking evidence."

"I know that," Ramsay said. "However, it isn't evidence the police have right now and, anyway, we think it had more to do with the smuggling than the murder."

Mrs. Golightly snorted. "More to do with Harry Peacock's temper, I'd say. And I'll guess it's what Percy Storm says too. There were times just wishing Harry good morning could get you a tongue-lashing."

"Well, that's what we did and thought," Ramsay said pacifically, smiling at Bracken who was finally loosening up. "Time for our walk?"

Bracken sprang to his feet and headed for the hallway. "We won't be too long," Ramsay said to his landlady. "It's another cold night."

* * *

RAMSAY'S MEETING with Constable Storm as he made his rounds of the village the following morning went exactly as Mrs. Golightly had predicted.

"Mr. Ramsay," Storm protested, "Harry Peacock argued with everyone. This isn't news, let alone evidence."

Ramsay outlined what he'd been told by Hazel about the conversation she'd overheard.

"That could refer to many things, though," Storm responded, "and Len Pritchard would soon give us a good account that Harry isn't here to contradict."

"I understand it's thin, Constable," Ramsay agreed, "I just want it known I shared some suggestive evidence with the police. If anything comes to light later that should have come to light earlier and I hadn't shared this, I'd be the one being blamed. Please tell Inspector Baldock what I've said, or I will."

"Maybe you should tell him, sir," Storm replied coldly. "I'm sure it will come better from you."

"I'm sure it won't," Ramsay said, "which is why I told you. However, if he has as little confidence in you as he has in me, perhaps I should be the one to tell him."

"I didn't say that," Storm retorted, clearly upset at the suggestion he wasn't regarded by senior officers. "I'll tell him, if you wish. I just don't think it will be considered as important as you think it should be."

"Thank you," Ramsay said. "What weight Inspector Baldock gives the information is up to him. I just think he needs to hear it." With that, Ramsay and Bracken left Storm and headed back up the hill and onto Station Road.

"We'll walk in the country for a short while, Bracken," Ramsay said, "then we'll see what Len Pritchard has to say about his arguments with Peacock. Something he's failed to mention each time he and I spoke, I should add."

Bracken was too busy hauling his friend up the hill toward the country to care about what he was being told.

An hour later and Ramsay was, once again, knocking on Pritchard's front door. He was invited in and offered refreshment, which he refused.

"I can't stop long, Len. I've a busy day today." Ramsay recounted what the two witnesses had said and asked, "Do you remember these conversations?"

Pritchard frowned and nodded. "I do and they weren't what you're thinking."

"You never mentioned them before."

"I didn't because nothing came of them," Pritchard responded. "I never got out to sea and Harry and I didn't fight, and nor did I kill him."

"Why did you want to go out on Harry's boat?"

Pritchard considered what he wanted to say carefully for a moment. "I wasn't entirely truthful when I said I quit investigating years ago. In fact, I never stopped until Harry disappeared. I thought it best to lie low until that was laid to rest."

"I guessed as much," Ramsay said, dryly.

"I wanted to go out because I wanted to see what the boats did out there at night and watch them return to shore," Pritchard said. "I wasn't expecting to see actual smuggling, only to understand the way a night's fishing went."

Ramsay nodded. "I know what you mean. Fishermen have told me what they saw but I'd like to understand events so I can gauge how reasonable what I'm being told is."

"Harry was adamant," Pritchard said. "No inexperienced people on his boats. And I could see his point of view. If I'd fallen overboard and drowned, the law would be involved."

"Is that what you thought was putting Harry off? The law, I mean?"

"It's what he said but it did make me wonder. You see, I asked Harry because I thought he was an honest man. After these discussions, I was beginning to doubt. When he disappeared, I thought that proved it."

"You think Harry was the leader of it all?" Ramsay asked.

"I do and now I know he's dead, I'm sure it's that business partner who's in charge."

Ramsay considered this. Was this genuine or had Pritchard just found two convenient scapegoats? One a dead man and another too new and inexperienced in the business to effectively defend himself?

"Baldock had to let Armstrong and that skipper go," Ramsay said, "but if they get enough to charge them, that will likely end any smuggling from here."

Pritchard nodded. "I agree. I think the smugglers will move on to a different port. Like they did in Whitby."

"Didn't you think it strange," Ramsay asked, "that they should move elsewhere when they'd removed you, the major threat to their business."

Pritchard's demeanor became defensive as he replied, "I didn't know they had until years after. Even then, I was told by someone I didn't entirely trust. Later, I learned there's no hint of smuggling there so it must be true, wouldn't you think?"

Ramsay wondered about the change in his old colleague's manner. "You must see how it looks, Len," Ramsay said, after a long pause.

"I know how it looks to the police," Pritchard replied. "But I repeat, if I'm the head of this smuggling ring where are my profits? How do I move the goods? How do I contact the people abroad? How do I pay them and what with?"

Ramsay let a silence build as he thought about this. He was sure Baldock or others would have searched for secret bank accounts or contacts that a retired police officer shouldn't have. Not finding something wasn't proof it didn't exist, but it did make it unlikely. Still, a police officer sees and learns things civilians didn't. Had Pritchard learned how to hide from the police all the things he'd just mentioned?

Pritchard decided to continue without waiting for Ramsay to speak. "I know you'd like to prove me innocent, Tom, but you and I both know how hard it is to prove anyone innocent. There are always doubts. All I'm saying is you may have to live with your doubts unless you can find the culprit."

Ramsay laughed. "The thing is, I can't even see how any smuggling is done here, let alone find someone doing it." It was barely noticeable, but Ramsay was sure Pritchard relaxed. *There's something I'm not seeing.*

"Did you give any thought to my suggestion of industrial secrets?" Pritchard asked.

"I did because it's a good idea. The problem is the police have all the evidence from the crime scene and Harry's house. There's nothing to say what might have been hidden there."

Pritchard nodded glumly. "I visited Harry at his house once, hoping to be invited in so I could check it out. He wouldn't even let me in the door."

"That would make me suspicious."

"And me," Pritchard replied. "Still, if I'd gone to the police, they'd have said it was Harry being himself and that would be that."

Ramsay decided to return to the earlier subject. "Did

you ask any of the other boat owners for a ride out to sea while they were fishing?"

"Only after Harry turned me down, and they were equally adamant they wouldn't have landsmen on their boats while working at night," Pritchard replied.

Pritchard's answers were all what Ramsay had expected and they didn't convince him either way. He bade his old colleague good day and left.

As they returned to the guest house, Ramsay asked Bracken, "Were you convinced?"

Bracken, who'd been bored throughout, gave his friend his usual, 'are you kidding me?' expression and trotted on ahead.

"Me neither," Ramsay murmured. "But innocence can look exceedingly guilty, if you want to see it that way. We need someone from those fishing boats who'll spill the beans, if there are any beans to spill."

At the point where they would turn off for the guest house, Ramsay stopped and looked out over the village rooftops to the sea and bay. It was a clear, crisp day and the hotel and golf course at Ravenscar seemed so near he could reach out and almost touch them. Seagulls wheeled above the fishing boats in the bay, their raucous cries the only sound. Smoke rose lazily up into the pale blue sky from chimneys in the village and from farms on the land above the bay, a peaceful scene. *The English Countryside in Autumn* it would be called, if a painter was capturing it. Yet somewhere among all those quiet cottages a murderer was living, not hiding, walking about in plain sight.

"Are you hungry, Bracken?" Ramsay asked, guiltily. Bribing Bracken so he could see Eliza wasn't quite right, he felt. But Bracken was always hungry and they were soon at the teashop door.

28

SETTING A TRAP

INSIDE WAS EMPTY, which meant Eliza could immediately say, "What did you learn?"

As he seated himself at his usual table, Ramsay told her.

Eliza seemed pleased. "Now I'm sure we didn't find the murderer or the smugglers. Baldock was right to let them go."

Ramsay nodded. "Which means we're starting again, and Len Pritchard is the most likely candidate, though I'm not happy about it."

"Not happy it's him because he and you are old acquaintances or because you don't think the evidence suggests he's the one?"

"Both, I'd say," Ramsay replied. "Everything we have against him is simply circumstantial. And there's real evidence pointing against him being guilty."

"Like what?"

Ramsay told Eliza of the points Pritchard had itemized when they spoke, ticking each point off on his fingers as he did so.

"It's true," Eliza said, ruefully. "He doesn't live like I'd expect a successful criminal to live."

"I'd like to create a trap where we could confirm one way or another if Pritchard is our villain," Ramsay said, thoughtfully. "Sometimes, you have to smoke the perpetrators out of hiding."

Eliza slipped her hand around his arm, and said happily, "Now you're talking. How?"

"I haven't found the answer yet," Ramsay admitted, as Bracken tugged at the hem of Eliza's skirt. "Down, Bracken."

Eliza let go of Ramsay's arm and bent down to fondle Bracken. "Poor thing. You must be starving." She hurried off, leaving Bracken gazing longingly after her. Moments later, she returned with a bowl of water and one of scraps, placing them at Bracken's paws before smiling at Ramsay. "You were saying?"

Ramsay said, "We don't know when the illicit packages, whatever they are, arrive, we don't know how the signal of their arrival is sent, we don't know if Harry was involved or whether it was just that ugly skipper. We just don't have enough to successfully fool the villain into coming out into the open."

"What about sending Pritchard a blackmail note?" Eliza asked. "Saying the writer now knows he murdered Harry?"

"Or one saying the writer now knows he's the head of the smuggling ring," Ramsay countered. "We need a good reason why the writer now knows, and I can't yet see that."

"Easy. Either Armstrong angrily said something or the ugly skipper got drunk and said something." Eliza stopped. "Hey, where does that fellow drink? If we knew that, we could build a good story."

"The *Dolphin* will soon be open," Ramsay said. "We can start by asking there."

"Wait for me," Eliza said, unfastening her apron. "I'll tell mam I'll be back to help her close."

"We can wait until you close," Ramsay said, firmly. He didn't want Eliza's mother upset with him for leaving her without help at closing time.

* * *

A HOUR LATER, with Eliza washed and changed into pub crawling clothes, they set out. The pub was in the quiet period before the evening rush when they entered. Ramsay bought drinks and, as he paid, asked the barman if the *Ravenscar Lady 4* skipper drank here.

"He's here some evenings," the barman replied, "generally with the crew. Why?"

"I wanted to ask him something," Ramsay said, neutrally. "I'll hang about in case he comes in. Thanks."

"So," Eliza said, when Ramsay told her what he'd learned, "we have the beginning of our trap."

"Damn," Ramsay cried. "We need to know if Pritchard also drinks in here. If he does, our trap will be soon exposed." He rose from his seat and quickly crossed the floor to the bar, thanking providence the place was still almost empty.

"Excuse me," he called to the barman who was placing a bottle of pickled eggs on the counter, "do you know if my old friend Len Pritchard ever comes in here?"

The man laughed. "Mr. Pritchard doesn't approve of pubs. He says his life in the police taught him that bars aren't good places to have in a community."

"But you do know him?"

"I do, from cricket," the barman said. "He turns out for us when we're short a man or two."

"I see, thanks," Ramsay said, and returned to his seat.

"Well?" Eliza asked.

"We're safe. Our writer's story goes like this: while drinking in the *Dolphin*, he saw the ugly skipper celebrating his release from police custody. The man began hinting what he knew about the real perpetrator of the crime. The writer recognized at once who the man meant and if Pritchard doesn't hand over a lot of money, he'll inform the police."

"When Pritchard brings the money to the arranged place, we do a citizen's arrest?" Eliza said, chuckling.

"Or we have Constable Storm with us, and he makes the arrest," Ramsay replied. "I'm sure he'd be happy to oblige."

"We could send the same note to Armstrong," Eliza suggested. "It still may be him."

Ramsay considered this but decided against. "He and that skipper must have had sound stories, or the police wouldn't have let them go. And I don't think Armstrong would bite at the bait. I think he'd have it out with the man."

"Maybe you're right," Eliza agreed. "I just don't like those two and would happily get them into trouble, if I could."

"I'll go back to the guest house and write the note," Ramsay said, finishing his whisky with relish. "And slip it through his letterbox right away."

"You don't want to mention the murder in the note?" Eliza asked.

Ramsay shook his head. "Our circumstantial evidence points to his involvement with smuggling, we'll confine ourselves with that for now."

Eliza handed him her glass as they rose to leave and suddenly whispered, "If Caldbeck is the smuggler, Pritchard will likely know him. He's more likely to search him out and confront him than hand over cash."

Ramsay, who was juggling two glasses, his hat, and Bracken's leash, was too busy to reply.

"Here," Eliza said, seeing the difficulty, "let me take Bracken." She took hold of the leash allowing Ramsay to finally reply as he took the glasses back to the bar.

"From the moment he gets the note, I plan to be watching him. Whether he goes to the bank for the money or to Caldbeck's lodgings for a fight, I'll know he's the one we're after."

"I'm coming with you," Eliza said. "He'll likely make his move on Caldbeck, before the man leaves for work."

Ramsay wasn't about to argue. In some ways, if Pritchard did leave the house and he saw Ramsay, Eliza, and Bracken walking he'd be re-assured by the normalness of it. "We'll reconnoiter the land at the top of the hill and find a spot to watch and wait."

* * *

By the time the note was delivered, low heavy clouds were dropping a steady torrent of rain, making Eliza and Ramsay huddle together under his golf umbrella at the vantage point they'd settled on.

"I don't believe anyone will leave their houses tonight," Eliza grumbled as she pressed closer to Ramsay. Bracken too was snuggling close to Ramsay's feet, shivering.

"Unfortunately," Ramsay replied, wrapping his free arm around Eliza's shoulders, "we've set the trap in motion, and we have to see it through."

"All future cases must be in the South of France," Eliza replied. "I'm cold and wet and we've only just started."

"You'd best get on home," Ramsay told her. "You could

take Bracken as well. He needs to be dried in front of the fire."

Eliza considered this, wanting to refuse, but Bracken was shivering more than she was, and having them all ill wouldn't help the investigation.

"I will," she agreed, "but only because Bracken will be ill if we keep him here any longer. I wonder at you bringing him out on a day like this."

"Like you, Bracken doesn't always know what's best for him," Ramsay said, chuckling. "He couldn't wait to get out for a walk. Of course, the rain wasn't so heavy then."

Eliza decided not to argue with his jibe about her character but took Bracken's leash, pulled her hood back over her head, and they set off at a fast trot back to her home.

Ramsay watched them go, with a wry smile on his face. If he wasn't careful, Bracken would become another draw for Eliza, and his task of untangling himself would be even harder. He was almost certain he wanted to untangle himself, only whenever he thought on it, something inside said no.

When they were out of sight, Ramsay settled down to wait. He'd dressed warmly and was still cold. Eliza's point about no one leaving the house was a valid one, he thought, only that's exactly when someone who didn't want to be seen would leave the house. He didn't dare leave.

After thirty minutes and Ramsay walking back and forth along the path to keep warm, while staying out of sight of Pritchard's window yet never taking his eyes off the garden gate, the rain began to ease. Ramsay grew more hopeful. Maybe, this would be enough to bring out Pritchard, if Pritchard was indeed the leader of the rumored smugglers.

His hopes were once again draining away when he saw Pritchard leaving his gate and turning to make his way into the village. Excitement mounting, cold forgotten, Ramsay stayed out of sight. As he watched the man making his way along the street, Ramsay tried to read his expression. It wasn't easy because Pritchard's umbrella flapped, obscuring his face and when it wasn't covered, there was a peaked flat cap and upturned coat collar making a difficult assessment even more difficult. However, Ramsay thought, based on the angry, determined stride and what little he could see of the man's face, he was certainly upset about something. Ramsay waited until Pritchard was past the point where he might see him and being careful to ensure Pritchard was not looking behind himself, Ramsay set off in pursuit.

The walk downhill into the village was a short one and had very few points along its way where Ramsay could hide if his quarry did look back. Consequently, it was a nervous ten minutes before they entered the village where hiding places were plentiful enough to calm Ramsay's nerves. Halfway down New Street, Pritchard turned to a doorway and rapped on it loudly enough for Ramsay to hear from his hiding place a hundred feet away.

A woman answered the door. There was conversation. She stepped inside, inviting Pritchard to follow and the door closed, leaving Ramsay once again watching and waiting. He was still waiting when Eliza appeared at his side.

"I saw you and Pritchard go by," she told him, shutting her own umbrella and huddling under Ramsay's.

Ramsay pulled her further into the gap between bushes. "You have to stay out of sight."

"If he returns straight home after talking to Caldbeck, I presume that's why he's in there, he'll see us anyway," Eliza replied.

"I want him to see me," Ramsay said. "I want to ask where he's been on this wet evening."

Eliza laughed. "He's more likely to ask you the same question. You haven't Bracken with you now so you've no good reason to be out."

"I've just stepped out for a drink, is what I'll tell him," Ramsay replied.

Further discussion was ended for the door further down the street opened. Ramsay and Eliza stepped out into the street and began walking down the hill.

"He'll think we're a couple," Eliza said, giggling as she linked arms with Ramsay.

"We're huddling under an umbrella," Ramsay replied, "a perfectly respectable thing to do in weather like this."

Ahead of them, they saw Pritchard leave the house, turn up his coat collar and begin walking down the hill, seemingly without seeing them.

"Even better," Ramsay replied to Eliza's comment they weren't going to catch him by surprise. "We can see where he's going now. I wish we knew that Caldbeck lodged in that house."

"I can get that from the regulars tomorrow," Eliza said. "Mind you, I don't expect we'll have many people in if this rain doesn't stop."

Their surveillance ended when Pritchard entered the Ravenscar Fishing office, where lights were on. Someone was working late.

"It'll be my dad and he can tell us what Pritchard came to say there," Eliza said. "I was right about you needing me as a partner. I'm doing all the work today."

29

RAMSAY HAS A HUNCH

Ramsay viewed the Ravenscar Fishing office building for a moment, deciding whether they should follow Pritchard in or 'accidentally' bump into him on the street when he came out.

"The café is still open, we'll get a cup of tea there," Ramsay told Eliza. "It will be dryer and warmer than waiting out here."

Eliza gave him a disapproving stare in return. "Their tea is terrible," she retorted, "and their cooking worse."

"You're prejudiced because your family owns a competing teashop," Ramsay retorted. "Come on and be polite."

Ramsay was right. The café was warm and the room buzzing with conversation that stopped when they walked in. Ramsay ordered tea, a coffee, and a buttered teacake at the counter, saying to the elderly woman serving, "It's like November out there."

"It soon will be," she replied, carefully. Ramsay noticed the conversation in the room was now subdued. If he'd thought it was because he was a police officer, he'd have been suspicious, but he knew it was much more likely they just didn't like outsiders invading their space. By now, everyone in the village must be aware Ramsay and Eliza were ferreting around in things that weren't their business.

He paid the woman and carried the tray back to the table Eliza had found for them. Ramsay grinned at Eliza's outraged expression as she fingered the plastic tablecloth and noted the mugs in which their drinks were served.

"Not your teashop standards," Ramsay said, grinning. "But very welcome to this frozen traveler nonetheless." He clasped his hands around the mug to warm them.

"Look how busy it is," Eliza whispered. "We never get anyone much outside of lunchtime at this time of year."

"But you cater to a different clientele, Eliza. And who would walk up that hill to your teashop from the slipway for a snack every day? Their tea break would be gone just getting to your place. And, anyway, they wouldn't be comfortable sitting in the teashop in their working clothes."

"Maybe," Eliza admitted, still frowning. "And mam wouldn't like our chairs covered in fish scales, I suppose."

Sensing that Eliza was beginning to see the justice of his comments, Ramsay said, "As you're the only one of us who can see to the office, I hope you've been watching for Pritchard to leave."

"What do you take me for?" Eliza exclaimed. "Of course, I have."

"Then keep watching while I eat my teacake," Ramsay said, biting into the still warm, buttery bun. It was good. Eliza's views on the café's customers, owners, and furnishings might have some merit, but she was completely wrong about the woman's cooking.

"How are we going to pounce on him if we have to wait for you to stop guzzling tea cakes," Eliza retorted.

"It's one tea cake and I'm eating it heartily, not guzzling," Ramsay told her, with a lofty air. "I've paid so we can spring from our chairs and be outside before he's crossed the street."

Eliza snorted in disbelief, before grumbling., "My coffee is practically cold."

"I'm sure they'd add some hot water or coffee, if you asked nicely," Ramsay replied. "My tea is just the right temperature for drinking. I think it might be your frosty expression that chilled your drink."

"They don't even give a pot of hot water with your tea," Eliza continued.

"Perhaps because they serve in a large mug and not a tiny teacup," Ramsay responded, sweetly. He was rather enjoying Eliza's discomfort. It took her mind off lecturing him.

"What can he be doing in there?" Eliza exclaimed in exasperation.

"Talking to your father or Armstrong," Ramsay replied. "The question is, why?"

"Because Armstrong is in it with him," Eliza retorted.

Ramsay nodded. "Possibly," he agreed. "Or maybe he's angry at one of Armstrong's employees hinting to anyone who listened that he, Pritchard, was the leader of the smugglers."

"Why should Armstrong care about what his employees say when they have too much to drink?" Eliza asked.

"Well, he might if it was company secrets being given away."

Eliza shook her head. "It wasn't though, was it."

"Who knows how Pritchard interpreted what I wrote," Ramsay said, before adding, "None of this looks like a man frightened he'll be exposed though, does it?"

Eliza admitted it looked more like a man angry at having his name dragged through the mud than a frightened criminal.

"Our trap seems to be failing," Ramsay whispered.

"Here's our chance to find out," Eliza said, jumping to her feet. "He's just left the office."

They hurried to the café door, where Ramsay paused, judging the best time to exit and 'see' Pritchard.

"Now," he whispered, and Eliza practically flew out the door. Ramsay followed. He caught Pritchard's eye and called, "Len, how are you? What are you doing out on a grim evening like this?"

Pritchard eyed them warily. "I might ask you the same question, Tom. Good evening, Miss Danesdale." He doffed his cap to Eliza.

"I was taking my constitutional when I ran into Eliza," Ramsay said, "who was supposed to be shopping but kindly accepted my invitation to refreshment."

"Spying out the competition," Eliza added with a disarming smile.

Pritchard tipped his umbrella to see them better, before saying, "I'm out for the air too. Salt air is just the thing, I find. I'm sure all the sea shanties will say so."

"Perhaps we can walk back up the hill together," Ramsay said, steering Eliza to fall in with Pritchard.

"Company would be very welcome," Pritchard replied.

"Did you see my father when you were in the office?" Eliza asked.

"Only to say hello too," Pritchard replied. "It was Armstrong I wanted to see. I've been wondering if he's even aware of the smuggling, Tom."

"And is he?" Ramsay asked.

"He says there isn't any, but then, he would, wouldn't he."

Ramsay smiled in agreement. "Of course, but I thought you'd given up on all this, Len."

"I try, only I'm reminded of it all the time," Pritchard said. He sighed. "Some days I think I really should have moved inland, Harrogate perhaps. I like Harrogate."

Ramsay laughed. "You've still time to move and it would put an end to the rumors about your involvement in smuggling."

"Would it? Or would people say I'd made my money for the move from smuggling?" Pritchard replied, unhappily. He lapsed into silence.

Ramsay glanced at his old colleague's face. It was bleak, his eyes seemed focused on eternity and a grim smile hovered around his lips. A smile that had no answering light in his eyes. *Will he tell me about the letter, or not? And, if he doesn't, does that mean he knows it's true or that he doesn't trust me? Or, maybe, he believes I sent the letter?*

"Here's where I leave you two," Eliza said, as they reached Wilson's greengrocery. She squeezed Ramsay's arm as she unlinked from his. "I hope we'll see you tomorrow in our teashop, Mr. Ramsay."

'I'll be there," Ramsay replied.

Pritchard wasn't any more forthcoming as the two men climbed higher up the street, heads down against the swirling wind and rain.

"You would miss this seaside weather, Len," Ramsay remarked, when a particularly violent gust threw what felt like a pail of cold water in their faces. "If you moved to Harrogate, I mean."

Pritchard nodded and head down, continued grimly

marching up the hill until they reached the junction where Station Road and Whitby Road separated. Then he said, "Sorry to be so glum today, Tom. I've a lot on my mind."

"Anything I can help with?" Ramsay asked.

Pritchard shook his head. "It's nothing really but when you live alone, things get all out of proportion." He laughed. "And you forget how to make conversation to old friends. Apologies again, Tom. I promise to be in a better mood when next we meet." He turned and strode off toward his home.

Ramsay too set off in the direction of the guest house but when he judged that Pritchard would be arriving at his house, he turned and headed back to the Danesdale's house. At the junction of the two roads, he checked to see that Pritchard was nowhere to be seen before continuing to Eliza's home.

Bracken was overjoyed to see him, which made Ramsay feel better. He rather expected a cold shoulder from his friend because of the soaking they'd both endured earlier. Eliza too was eager to know what Pritchard said. Ramsay told her.

"He didn't mention the letter at all?" Eliza asked.

"Not at all. Worse, he was clearly worried about something, and I think that has to be the letter. I don't know how but he must be involved."

"We can't watch his house all night in this weather," Eliza said. "We'll all be down with pneumonia before morning."

"Unless he has a lot of money in his house," Ramsay replied, "he will go to the bank in Scarborough or Whitby in the morning. We'll ask the stationmaster tomorrow evening, if Pritchard took a train."

"I'll do that," Eliza said. "Mr. Coulson is a friend of mine."

"Is he another cranky old man?"

Eliza grinned. "No. I used to babysit his kids when they were small, and they liked me, so he does too."

"I'm amazed you didn't murder them," Ramsay replied, grinning. "I wouldn't have expected you to have the patience to manage small children."

"Oh, I have patience with children," Eliza said. "It's people who should know better, like adults, that drive me nuts."

Returning to the matter in hand, Ramsay said, "If he takes the train, I'll slip a note through his door telling him where and when to leave the money."

Eliza's mother appeared in the doorway to the living room. "Evening, Tom."

Ramsay greeted her and, after a brief discussion about the weather, added, "Well, I must be going, or Mrs. Golightly will throw dinner at my head. I'll take Bracken home and finish drying him."

He picked up Bracken and placed him under his left arm. Mrs. Danesdale opened the door and helped Ramsay open his umbrella, saying, "Will we see you for lunch tomorrow, Tom?"

Ramsay assured her they would and set off quickly for the guest house, with the indignant Bracken complaining all the way. "I'm not putting you down," Ramsay told him. "You'll just get soaked again."

* * *

ELIZA WAS right about the teashop, Ramsay found when he arrived next day to take his usual table. No one wanted lunch so badly they were prepared to walk through the rain to eat it here, which meant Eliza could join him at his table the moment she'd brought the Scotch Broth he ordered.

"Mam did it especially for you," Eliza said, as he dipped his bread in the bowl. "She thinks you need fattening up."

This surprised Ramsay. He was so used to remembering himself as he was before he retired, he had failed to notice all the walking was shedding pounds. He looked at his small 'beer belly', which had nothing to do with beer, and replied, "I think there are still pounds to go yet."

Eliza nodded. "It's your face where you can see it. You're looking peaky."

"That's being outside so much in this awful climate," Ramsay objected. "Not my diet."

"Well," Eliza said, stroking Bracken's head as he begged for more scraps, "what are our next steps, boss?"

"You're going to continue asking your customers, if you have any today, about Pritchard and then after work your stationmaster friend about Pritchard and the train," Ramsay replied. "I'm going to talk to Constable Storm and, if I can, your dad and Arthur Peacock, if Armstrong isn't about."

"Why?" Eliza cried. "We've talked to both of them over and over and learned nothing useful."

"They may tell me what Pritchard had to say last night," Ramsay replied. "Did you grill your dad when he got home?"

Eliza nodded. "Apparently Pritchard and Armstrong were talking in Armstrong's office with the door shut. They talked quietly and Dad heard nothing."

"Then I think Armstrong is in on it too," Ramsay mused. "Or why the secrecy?"

"What do you hope to get from Percy Storm that you couldn't get from a babbling brook?" Eliza asked, derisively.

Ramsay smiled. "I'm not sure I'll get anything, only I've a hunch I need to follow up on and he's the man to confirm or deny it."

30

THE TRAP IS WORKING

RAMSAY by now was familiar with Constable Storm's routine and once again managed to accidentally meet him on his afternoon patrol of the village. Storm, who was wearing the old-fashioned police waterproof cape and carrying an umbrella, looked much as Ramsay felt -- sodden.

"Good afternoon, constable," Ramsay greeted him brightly. "Police and dogwalkers are the only people mad enough to be out today, I see."

Storm nodded. "Aye, it's true. I haven't seen a soul."

"I remember you saying I should see the Fylingdales Early Warning Station while I was here," Ramsay said. "I thought if I went inland tomorrow, I might escape this awful rain. How would I get out there to see it?"

"Take the train to Whitby and get the Goathland bus," Storm said. "You can't go inside the facility, of course. It's top secret. But just seeing those three giant golf balls on top of the moor is a sight, I promise."

"Have you been inside?" Ramsay asked.

"Twice. We were given a tour the first time we were up there keeping the protesters out," Storm replied. "The second time was with the Territorials when we were doing an exercise on defending the place from attack. It's fascinating."

"I imagine," Ramsay said, ruefully. Though he felt he'd probably dislike the whole place on principle. "Well, if tonight's weather forecast on the radio isn't any better, that's what I'll do."

"There's a nice old hotel and waterfall at Goathland," Storm said. "Look in there after you've gazed your fill at the early warning station."

"I will, thank you," Ramsay said. "Do you know anyone that works at the station?"

Storm laughed. "Even if I did, they still couldn't let you in. I'm just a lowly village copper and a little less lowly sergeant in the Territorials. I don't have friends who have that kind of authority."

Ramsay smiled. "I wasn't expecting a grand tour, more someone who could tell me what I'm looking at. I know it's to detect soviet missiles as soon after launch as is possible but beyond that, I'm clueless."

"Some of the airmen drink in The Mallyan Spout Hotel, that's the waterfall I mentioned by the way, the Mallyan Spout. Go there for lunch and keep your ears open."

"Thanks," Ramsay replied. "Next miserable day, I'll do that." He nodded farewell to Constable Storm and headed for Station Road, where Bracken could indulge himself by pretending to be a sheepdog. Not that Ramsay would ever let him off the leash to test out his friend's skills. Farmers tended to shoot dogs that worried their sheep.

"What say you, Bracken?" Ramsay asked. "Some moorland hiking for a day? Or keep the pressure on our suspects here?"

Bracken gave a low growl that Ramsay at first interpreted

as an answer to his question but, looking where Bracken's eyes were focused, he saw Pritchard leaving his gate.

"Hello, Len," Ramsay called. "I thought it was only dogwalkers outside this afternoon."

Pritchard looked uncomfortable. "I have to go to Whitby. Can't stop, I must catch this next train." He hurried past Ramsay and Bracken on his way to the station.

"I think we're going to be proven right, Bracken," Ramsay said, quietly. "And I'm sorry about it. Deep down, I thought Len Pritchard was a good man." He lapsed into a sad silence for a few moments before brightening, saying, "At least now we haven't left Eliza to do all the work. She won't be pleased." The thought kept him grinning throughout the walk and his return to the teashop for mid afternoon tea.

* * *

"You look pleased with yourself," Eliza said, suspiciously, when he entered the café and hung his dripping coat on a hook at the door.

"Just fresh air and good company," Ramsay lied, his smile growing broader.

"High Tea?" Eliza asked.

"Yes, please and one for me too," Ramsay said, teasing her.

"Just for that, I'll get Bracken a towel and food first," Eliza responded.

Ramsay didn't reply. He took his usual table; it didn't look like anyone had been in all day to his untutored eye.

Eliza returned and handed him the towel. "You can dry Bracken. You're the one who got him wet. This poor dog will die of cold before your holiday is out. He needs a raincoat. Mr. Wilson will have one in the Village Store."

Ramsay frowned, guiltily. "I never thought of that..."

"You wouldn't," Eliza interjected.

"...I'll go straight there after we've warmed and dried a little," Ramsay added, before she could continue her theme. What he'd meant to say was Bracken had a raincoat and he hadn't thought of putting it on his companion.

"Be sure you do," Eliza said, sitting on the chair opposite and stroking Bracken's head. Bracken didn't look up from the bowl of meat scraps he'd been given until it was gone. At which point he began his 'puppy dog lost' routine of sorrowful eyes and baby-like mewing.

"I'll get you some more, you poor thing," Eliza said, picking up the bowl and marching off to the kitchen.

"One day, Bracken," Ramsay said, amiably, "you'll go too far, and you'll be marched off by a do-gooder to a puppy shelter where you'll be sold to a shepherd and you'll chase sheep every day, come rain or shine, until you're worn down, sold to a factory, turned into animal feed and your bones boiled for glue. And it will serve you right!"

Bracken ignored him loftily, giving Eliza a beaming smile and a wagging tail of approval when she arrived back with his bowl. "Yours is still being made," she told Ramsay.

"You don't help your mother in the kitchen?"

"She'd murder me, or I her, if I did that," Eliza said. "She's very particular about how things are made and presented."

"As a customer, I'm pleased to hear that," Ramsay said, chuckling.

"If you were really hungry, you wouldn't," Eliza retorted. "Have you done any useful investigating today or have you just been mistreating this poor animal?"

"I learned Pritchard has taken the train to Whitby," Ramsay said, smiling sweetly at her outraged expression. "Or, at least, he said he was going to. I didn't watch him get on."

"That was my job," Eliza said, if a perfect impression of an irate union worker discovering a scab at his workplace.

"It still is," Ramsay replied, soothingly. "I met him in the street, and he told me he couldn't stay to chat because he had a train to catch. Only the stationmaster knows for sure he did catch a train and, if he did, was it to Whitby, as he told me, or Scarborough, which he didn't want me to know."

Eliza was mollified by this and asked, "Was there time for him to get to the bank if he caught the train he was rushing for?"

"I should say so," Ramsay replied. "Certainly, if it was Whitby and possibly if it was Scarborough."

"It seems he didn't get the answers he wanted from Armstrong and Caldbeck then," Eliza said, triumphantly. "We've got him."

"It looks like it," Ramsay agreed. "I can't think of any reason he would pay blackmail if he wasn't guilty."

"I was always told you don't pay blackmail at any time," Eliza said. "I would have thought an ex-cop would know that too."

Ramsay laughed. "It's like a lot of good advice. Easy to give, not so easy to act on. People regularly pay up because instant exposure is more terrifying than slowly handing over everything you have."

"The principle behind taxes," Eliza said. "At least, that's how my dad describes it."

"Your dad didn't strike me as being a radical," Ramsay said, mildly puzzled.

"He isn't," Eliza replied. "He just hates paying taxes on

the little we earn. He does our books, you see. It strikes him more clearly than it does mam and me."

"To return to our plan of unmasking the smuggling ringleader," Ramsay said. "If Pritchard is really in Whitby today drawing money from his bank, we should expect to see him dropping it off where we told him before tomorrow morning. How do we split the nightshift?"

"I'll finish here by five o'clock," Eliza replied. "I could nap until two in the morning and relieve you to get some sleep."

Ramsay considered and then said, "That would be best. I can't believe he'll drop off the package until morning anyway. Too much chance of an early rising dogwalker finding and taking it. Your parents might object to you sitting outside half the night, though."

"I'm not going to tell them what I'm doing."

Ramsay shook his head. "They'll hear your alarm go off."

"No, they won't because I won't set an alarm," Eliza retorted. "If I tell myself what time to get up, I'm always awake then."

Ramsay assured her if she wished to get out of the house unnoticed that would be best. Secretly though, he felt sure she wouldn't be relieving him at two o'clock and even if she did, he wasn't leaving her alone in the middle of the night on the outskirts of the village.

After he'd eaten, Ramsay rose to leave, saying quietly, "I'll see you at the drop spot early tomorrow."

"You'll see me before," Eliza reminded him. "If Mr. Coulson doesn't confirm Pritchard left and returned on a train, there likely won't be a package to collect."

"I'd forgotten," Ramsay admitted. "It's old age, I expect. And I must persuade Constable Storm to be with us when the time comes. I'll go soften him up and confirm it after I hear from you. Until later, then."

* * *

LATER, when he felt sure Eliza would have spoken to the stationmaster, Ramsay walked Bracken down the hill to Eliza's home and knocked on the door. It was opened before he'd let go of the knocker.

"He did and it was Whitby," Eliza whispered, ushering them both in. "I told mam and dad you'd be dropping by. Go right in."

Ramsay removed his wet coat and shoes and Bracken's waterproof coat before they entered the snug living room. It was over an hour before he felt he could politely leave.

"Till two," Eliza whispered, as she closed the door behind him.

31

THE BITER BITTEN

A LITTLE AFTER two the next morning, Eliza joined Ramsay at the bench they'd arranged as their observation post.

"Brr," she stuttered. "What a time to be outside. It's freezing."

Ramsay offered her some hot tea from the Thermos flask he'd brought with him. Years of similar vigils had taught him comfort, even something as mundane as a hot drink, boosted morale enormously. Eliza hesitated then accepted it. She'd come out without breakfast.

"You can leave me the Thermos," Eliza suggested, grinning, as the hot drink warmed her inside.

"I'm not going anywhere," Ramsay said. "These next hours are when he's most likely to drop off the cash."

"When will Percy Storm be arriving?"

"He said around this time," Ramsay answered. "He's even harder to get out of bed than you are."

"I wasn't late!" Eliza cried.

"No," Ramsay said, soothingly. "You were fashionably on time."

Before Eliza could respond, Constable Storm arrived

and whispered a subdued 'good morning' before saying, "Nothing happening yet?"

"Not yet," Eliza replied, "but soon."

"I hope so," Storm said gloomily. "I woke the dog getting up and she woke my wife. This had better produce a result or I'm in trouble."

Ramsay and Eliza assured him it would, and they settled down to watch. Hours ticked slowly away, and a light rain began to fall.

"I'd hoped the clouds were all out of rain after yesterday," Ramsay grumbled, turning up his coat collar further and settling his hat lower on his head.

Just after five, they saw a dark figure approaching down Station Road. "That's him," Ramsay whispered.

They crouched lower behind the bushes that screened them and watched the figure through the branches. The man stepped out of the darkness into the light from a streetlamp and they could finally confirm it was Pritchard. As he drew nearer, all three watchers stiffened, making ready to pounce.

Pritchard reached the spot and crouched to hide the package in the spot he'd been told to. Ramsay stood up and called, "We see you, Len. Stay right where you are."

Pritchard rose and turned to face them. Even in the faint light, Ramsay could see he was grinning.

As Ramsay left the hideout, Pritchard said, conversationally, "I knew it was you, Tom. You're not a good enough actor to carry off a trap like this."

"Well, it caught you," Ramsay retorted.

Pritchard laughed. "No, it caught you." He gestured to the darkness behind Ramsay, who turned to see shadowy figures moving closer. "I told Inspector Baldock of your clumsy blackmail attempt and here we all are."

As Baldock approached the small group, he shouted, "Constable Storm, do the honors. Arrest Mr. Ramsay and his accomplice."

Storm read Ramsay and then Eliza the official words before placing handcuffs on Ramsay's wrists and then Eliza's.

"Well done, Mr. Pritchard," Baldock said, when the short ceremony was over, "you played your part well. I always knew this fellow had a hand in it somewhere and now I find he supplements his pension with blackmail. It's the best start to a day, I can remember."

"I had nothing to do with the murder or the smuggling," Ramsay said, evenly, though his heart was thumping. He knew how easily innocent people could be made to look guilty.

"Save all that for when we get back to the station," Baldock said. "Let's go."

At the police house, Ramsay was processed by a smug Constable Storm. "I told them you regularly questioned me for information on where the investigation was going," he explained to Ramsay, while filling out the forms. "We all knew what you were up to."

"And what was I up to?" Ramsay asked.

"Trying to deflect the investigation away from yourself," Storm replied. "First with Armstrong and then with Pritchard, both red herrings. And thinking by using me to channel the false information, you'd hide yourself from the inspector."

"It couldn't be I simply told you what we'd learned in order to keep you informed, could it?" Ramsay asked.

"That's what you wanted us to think," Storm said, signing a form with a flourish. "Only we country bumpkins aren't as green as you think, Mr. Big City Policeman."

"Why would I tell you about catching Pritchard dropping off cash, if I wanted to profit by it?" Ramsay asked.

"I'm sure you'll explain it all to the inspector when you make your statement," Storm replied. "And if you don't, Eliza Danesdale will, if she knows what's good for her."

"That sounds awfully like a threat, constable," Ramsay growled.

"Not at all," Storm said. "She can either cooperate and have the charges dropped or she can go down with you. Not a threat, just common sense."

Ramsay had already guessed they'd use this tactic, so Storm's words weren't a surprise. He only hoped Eliza wouldn't say or do anything foolish. A good prosecution lawyer could have her admitting to perjury, if she got it all wrong.

"There now," Storm said, putting down his pen. "That's you done. If you'll follow me to the linen closet we call a cell, I can start on Miss Danesdale's paperwork."

Storm was right about the cell. When the house had been a family home, the room was probably a place for drying clothes. With the door shut behind him, he took the only chair in the place and began planning his next steps. This was one outcome he hadn't dreamt of, let alone planned for. *What was Baldock thinking? He couldn't hold him on this charge, not when he'd told the police about the handover of cash and invited the police to be on the scene to witness it.*

Baldock, though, clearly thought differently for only an hour later, Ramsay was driven to Scarborough and an even less attractive cell, where he spent an uncomfortable night cursing Baldock and his insane resentment.

32

WHEELS IN MOTION

THE FOLLOWING MORNING, Ramsay was awakened by a police constable bringing breakfast. It was a measure of how unpleasant his night had been that Ramsay was grateful for the attention.

"Was Miss Danesdale allowed to go home?" Ramsay asked the man.

"I don't know any Miss Danesdale," the officer replied.

"She's not being held here then?"

"No one of that name is here," the officer replied, leaving the tray on a small table and exiting the cell.

As Ramsay ate his breakfast — he was famished after yesterday's missed meals and sleep — he pondered what that meant. Had they not charged Eliza? He hoped not. Or had they persuaded her to inform against him in exchange for not being charged? He suspected she wouldn't have agreed to that but knew how easily people were seduced by such offers when the reality of their situation was brought home to them. No doubt he'd learn more when he met with Baldock, which couldn't be too long. Ramsay realized another drawback to meddling in crimes away from his home. He didn't know any lawyers to call with his one phone call.

It was past mid-morning, when he was summoned to meet Baldock. Glad to be released from the cold cell, Ramsay followed the constable who'd brought him breakfast to an interview room where Baldock was smoking a cigarette.

"Thank you, constable," Baldock said, dismissing the officer. When the constable was gone, Baldock began, "What were you playing at?"

"I was smoking out a villain, or to be more accurate, trying to confirm whether or not Pritchard was a villain," Ramsay replied.

"What do you think now?" Baldock asked.

"I think not," Ramsay replied. "It was always a long shot, but it had to be done."

Baldock nodded. "I've been talking to your man, Inspector Morrison, up in Newcastle. He says you're a loose cannon but you're painfully honest."

Ramsay laughed. "Sadly, my superiors didn't think being honest was enough to offset my unconventional approach to crime fighting."

"That's also what he told me," Baldock replied. "But right now, I've a dilemma. I've one ex-police officer who was blackmailing another ex-police officer and both claiming the other is the head of the smugglers and just possibly the murderer of one of their gang members, as well. Which do I believe?"

"I no longer suspect Len Pritchard," Ramsay replied. "And I think my having invited Constable Storm to be in at the capture would suggest I'm not really any kind of criminal."

"Why did you inform Storm and not me, by the way?"

"I felt he should get some credit out of this," Ramsay replied.

"He's not looking for promotion," Baldock said. "He wants to stay in the village."

"He told me," Ramsay said, slowly, before continuing, "I spent a lot of last night thinking..."

"I'm glad to hear it," Baldock replied. "I meant you to."

Ramsay bit his lip and continued, "Can I suggest another small charade we might try?"

"If it involves blackmailing people," Baldock replied, "Then the answer is no. Not even a dodgy character like Pritchard."

"You still think Pritchard was the smugglers' inside man?" Ramsay asked. "Even as he contacted you to set up the trap for me?"

Baldock laughed. "Even if he's as guilty as sin, he'd have done that to get on my good side and point the finger at you."

Ramsay couldn't help but suspect that may well be true. "I'd hoped I'd disguised my writing and character enough in the note to fool him. I should have had a fiction author write it."

"Do you know any of those?" Baldock asked.

"No, which is why I had no choice but to do it myself," Ramsay admitted. "Anyway, do you want to hear what I suggest for bringing an end to this nonsense?"

"Tell me," Baldock replied. "Only don't assume I'm going to jump at it. Your friend Morrison may be happy to vouch for you but there were plenty in the Whitby force who'd have done the same for Pritchard until we had the evidence proving he was bent."

Baldock listened while Ramsay outlined his idea. When Ramsay finished, Baldock nodded, "Okay but you'd better be right this time because you're still on the hook for attempted blackmail if you aren't."

"I'm sure I'm right," Ramsay replied, handing over the sheet of paper he'd picked up from Harry's wardrobe.

"Very well," Baldock said. "Based on your old colleague's almost glowing reference for you, I'll organize bail and follow up on your request. We'll speak again when I hear from the Ministry."

* * *

Two days after his release on bail, Ramsay was preparing to leave the guest house for his, and Bracken's, midday walk when there was a sharp knock on the door. He returned his coat to the rack and opened the door to find Constable Storm about to knock again.

"Good day, Constable," Ramsay said. "What can we do for you on this fine October day?"

"I'm to escort you to the police house where Inspector Baldock has more questions for you," Storm replied.

Ramsay sighed. "Sorry Bracken, you'll have to run around in the garden." He poked his head around the living room door where Mrs. Golightly was knitting and told her of his change of plans and Bracken's whereabouts while he was away.

She smiled. "I guessed when I saw Constable Storm through the window."

With his companion left to fend for himself, Ramsay put on his coat and was escorted to the police house by Storm.

"What's all this about?" Ramsay asked, conversationally, as they walked. He'd always had success in drawing Storm out in the past.

"I couldn't say, sir," Storm replied, in a tone that suggested he didn't intend to discuss the matter further.

"Has new evidence come to light?" Ramsay continued probing.

"I couldn't say," Storm replied.

There seemed no more to be said and they remained silent until Storm ushered Ramsay into the small office of the police house when Inspector Baldock sat in silent contemplation of the other three men in the room, Armstrong, Caldbeck, and Arthur Peacock.

"Good day, Inspector, Arthur, Mr. Armstrong," Ramsay said, nodding at Caldbeck, before adding, "Isn't one of your suspects missing?"

"He'll be here soon enough," Baldock growled. "My sergeant is inviting him as we speak."

"You think between us we can all sort this out?" Ramsay asked.

Baldock was saved from answering by the sound of the front door opening, heralding the arrival of Len Pritchard with Baldock's detective sergeant.

"Afternoon, Len," Ramsay said, as Pritchard entered the room. Ramsay was enjoying himself. Things were going to plan. Everyone in the same room and no hope for the guilty party to escape. Even better, Eliza wasn't invited. She'd be angry for, like many young people she thought she could take on the world and win. Ramsay knew however, you rarely did and the world was not a forgiving place.

"Right," Baldock said, "Now we're all here, I want some answers from the lot of you and this time I want the truth. Something you've all been economical with until now."

There was general murmur of dissension at this accusation, which Baldock waved aside.

"I'll start with you two," Baldock said, pointing at

Armstrong and the unkempt man beside him. "You had the most pressing motive, Mr. Armstrong. You wanted money quickly and it was tied up in a company where the owner wasn't willing to release funds to you."

"I needed money but not in the way you're implying," Armstrong growled. "As I've already told you many times."

"You took money from the company's working reserves," Baldock continued, until he was interrupted again.

"With Harry's permission," Armstrong replied. "Again, as I've repeatedly told you."

"You say it was for your sister," Baldock continued, "but your sister never received the cash."

Armstrong sighed, shaking his head. "How many times do I have to say this? My sister didn't need my help in the end. And I didn't give it to Mr. Caldbeck, here," he added, gesturing to the man standing next to him.

"Here's the thing, though," Baldock added, "You say you didn't, Mr. Caldbeck says you didn't but there's no proof either way."

Caldbeck interjected, "I haven't a bank account, you checked my post office savings account, you searched the house I rent, and found nothing. How much 'proof' do you need?"

Ramsay, who'd been wondering what Armstrong, and his accomplice, were telling the police was fascinated by the tale unfolding before him.

"Unfortunately for you," Baldock replied, "no proof of wrongdoing isn't the same as innocence."

"What do you do with your money then, Mr. Caldbeck?" Ramsay asked, momentarily forgetting he wasn't the police any longer.

"If I have spare money it goes into the post office or I

spend it," Caldbeck replied, angrily, before Baldock could stop him. "Why? What do you do with yours?"

"I save it for a future rainy day," Ramsay said, speaking quickly as he saw Baldock about to re-assert himself into the conversation.

Caldbeck snorted. "I'm a fisherman. It's a dangerous occupation. How likely is it I'll have these future rainy days you all talk about."

"Enough!" Baldock shouted, slapping the desk with his hand. "That's where we stand with these two gentlemen," he continued, gesturing at them while speaking to Ramsay and Pritchard. "Can you two add anything to further this story?"

Ramsay and Pritchard shook their heads before Ramsay said, "I've never met Mr. Caldbeck and I've only met Mr. Armstrong on three brief occasions. I know nothing about them."

"I have much the same experience," Pritchard said. "I've seen these men about the village and that's all."

"Then I'll come to you, Mr. Pritchard," Baldock said. "You left Whitby and the police force under a cloud of suspicion of involvement in smuggling. However, you didn't go very far, did you?"

"I'm from this part of the world and the few remaining family members I have are all here. Why would I go farther?"

"So, you say," Baldock replied, "however, I might assume you simply moved somewhere more central to your activities. From Robin Hood's Bay you're in easy reach of the ports of Whitby and Scarborough, where your contacts in the smuggling world may exist."

"I have no contacts in the smuggling world," Pritchard replied angrily.

"Yet you were frequently seen in, shall we say, animated

conversations with Harry Peacock right up until his death. What was that if it wasn't a contact?"

"I've told you before," Pritchard said, his voice even and low yet filled with rage. "When I first retired, I couldn't quite give up investigating the smuggling ring operating out of Whitby. Harry Peacock regularly met with Whitby men. He was a school friend, and I was badgering him for information, hoping he'd tell me honestly because we knew each other or he'd become so angry he'd make a mistake and give the game away."

"He didn't?" Ramsay asked.

"Not at all," Pritchard replied. "He'd get angry all right but always insist they were bringing nothing illegal into the country. He even recommended I speak to Constable Storm for confirmation."

"I would have confirmed it, if you had," Storm said.

"That's enough," Baldock shouted. "I ask the questions and you all answer them."

Armstrong groaned. "We do, Inspector, but you don't listen."

Baldock ignored him and continued, "To continue, you, Mr. Pritchard, have no alibi for the days of August fourteen to sixteen, the days immediately following a 'blazing row', as our witness described it, with Harry Peacock."

"All my conversations with that man ended in a blazing row, it's what I wanted. I was not, however, giving him instructions that he didn't want to follow, as you accused me of."

"But you 'can't remember' what the conversation was about?" Baldock said, sarcastically.

"I can't remember the specific details," Pritchard replied, "only that I was pressing him for answers about where his boat went when it left the others and why?"

"You made frequent trips to Whitby at this time as well," Baldock continued.

"As I said, I couldn't let the investigation go," Pritchard replied, wearily. "Then Harry Peacock disappeared, and I realized somebody had come to suspect him and that may have been my fault. If so, I was likely next."

"You were never threatened, though?" Baldock asked.

"I wasn't threatened. That's true."

"Well, gentlemen," Baldock said, looking around the room, "can any of you add anything to this unlikely tale?"

Armstrong, Caldbeck, Peacock, and Ramsay shook their heads.

"Come, Mr. Ramsay," Baldock said. "You can't pretend you don't know Mr. Pritchard from before or that you've met him since arriving in the village. Have you nothing to say?"

"My visits to Len have been social, looking in on an old acquaintance and colleague," Ramsay said. "What he has just told us lines up with what he told me when I asked what he's been doing since he retired."

"Very well," Baldock said, "then we can consider your appearance in this drama, Mr. Ramsay."

When Ramsay said nothing, Baldock continued, "You just happened to pick this spot for a walking holiday before the winter sets in. Is that right?"

Ramsay said it was.

"You had no idea your 'old acquaintance and colleague', as you so eloquently put it, was living here or that a man generally considered to be smuggling goods into the country was missing? How am I doing so far?"

"What you've said is true, Inspector," Ramsay replied.

"Then, following hard on the heels of your recent successful case in the Lake District where you coincidentally met a runaway teenage girl, here you coincidentally find the missing fisherman's body. Is that still correct?"

"It's correct but misleading. The two incidents are in no way related," Ramsay replied.

"So, you say," Baldock responded before continuing, "and since then you too have been unable to stop yourself investigating."

"I have a vested interest in the truth coming out," Ramsay replied, caustically, "and I've given you any information I learned that I thought you may not know."

"Very civic minded, I'm sure," Baldock said. "Another interpretation could be you were misdirecting us to keep your role hidden, but I'll let that pass for now."

"Forever not 'now', Inspector," Ramsay replied, sharply.

"I open up the floor to the rest of you," Baldock said, looking around the room. "Have you anything to add to what I've said, and Mr. Ramsay has kindly clarified?"

"Ramsay's been hounding me since the day he arrived," Armstrong said. "He says investigating, I say he was looking to place the blame on someone other than himself. Though we'd never met, and he knew nothing about me, he was sure I killed Harry."

"I asked you questions on three occasions," Ramsay said. "Hardly hounding."

"He was questioning me too," Peacock cried. "Insinuating I murdered my dad for the company."

Baldock intervened, saying, "But Mr. Ramsay, you're a private citizen. You have no authority to question people."

"You don't need authority from anyone to ask people questions," Ramsay replied. "I was simply trying to make sense of what I stumbled upon."

"It's not your place to interfere in police business and Mr. Armstrong's and Mr. Peacock's point is a valid one,"

Baldock continued. "Your behavior does look like someone trying to deflect blame onto others. When you were a police officer, you would have thought that, I'm sure."

"I would," Ramsay agreed, "and now I know how wrong I would have been."

"There are a number of laws that say your new view of the world isn't a lawful one," Baldock responded. "Now, do you have anything more to say in your defense?"

33

A CONFESSION

RAMSAY PAUSED to collect his thoughts before answering. "My thoughts as an ex-policeman are as follows. You've brought us all here in the hope that, as we squabble, one of us will slip up and give away our guilt. It's a good tactic in movies. In real life, I find, it's people who are innocent who incriminate themselves because they aren't used to the game of deceit."

"If they're innocent, they can hardly incriminate themselves," Baldock interjected.

"If that were true there'd be no innocent people in jail and we all know that isn't true," Ramsay replied. "To continue my thoughts, your summation of the potential case against those you highlighted were perfectly reasonable. I don't deny that. However, as I pointed out once before, a similar case can be suggested against you and with as little evidence to back it up."

"It's gross slander," Baldock growled.

"And so was your suggestion about me, and I strongly suspect, the case against Len Pritchard was too."

"There is plenty of evidence," Baldock shouted, "and if he says there isn't, he's lying."

"But it would be too embarrassing for the police if it went to court," Caldbeck sneered, "so you pushed him out and gave him his pension. We all know what happened."

Ramsay was pleased at this turn of events. One by one, each of the participants in the drama was being dragged into the shouting match. The movie strategy could work, if the right man spoke.

"Hey," Ramsay said, raising his voice, "I haven't finished giving you my thoughts based on my experience of crime."

For a moment there was silence and he continued, "There's another possibility to be considered. Constable Storm checked the boats as they came in and never found any contraband, he says. Maybe he did, was paid off, but became greedy and when Peacock wouldn't pay more, there was a fight, and Peacock was struck by a police truncheon."

"You forget," Storm shouted. "You yourself said he was struck by a lefthanded man. I'm very clearly right-handed." He waved his right hand to reinforce his point.

Ramsay nodded. "I did, which was slow-witted of me. I should have said a lefthanded man facing Peacock or a right-handed person striking his head from behind. You see how easy it is to make a case without any real evidence, only conjecture?" Ramsay smiled at Storm reassuringly.

Constable Storm was not reassured. "A superior officer, even a retired one, passing the blame to an honest working man on the beat is contemptible," he shouted.

Ramsay looked at Baldock and saw the inspector was taking in these additional possibilities. "Do you feel your strategy is working, Inspector?" Ramsay asked.

"I'll say back to you what you said to me, Mr. Ramsay," Baldock replied. "Pointing the finger at everyone in the room may work well in films but, as you see, no one here is fooled. We all see what you're doing and every time you speak, you make them, and me, surer that somehow, you're at the bottom of this."

"Then I'll continue because I think it's going well," Ramsay said. "Mr. Caldbeck was brought here to captain a boat when there were plenty of local men with the experience and character to be its skipper. Why was that Mr. Caldbeck? What quality did you bring that the local men couldn't?"

"I know these waters as well as anyone," Caldbeck replied, angrily. "I've fished out of Whitby all my life and I've experience skippering bigger boats."

"And that was important because the new *Ravenscar Lady 4* goes out a long way, doesn't it?" Ramsay asked.

"Of course, bigger boat, better to manage the rougher waters farther out," Caldbeck replied. "I shouldn't need to point that out to anyone, not even you."

"Will you be sending the boat that far out, Mr. Armstrong, or was that just Harry's strategy?" Ramsay asked.

Armstrong shrugged. "I don't know anything about fishing. I'll be guided by Vernon on the best way of managing the work."

"You've no plans to stop the boat sailing farther out?" Ramsay asked.

"No. Why should I?"

"I wanted to be clear who was *in* and who was *out* of the loop," Ramsay said. "It seems you're in."

"I have no idea what you're talking about," Armstrong said, shaking his head. "Inspector Baldock, this man is desperately trying to throw you off the scent, and you should rein him in."

"Where are you going with this, Ramsay?" Baldock asked.

"Ravenscar Fishing is a genuine business but some of the crewmen and a skipper, it used to be Harry, have a side occupation of smuggling," Ramsay said.

"Constable Storm has checked the boats when they come in," Caldbeck said. "He told us."

Storm angrily said, "That's right. I've never seen anything on the boats when they return."

Ramsay smiled. "That's the beauty of this kind of smuggling. Checks are made on the return but not when they leave."

"Nobody smuggles stuff out of this country," Baldock said. "Everything here is too expensive to sell abroad."

"There are some things some people want that they'll pay a king's ransom for. Isn't that right, Constable Storm?" Ramsay asked.

Storm's face registered total shock. "Why are you asking me?"

"Maybe I should ask Mr. Armstrong?" Ramsay said, looking at the man's horrified expression. Ramsay paused, "or you, Mr. Caldbeck?"

The three men lunged forward and only quick thinking from Baldock's silent detective sergeant stopped them. Stepping between Ramsay and the men, he growled, "That's far enough. Answer the gentleman's questions politely."

It was Armstrong who spoke first. "If Mr. Ramsay knows something about the company that I don't, he should say so and stop this insinuating we're guilty of smuggling."

"You're in the Territorial Army, aren't you, Constable Storm?" Ramsay asked.

"Is that against the law now?" Storm demanded.

"It's very commendable," Ramsay said. "Ready to defend

your country if an enemy should land here. And you've protected the Fylingdales Early Warning Station from protesters too. Such fervent patriotism is rarely found these days in one so young."

"I think I see where you're going with this, Ramsay," Baldock said. "I hope you have proof."

Ramsay said, "I'm sure by now you have the proof in the paper I found at Harry's farm."

Baldock nodded as he removed the sheet of paper from an envelope. "I do indeed. You were right. To an honest man, a simple list of fish prices at nearby ports. Totally unremarkable in the possession of a man running a fishing company, I think you'll all agree." He held it up for them all to see. "Except, as Mr. Ramsay realized, it isn't in the usual format."

Armstrong shrugged, puzzled. "All that says is Harry didn't want to take the official documents to sea with him. A not unreasonable precaution to take, I'd have thought."

"Earlier today, I asked the other crew members if they'd ever seen Harry with this document or one like it," Baldock replied, smiling faintly. "None of them had. Now why was that, do you think?" He looked at each of them in turn before saying, "Mr. Ramsay?'

Ramsay turned to the group of men and said, "Because this was what told one of you how much the payments were and where and when he could go and receive them."

"Harry's dead, Inspector," Armstrong said, quickly. "Whoever killed him no doubt learned of his treachery and made sure it was stopped. They did the country a favor, whoever it was."

The room was silent after this speech. Ramsay silently prayed one of them would take this opportunity to confess. A clear motive a jury would accept for the killing.

Suddenly Storm said, "Mr. Ramsay and Mr. Armstrong

are right. I killed Harry Peacock when I realized he was smuggling secrets out of Fylingdales. One of the Security Guards there told me papers were going missing. I followed Peacock to that cave and questioned him about it. I wanted to know who the other spies were."

"And he turned his back on you?" Baldock asked, incredulous.

"He treated me like dirt," Storm said. "Told me I was mad, and I should leave before he gave me a good hiding. He turned away. Dismissing me like an errand boy, a schoolboy. I lost my temper. I was being dismissed by a traitor. I thought of all the people whose lives he was putting at risk, and I hit him with my truncheon. I meant only to render him unconscious, but in my rage, I hit him too hard."

"Your duty was to report this," Baldock said. "Not cover it up."

"I panicked," Storm cried. "My wife, my family, my job, the people I know, they would all condemn me. I should get a medal and yet I was looking at a life sentence. Closing the cave and leaving the traitor's body to rot seemed like justice and that's what I did. It was wrong, I know, but believe me, I'd never have let anyone suffer for what I did. If we laid charges against anyone, I promised myself I'd confess and explain."

Baldock gave Storm a look that said plainly he wasn't believed. "Sergeant," he ordered, "arrest Constable Storm on suspicion of murder and Vernon Caldbeck on suspicion of spying for a foreign country. Mr. Armstrong, you will not leave custody until you've answered questions concerning your knowledge about this."

"That's easily done," Armstrong protested. "I knew nothing about it."

Baldock didn't reply. "Sergeant, take them away."

"Mr. Ramsay, I'd like a word with you outside, if you please," Baldock said, grimly. "You too, Pritchard."

The three men left the house and congregated behind the stone shed where Constable Storm kept his bicycle.

"Yes, Inspector?" Ramsay asked, when it seemed no one was about to start the conversation.

"How likely is it the spying stopped when Harry Peacock was killed?" Baldock asked.

"Not likely at all," Ramsay said. "I didn't want to say more while Storm was confessing because he was nicely tying up the case with a bow. However, he's the link between the traitor in Fylingdales and the boat. In fact, I'm not sure he isn't the instigator of the whole rotten plot."

Baldock snorted. "Not him. He hasn't got what it takes."

"I think we all underestimate Mr. Storm," Ramsay said. "He's a sergeant in the Reserves, you know. He has leadership abilities; he just doesn't choose to display them in the police force."

"So, he doesn't get moved out," Pritchard said. "Still, that Caldbeck came here from Whitby where they do smuggle so you shouldn't rule out a bigger fish somewhere behind it all."

"Perhaps that's Armstrong," Baldock suggested. "He came from Newcastle, and they have smuggling there too."

Ramsay shook his head. "They smuggle contraband *into* the country, not state secrets out of it. It's different. Caldbeck and Armstrong may have come on board because they wanted a piece of the loot but not, I think, to manage the operation."

"What did you think of Storm's explanation for killing Peacock?" Pritchard asked. "I think more like a falling out among thieves."

Ramsay shook his head. "This wasn't about money, at least not for Peacock, though I'm sure they were paid."

"We arrested Storm's cousin earlier today," Baldock added. "Mr. Ramsay got it right. During one of those Ban the Bomb protests, Storm was persuaded that the only way we could all be safe in a nuclear world was if both sides knew what the other possessed and what they knew. Mutually Assured Destruction they call it. It sounds crazy but many people believe the only thing that will stop the politicians of both sides from blowing us all up is if they know for sure they will be incinerated too. Storm and his cousin agreed. Maybe Harry Peacock did too, at first. Maybe he changed his mind and was killed for it."

"Or maybe he thought it was just industrial secrets," Ramsay said. "You'll learn more as you question them. We should let you get on with that."

Baldock smiled and thanked Ramsay with a wry smile. "Maybe you'd like to temporarily rejoin the force and do that yourself."

Ramsay grimaced. "No but I would like to tell the people who've helped me these past days. I'll wait until you tell me I can. Perhaps we can all meet in Mrs. Golightly's front room, and we can lay it out to them in a way that stops the tale becoming twisted on the village rumor circuit."

"When I can," Baldock said, nodding. "I'll tell you and you can gather the appropriate people."

34

CLOSING THE CASE

It didn't take long. Baldock was on the phone to Ramsay the very next day, saying, "Special Branch and the Secret Service mob have the evidence they need to charge Storm with espionage."

"What does Storm say?" Ramsay asked.

"At first, he wanted to continue with his fiction about discovering Harry Peacock was a spy but then suddenly shifted to, 'I'm proud of what we did.'"

"Proud?"

"As you suggested," Baldock responded. "One of those university speakers at a protest got inside his head. He maintains that if an enemy landed on our beaches, he'd happily fight them off as a patriot. However, as a patriot, he wanted to be sure our lunatic politicians would do everything in their power to avoid a nuclear war where they too would die."

"Sadly, for him, those lunatic political leaders won't want that coming out in court," Ramsay said.

"You think they'll kill him?" Baldock asked, nervously Ramsay thought.

"Maybe exchange him for one of our spies that the other side are holding," Ramsay said. "Captured spies are valuable assets."

"I'm not sure how I feel about that," Baldock said. "I wouldn't have thought Storm had what it takes for something like this."

Ramsay gathered his thoughts before beginning. "The most important thing was when I was told Constable Storm is a sergeant in the Territorial Army. It didn't mean much at the time but did later."

Baldock interjected. "I'm being summoned by the Chief Constable; I must go. Let's discuss it this afternoon over tea at the guest house where you're staying. Invite your helpers if you wish but you need to agree on what can and cannot be said."

Ramsay accepted his terms and set a time he was sure they could meet.

* * *

MRS. GOLIGHTLY, though put out at having a small crowd descend on her with little warning, nevertheless managed plenty of sandwiches, baked goods, and tea for those hungriest of men, Yorkshiremen.

Baldock began. "I'm going to tell you what's happening with the people the police have detained. I'll let Mr. Ramsay explain the rest. Constable Storm is under arrest for killing Harry Peacock, which he admits but claims it was accidental death, and he and Mr. Caldbeck are being held on suspicion of espionage. The Security Services will take over that case. Mr. Armstrong has been released because we have no reason to doubt his word that he knew nothing about any of this."

He briefly answered questions about Percy Storm before saying, "Mr. Ramsay, the floor is yours."

Ramsay looked around the room and those in it: his team, Eliza and Bracken, Mr. and Mrs. Danesdale, Arthur Peacock, and Mrs. Golightly who was enjoying the event so much she could hardly sit still.

Ramsay was preparing to speak when Eliza burst out, "When did you realize they weren't smuggling anything *in*, but they were smuggling things *out*?" She knew this already and wanted that known by the others.

Ramsay smiled at his eager assistant. "I was taken in by the smuggling red herring for too long. Constable Storm, like many others, led me astray. All this talk of smuggling in days of old and hints it was going on at the present time. I had sleepless nights trying to imagine how smuggling could be done here. It can't. Whitby and Scarborough, yes, but not here. I'm tempted to say that, apart from the odd bottle of spirits, it's never been done here. It's true, it's isolated enough to escape scrutiny but the cliffs and the way the village looks out along the beach make it impossible to secretly land anything. That's when I realized I'd been looking at it backwards. They weren't smuggling into the country but out."

"And that's when you remembered the Fylingdales Early Warning Station?" Eliza's father suggested.

Ramsay nodded. "That too should have registered earlier. Its name is on signposts, and it's often in the news because of the Ban the Bomb campaigns that have picketed the place. How easy would it be to have someone smuggle papers out of the station to a courier who could take them out to a waiting trawler."

"The whole crew of Harry's boat must have known what

was happening though," Eliza's mother said, frowning. "I can't believe it of the local men."

"I find it hard as well but as someone told me, people have families," Ramsay said, "and they have hopes and dreams that can't be met nowadays on the money from fishing."

"And they all believe the fish will soon be gone and there'll be no work," Eliza added, "so I can understand it a little."

"Was Storm the leader of this spy ring?" Eliza's dad asked.

"Him or his cousin who worked as a technician inside the facility," Baldock replied, "but he may be the local leader. It may even have been him who saw the opportunity."

"Why would Constable Storm kill Harry, his chief man?" Eliza's mam asked. "What made them fall out?"

"I think Harry wanted more," Ramsay said. "Maybe wanted to be the boss."

Eliza burst in. "That's my belief. I can't imagine Harry being happy taking orders from Percy Storm, even if Percy is a sergeant in the Territorials. Harry was such a domineering man and Percy isn't. However, good an organizer he appears to have been."

Ramsay nodded. "We'll only really know for certain if Storm tells the whole tale to the Secret Service interrogators, or Inspector Baldock as part of the murder inquiry."

"From the little he's said," Baldock added, "Miss Danesdale has it right. Harry, apparently, could be verbally abusive, brutal even, when he lost his temper."

"Why would ordinary people suddenly start spying for the Soviets?" Eliza's dad asked.

"In Percy's case he believed he was doing the right thing

and he's proud of it. Told us so himself. You'd think a man who'd given so much of his time in preparing to defend the realm wouldn't be actively ensuring our most plausible enemy, the Soviet Union, would have the upper hand on us if it came to war but the way he sees it, he's making a war less likely."

"More likely we'd be caught out in a surprise attack if the Early Warning Station was put out of commission," Eliza's dad said, indignantly.

Baldock nodded. "Most people would agree with you, but Storm and Peacock thought otherwise and, perhaps because they wanted to have things their legitimate earnings couldn't provide, they persuaded themselves and others to ferry information abroad."

Arthur Peacock, who'd been silently listening suddenly said, "It wouldn't be money in Dad's case."

They all stared at him as if they'd forgotten he was there.

"Dad's brother was killed in the war," Arthur continued. "He was on a ship that was torpedoed. Dad worshipped his older brother and was still angry about what happened to him. He'd be easy to convince that what they were doing would put an end to war."

"I'd forgotten," Eliza's father said, quietly. "Yes, Oliver Peacock was almost godlike in Harry's eyes. And he did seem to do everything effortlessly; the fastest runner, best footballer, top of the class in almost every subject, and even kind to we younger children as well."

There was a silence, broken by Eliza asking, "Is that why Harry was so angry all the time, dad?'

Her father nodded. "It started then, and it also set Harry on his path to success. He wanted to take Oliver's place, if you see what I mean?"

"I think we can understand," Ramsay said. "A loss of that

kind drives you to do better, be better, than you maybe were going to be before."

"Maybe at first Dad didn't know Storm was being paid," Arthur said. "Maybe it was finding out that Storm and his cousin were being paid was what led to the fight where he was killed."

Ramsay had been considering this too as he'd been speaking. "On balance, I agree with you Mr. Peacock. I think that more likely than him wanting more money."

"But Percy Storm couldn't have killed Harry in a fair fight," Eliza said, scornfully, "even if Harry was years older."

Baldock nodded. "Storm says Harry challenged him about money and used vile language. I took that to mean Harry wanted more. Mr. Peacock's evidence puts a different interpretation on it. Anyway, Harry's abuse grew too much for Storm and when Harry turned away in disgust, Storm was so enraged he lashed out with his police truncheon." Baldock paused, before adding. "It's been scrubbed clean so effectively, we can't confirm that."

"Those batons are heavy," Ramsay said. "I should have thought of that possibility earlier when I saw the shape of the injury."

"No one would have suspected Percy Storm," Eliza's mother cried. "He's the most easy-going, mild-mannered person in the village."

"It's often those kinds of people who snap when life takes an ugly turn," Ramsay replied. "And don't forget his army training means he's probably stronger than he looks."

"Why didn't he dispose of the body or move it where it could be found, by him or someone else? That would be the decent thing to do," Eliza's mother asked. "Leaving Arthur Peacock not knowing if his father was alive or dead for months. I mean, really."

"I can only guess at his motives," Ramsay said, "but I suspect it was knowing the tunnel had been lost in the local memory led him to try his luck. Instead of risking years in prison, which was the most likely outcome of a murder investigation when the trail was hot, he could let the trail go cold. After all, if the tunnel wasn't known, and it didn't seem to be, then Harry's body might never be found."

"And if it was, it might be years in the future when he was no longer living here or even alive," Baldock added. He continued, "As it was, by not telling anyone of Harry's death, Storm and Caldbeck were able to continue smuggling out secrets for a further two months."

"What will happen to them, Inspector?" Eliza asked.

"That's out of my hands," Baldock said. "We've let it be known we've arrested Storm on suspicion of murder and said nothing about the spying. That side of this case was handed over to the appropriate organizations who track and stop spies. The Fylingdales technician and Caldbeck have been offered lighter sentencing if they cooperate. They're under observation until the whole chain of this spy ring has been identified."

"Won't the crew realize that, if Percy has been arrested for Harry's murder, the reason will come out?" Eliza's mother asked.

"We've told the press his motive was personal," Baldock said. "And Mr. Peacock has agreed to run the business long enough for us to get the evidence we need. You here today, of course, have agreed to sign the Official Secrets Act forms I have with me. I hope you understand how serious it would be for you, if any of this came out before we're ready?"

As they'd been advised of this before the meeting, they signed the documents he placed before them.

"I still can't believe it of our local men," Eliza's mother

said, even more appalled than she had been when she believed the smuggling story.

"They may not know exactly what is being done," Ramsay said. "They may have been told it was something relatively harmless, like hard currency. Russian sailors need Western currency to spend in foreign ports and it isn't an offence to give it to them."

"And be given bottles of vodka in exchange, maybe?" Eliza suggested.

"Something like that," Ramsay replied. "We won't really know until Special Branch and the Secret Service have rounded them all up."

"Their poor families," Eliza's mother said, unable to get the plight of the local men out of her mind.

Ramsay hesitated before replying. "Storm would ask you to consider *all* our families. If putting the Early Warning Station out of service prevents a war starting, we're all safer not just the armed forces. Still, I'm as against wars as much as any peace campaigner but I can't approve of anyone giving potential enemies assistance. They may have hoped what they did would be used wisely by good people, but they can't know that it will."

Baldock interjected. "As I said, Storm believed he was leveling the playing field, which would ensure neither side was so strong it would take the risk of using their First Strike nuclear weapons. Like Mr. Ramsay, I don't like to think of our people assisting potential enemies, but I do see where Storm and the others are coming from."

"Inspector!" Eliza cried in outrage.

Baldock held up his hand to silence the growing cries of outrage. "I'm not arguing for treachery, or that I have sympathy for those who commit it, I'm just saying I understand their argument."

Ramsay stayed silent. His own experience of policing had taught him how people could believe and act on activities he would never consider acceptable. And his own limited experience of the spying world made him wary of the good intentions of any side in a war, cold or hot.

"What about poor Mrs. Storm?" Eliza's mother asked. "Will she get Percy's police pension?"

"I don't know," Baldock replied frankly. "I doubt we've ever had a policeman engaged in espionage before so who knows what the Pension Board will rule. However, I'm sure everything that is done will be done by the rules."

"Wait a minute," Eliza cried, "How did they get paid?"

Baldock glanced at Ramsay who said, "Didn't we say? Most of the papers we found were cover documents for the drawings and technical papers attached but some were coded messages and instructed a Soviet contact how to hand over their payment."

"When he killed Harry, why didn't Percy take them?" Mr. Danesdale asked. "Leaving them would mean not getting paid, wouldn't it?"

"To convince the crew Harry had run off with the cash, I imagine," Ramsay replied.

Baldock nodded. "He took the sheets he needed to release the money and got the cash. The sheets of paper that were the cover for the important message, he left behind to implicate Harry in smuggling and point the finger away from himself."

"Not such a pure peace worker, after all," Eliza said, sarcastically.

"I imagine there were mixed motives from the start," Ramsay said, adding, "Storm was on duty for many of those Ban the Bomb protests at the Early Warning Station."

Baldock interjected. "Which is where he first heard the

arguments that set him on his life of treachery. Some of those dotty old academics who turn up at these events can be very persuasive, especially to a naïve young man who's struggling to make his way in the world."

"If there's nothing else, we should let you go, Inspector," Ramsay said, looking around the faces in the room for more questions. "Thanks for coming here and filling us in. This case meant a lot to me as a mere visitor, I can only imagine what it meant for the villagers."

35

WRAPPING UP

When Baldock was out of earshot, Pritchard asked, "Do you think they'll get the whole spy ring?"

Ramsay shrugged. "I don't imagine we'll ever know. Special Branch and the Secret Services are running that operation. Storm, his cousin, and Caldbeck can make deals to save their lives."

Pritchard pulled a wry face. "Caldbeck has little to bargain with."

Ramsay replied, "If he cooperates and is useful, he may escape the death penalty."

With the excitement over, the group was breaking up, preparing to leave. Ramsay rose to escort them to the door. As they put on their coats and hats, Len Pritchard asked, "Is it just a coincidence you were in the right spot twice in the past six months?"

Ramsay laughed. "Unlikely as it may seem, it is a coincidence. They happen often in my experience."

"I thought of becoming a private investigator after I retired," Pritchard said. "The memory of all the ones I met when I was in the force held me back and I'm glad it did.

What about you? Now you've made a name for yourself, you could pick only the best cases. No divorces or anything unsavory, I mean."

Ramsay considered this for a moment, before saying, "I'm sticking with my original plan to walk the scenic parts of this beautiful island. Because of these mysteries, I saw very little of the Lake District and now I've seen nothing of Yorkshire. I start afresh next spring."

"If you return here next year," Pritchard said, "I'd be happy to accompany you on a walk, so long as you don't find any bodies along the way."

Ramsay laughed. "I can't promise that, but if I come back here for hiking, I'll drop you a line."

Eliza's dad broke into the conversation saying, "Caldbeck and Storm would have fallen out eventually, don't you think? We'd have had another murder here."

Ramsay nodded. "I do. Storm needed Caldbeck to continue Harry's role. Caldbeck wouldn't need Storm if he could discover how the system worked and he strikes me as the kind of man who would find out. I'd say Constable Storm had only months to live."

Pritchard chuckled. "My thoughts too, which is good because it makes me less sympathetic toward Caldbeck. I think he'll be the one for the high jump."

"I still think it was mean of you not to share what you'd decided about Percy Storm," Eliza said, when he closed the door behind their visitors. "I was ready to fight them tooth-and-nail when they arrested us, and you'd been holding out on me all along."

"Because I was only sure when I heard from Baldock about Storm's cousin working in the station," Ramsay said, putting his arm around her.

Eliza gave him 'the look', saying, "I don't believe you. We're partners remember."

As anything he said would lead them into a pantomime routine of 'I didn't' and 'you did', Ramsay changed the subject. "Now it's over, we should have a celebratory drink."

"A last drink in the *Dolphin*?" Eliza asked.

"I'm not leaving the village yet," Ramsay replied, "but let's go there. It'll be a good way of letting people know I'm not still in a police cell."

As they put on their coats and hats, Eliza said, "I think they'll all know by now. Mrs. Storm will have told everyone about everything," she continued, laughing, "even though it's her husband in jail."

"You survived your arrest without coming to any harm, I see," Ramsay said, opening the door to let Bracken and Eliza go out.

"I wasn't really arrested," Eliza said. "I was just detained. And I got tea and scones again, which was very welcome after sitting out there in the cold all night."

Ramsay, laughing, said, "And I was worried about you."

"You needn't be," Eliza said. "I'm tougher than I seem, and I can look after myself."

As they walked, arms around each other to keep out the cold, as Eliza reminded him, Ramsay asked, "Would you like one more opportunity to wear your best going out dress?"

"Of course."

"Then why don't we celebrate with dinner at our favorite spot tomorrow night," Ramsay said.

Eliza exclaimed, "Good idea!" Then added, "We can discuss the future of our partnership."

Ramsay shook his head. "There's only a partnership if I decide to help people with mysterious problems and I'm not certain I will right now."

"Grrr," Eliza growled, before adding, "You are infuriating. Look how well this turned out."

Ramsay squeezed her. "We'll make the reservation on the way to the pub and at dinner we'll talk about the future."

"You have to help people," Eliza said. "You know it and I know it, even Bracken knows it. Stop this dancing around and say yes."

Ramsay frowned. This was all reminiscent of his friend Miss Riddell's experience. There was a need for people to solve mysteries that the police and private detectives weren't providing. Should he, or shouldn't he? Eliza was right about his nature. He did come alive during an investigation, and it would be hard to have that experience walking in the countryside. "What say you, Bracken?" Ramsay asked, at last.

Hearing that he was finally being invited to have a say, Bracken gave his friend his widest smile.

"I told you Bracken agreed with me," Eliza said, as they arrived at the entrance to The Seaview Hotel.

Ramsay stopped and turned to face her. "It's not a democracy. I want more time to think. Not another word more shall pass my lips on this subject until I'm sitting at a dinner table with a starched white cloth and napkins, a glass of French wine, and an attentive waiter just itching to take my order."

"I don't know why I ever liked you," Eliza said, conversationally, as they entered the hotel. "My dad is less infuriating than you."

"Your father has been worn down by the constant irritation of having you as his child for nineteen years," Ramsay replied, approaching the reception. "I'm still too new."

The receptionist made their reservation for dinner, and they left the building, heading back up the street to the pub.

Once outside, Eliza said, "We are a good team, aren't we?

I mean apart from your inability to share the credit at the end, we did work well together."

"We did and your share of the partnership was crucial to my understanding of the place and people," Ramsay replied. "I couldn't have done it half as well or half as quickly without you."

"Hmmm," Eliza said, "I don't like the sound of that. It sounds awfully like goodbye."

"Goodbye to this mystery," Ramsay said. "Not goodbye to our friendship."

"Or our partnership," Eliza said, suspiciously. "I expect to be working with you on all future cases."

Ramsay looked puzzled. "You live and work here in the family business. Even if another mystery came my way, it wouldn't likely be here. How could you take part?"

Eliza snorted. "I work in the teashop because there's nothing else to do around here and I don't have any qualifications for a job working somewhere else. When the next mystery appears, I'll be on the first train to wherever it is."

Ramsay laughed. "I don't get paid for doing this, you know. It isn't employment. How would you keep yourself?"

"We'd find someone who needs to know the truth and negotiate a fee from them," Eliza replied. To Ramsay's wonderment, she appeared to feel they'd have no trouble doing that.

"Take this case," Ramsay suggested. "Who would be the interested party that might pay?"

"In this case, you," Eliza said, bluntly, "or Armstrong, if he's honest. Or my father, if he could be persuaded it might save his job. You see? I can make this a paying concern. You have no idea."

They were once again stopped, and the blustery wind was blowing their hats and coats like ragged flags. Eliza moved sideways so she was in his shadow. "You're lucky you still have all your hair," she commented, as Ramsay grabbed his hat, which had been blown off his head, and brushed his hair from his eyes. "Most men your age don't."

"Your mind does jump around a lot," Ramsay retorted.

"Better than running on a single track like yours," Eliza said, sharply. "We're working together on the next case, and you'll have to get your mind around that."

"We can talk as we celebrate," Ramsay said, opening the door for her.

"If it's a celebration, we should have champagne," Eliza suggested as they entered the bar.

"This is a pub. I doubt they have champagne," Ramsay reminded her. "We'll have champagne with dinner tomorrow night."

"That's my idea of teamwork," Eliza said, as Ramsay ordered their drinks at the bar. "Working together to get the right answer."

36

SAYING GOODBYE — OR IS IT?

It was blustery morning as Ramsay and Bracken waited with Eliza for his train to arrive. The open platform provided no shelter at all.

They said little, even Eliza seemed unwilling to speak until the train clanked and hissed into the station.

"Tom," Eliza said, tears prickling her eyes, as he turned to pick up his bags. "You will visit, won't you? This isn't goodbye. You promised."

Ramsay smiled. He hugged her, saying, "I'll visit on as many Tuesdays as I can."

"And I can visit you?" Eliza asked, before kissing him. She felt his body stiffen as he always did.

"Your parents would be unhappy if you stayed in my house alone," Ramsay responded. He should, of course, refuse outright but he knew he couldn't. He would have to wait until her infatuation wore off. And his too. What a ridiculous thing to happen at his age.

"I wouldn't be alone, would I," Eliza said, hugging him to her breast and refusing to let go. "There's a retired policeman in residence, and if you can't trust the police, who can you trust."

Ramsay laughed. "I doubt your father would see it that way. I have three bedrooms. Maybe you all could come when the teashop closes for the season."

"It's better than nothing, I suppose," Eliza replied, still holding him. "I've never been to Newcastle, you know. I don't remember being further than Scarborough."

"Then you'll all be very welcome," Ramsay replied, opening the carriage door and helping Bracken inside. Bracken stayed at the door until Eliza had properly kissed and hugged him goodbye. Even then, he was unwilling to make way for Ramsay's cases.

"Bye for now," Ramsay said, kissing Eliza on the cheek. "I'll phone you tomorrow at the teashop."

"You'd better," Eliza said, fiercely, and then kissed him on the lips. "Remember. I know now where you live."

Ramsay watched from the carriage door as the train pulled out of the station. Eliza waved, sadly, he thought, and his heart ached. He returned her wave; the train began to turn, and she was lost to sight. He closed the window and sat. Bracken watched him.

"You look as sad as I feel, Bracken," Ramsay said. "This isn't wise. It will end in tears."

37

HOME AGAIN... BUT RESTLESS

RAMSAY'S NEXT-DOOR neighbor was as good as her word. A glowing fire was burning in the hearth and the house was warm and dry, without that musty feel Ramsay so disliked when he returned from a trip.

"I'll unpack and we'll go for a walk, Bracken," he told his companion who was eyeing him hopefully. "Ten minutes at most."

Bracken lay down on the rug and watched, with soulful eyes, Ramsay removed his clothes from his suitcase. When Ramsay closed the lid, Bracken jumped to his feet eagerly.

"It was a long journey, wasn't it," Ramsay said. "The train waiting at Middlesborough for a lifetime was particularly bad. Because of that, we missed the express, which meant we had to take the slow train. We won't go anywhere in the future without the car."

Outside, darkness was falling, and a thin rain was soaking the garden. Ramsay opened his umbrella and they walked closely together under its shelter. "We won't do any more trips this year," Ramsay said, as they entered the park where he would always let Bracken off the leash. "It's too cold and wet for hiking the hills and moors. We could drown as we walked up on the heights." He let Bracken go and watched him check out each of the posts, tree trunks, and corners where dogs had been leaving messages while they were away.

Ramsay continued his slow walk along the gravel path through the park, keeping track of where Bracken was. The long train journey had been wearisome, but it had given him time to think about the future. In Ramsay's opinion, it would be four months before the land was dry enough for him to do the walks he wanted to do. How was he to get through the winter? The only decision he'd made was he'd go to a hotel for Christmas. Maybe in the Lake District, and visit Sophia and Alastair, or Yorkshire, and visit Eliza, or somewhere in Scotland. He might look up his Ramsay family. Christmas was a time for family.

Bracken trotted back, clearly satisfied he knew what had been going on while they'd been away.

"You learn more with your nose, Bracken, than I do with all my five senses."

Bracken looked at him scornfully and thought: 'I doubt you have any senses, let alone five. Still, I'm fond of you and your shortcomings only make me more anxious to help you.'

"I haven't seen my Scottish family for more than twenty years," Ramsay said. "I doubt they'd welcome me turning up now, out-of-the-blue. No, it's either Yorkshire or the Lake District for Christmas. What's your opinion, Bracken?"

Bracken's stony expression in response suggested: 'I'd rather stay at home.'

"What about a hotel near Cheviot? We could visit your family instead."

Bracken seemed as uninterested in this as the other choices he'd been given.

"I wish there'd been a reward for catching those spies," Ramsay said. "With a little bit of extra cash, we could have gone somewhere warm. As it is, we're going no farther than I want to drive on dark wintry days."

Bracken yawned. None of this sounded interesting.

"Miss Riddell's family lives near Robin Hood's Bay," Ramsay mused. "I wonder if she'd be home for Christmas."

Bracken sat up. He hardly knew Miss Riddell, but he did know Robin Hood's Bay. He was well fed there by his friend Eliza.

"Maybe The Seaview Hotel or The Mallyan Spout Hotel for Christmas, Bracken. What do you think?"

Bracken thought: 'That is a gr-r-reat idea!'

* * *

Now you've reached the end of the story, please help other readers by leaving a review. Here's where to do that: https://www.amazon.com/review/create-review/?ie=UTF8&channel=glance-detail&asin=B0CQKMRT7S

* * *

And buy the next in the series, Dark Deeds on a White Christmas

* * *

Or the first in the series, Hey Diddle Diddle, the Runaway Riddle, if this book is your introduction to Ramsay, Eliza, and Bracken.

MORE BOOKS BY THE AUTHOR

On Amazon, my books can be found at the

One Man and His Dog Cozy Mysteries page

And

Miss Riddell Cozy Mysteries series page.

And for someone who likes listening to books, ***In the Beginning, There Was a Murder*** is now available as an audiobook on Amazon and here on Audible and many others, including:

Kobo, Chirp, Audiobooks, Scribd, Bingebooks, Apple, StoryTel

You can find even more books here:

P.C. James Author Page: https://www.amazon.com/P.-C.-James/e/B08VTN7Z8Y

P.C. James & Kathryn Mykel: Duchess Series

P.C. James & Kathryn Mykel: Sassy Senior Sleuths Series.

Paul James Author Page: https://www.amazon.com/-/e/B01DFGG2U2

GoodReads: https://www.amazon.com/P.-C.-James/e/B08VTN7Z8Y

And for something completely different, my books by Paul James at: https://www.amazon.com/-/e/B01DFGG2U2

ABOUT THE AUTHOR

P.C. James is the author of the quietly humorous Miss Riddell Cozy Mysteries, the One Man and His Dog Cozy Mysteries, and co-author of the Royal Duchess and Sassy Senior Sleuths cozy mysteries.

He lives in Canada near Toronto with his wife.

He loves photographing wildlife in the outdoors yet chooses to spend hours every day indoors writing stories, which he also loves. One day, he'll find a way to do them both together.